St. John's
BESTIARY

A DETECTIVE NOVEL

by William Babula

A WRITE WAY PUBLISHING BOOK

Other books by William Babula:

St. John's Baptism

According to St. John

St. John and the Seven Veils

This one is for Lester Goran

PROLOGUE

It was a case I had a hard time taking seriously when I first heard it laid out. Maybe the client who brought it to me should have been wearing a sign that read: BEWARE OF THE CATS. What started out as the almost comic Great Cat Kidnapping Caper Case ended up as one of my most serious and deadly cases, and most personally tragic.

My name is Jeremiah St. John, eponymous founder of a San Francisco detective agency that had been in business for over four years when a prospective client came to me with a case that involved rescuing some felines. I never imagined that such a case, through a bizarre series of twists, would lead to my being shot. And not just once, but twice. Me, who had never been shot in those four plus years as a PI. No more comic cases, is my motto. Cat rescues should be turned over to the fire department, where they belong.

I am thirty-two years old, six-foot-one, one hundred seventy-five pounds, with straight brown hair that I wear neatly cut, and clear blue eyes that give me perfect vision. I am in pretty good shape, reasonably good looking, with regular features, except for a once-broken nose. None of the above charming characteristics saved me from stopping those bullets, however.

Lying in the hospital with a bullet wound, connected to IVs and monitors, I cursed the Catnapping Caper which got me into all of this, and then I cursed my PI occupation, as well. Until I remembered what I had been before: an attorney, a genuine passed-the-bar attorney.

After law school at Boalt Hall, I became a deputy district attorney in one of the Bay Area's most crime-ridden counties. The idealism I brought to the job was quickly undermined, not by the criminals I prosecuted, but by the staff in the DA's office. Everyone was trying to get out, looking for sinecures on special task forces, moving into lower pressure U.S. Attorneys' positions, switching to high-paying criminal defense, or joining private firms that specialized in civil suits.

I got out of there too. But not for the same reasons. I made some very wrong professional moves in the office. There were a substantial number of female deputy DAs, and with little time for socializing outside of the office, office affairs became the pattern of behavior. Several of these office romances led to the altar. Mine led me to bed with Sarah, with whom I believed I was in love. But when I started talking marriage, she let me know that she was planning to marry my superior in the office. Their affair, since he was getting a divorce at the time, was a well-kept secret. Especially from me. Unfortunately, my affair with Sarah was not equally secret from him. The result was a career disaster.

I was handed all the cases that were hopelessly deficient legally, with great potential to embarrass the prosecutor who handled them. After six months of dismal cases, I left Sarah to her soon-to-be-husband—the man had forgiven her for her indiscretion with me, but as for Jeremiah St. John, the word had been revenge—and quit the DA's office for a prestigious San Francisco personal injury law firm. After over a year of whiplash cases and accident reconstruction, I decided the law, any kind of law, was not for me.

I'd met a few private investigators during my time in the DA's office and the law firm, and I got interested in the business. I realized that most of them were ex-cops, but why not an ex-lawyer like me? What I knew about the law could come in handy. So I dropped out of the great flood of California lawyers that was spreading out over the state just like another natural disaster, and opened a PI agency with the money I had made from numerous billable hours with the law firm.

I hadn't lost interest in the law and justice, I just wanted a little freedom in how I went about dealing with those twin support towers of what remains of our civilization.

By the time the man seeking his missing cats walked into my office, I had long since moved from a decrepit building, now condemned and demolished, in the Mission District, to decent space. I now had two partners, one a beautiful ex-cop, the other a huge Seminole who had once been an alligator wrestler, and now had a pretty good reputation for results in the legal and PI community. Which meant I really didn't need to take the Great Cat Kidnapping Caper Case.

But I'm known for my mistakes. Especially to my partners, who are not exactly forgiving types.

I realized too late I should have asked the man how many of his cats were black.

1

"God*dam* the CFAF," Professor Vernon Krift shouted across my desk.

So far he had told me his name, his title, and his crying need for the services of a private detective. Now he was damning some people I didn't know anything about. All this before he even sat down.

I asked the obvious. "What is the CFAF?"

Krift looked at me with piercing blue eyes and explained the acronym. "The Committee for Animal Freedom. They stole my cats."

"Your what?" I asked, not sure I had heard him right.

"My cats," he repeated.

"Are these. . . uh. . . valuable cats? Exotic breeds or something?"

"No. They're American short-hairs. Alley cats, if you prefer."

"Sounds more like a job for the Humane Society," I said, thinking this was sounding absurd.

"No. I assure you it is not."

"Have you heard of the Sherlock Bones Agency? They specialize in missing pets." I was generous, willing to send some business the way of another agency.

"These are not pets."

Reluctantly I offered, "Why don't you sit down and we'll take this one from the top." I knew the clichés to get a good Q&A going. Usually.

"I'd rather stand," the man said. But he didn't stand; he started pacing.

"Whatever," I said. As long as he got to talking about his problem. Soon.

I leaned back in my chair and waited. I considered offering him some chilled Russian vodka, but decided against it. I was stuck wasting time on an apparently silly case; why waste good vodka as well?

We were in my private back office in the Stick-Eastlake Victorian I rented to house the agency on the ground floor—with living quarters for me upstairs. My office has a view of the backyard, and I was getting bored enough with Krift to turn away from him and look out of my window. The yard was winter-bare with most of the small trees looking like the skeletons of scarecrows. The sky above them was swollen with gray December clouds. The kind that look like snow in the Sierras on the state's eastern spine, but almost always mean cold rain in the City by the Bay.

Krift looked back to the front of the building at the two empty offices that led up to mine. "You do have partners?" It was more of a statement than a question.

"Yeah. But they're out. . . on a case." Actually I was alone in the office for a different reason, but there was no need to clue Krift in about it. Without much work to do, I had finished my Christmas shopping early. On the other hand, my two partners, Mickey and Chief Moses, had procrastinated. They would argue that it was because they had cases to attend to and I didn't. But now it was Tuesday the 20th of December, with only five shopping days left until Christmas; I gave them the afternoon off.

"This needs to be kept strictly confidential," Krift said, as he looked around again.

"Eventually you're going to have to tell *me* about it."

"Of course. But as few people as possible should be involved."

"I'll make it easy for you. Don't tell me anything. Just leave." That seemed the best of ideas to me.

"I need help."

Somehow I didn't feel particularly moved by his plea. I leaned forward. "If I were to take this case, I wouldn't keep it from my partners."

"But every detail?"

"Talking to them is like talking to me. And talking to me is like talking to. . . an attorney." Which of course I actually was in another life.

Krift stepped forward and put his hands on my scarred wooden desk. I estimated he was six-three and about two hundred pounds. He had a classically chiseled face with a broad but aquiline nose, and full lips. His longish blond hair was going to white and that, along with the crinkled lines around his eyes, put him in his mid-forties. He looked in good physical shape under the imported three-piece brown woolen suit he wore, with a matching silk paisley tie. My guess was that he was into racquetball or squash. For a professor, he dressed expensively, and well.

"I was told you could help me," he said.

"Who told you that?" I asked.

"I called my attorney, Brian Samaho, and he recommended you."

"Oh," I said, biting my lip and nodding. It was a reasonable explanation. We had worked with Brian and his partner Scott Forsander on the *Macbeth* murder case over a year ago, and they had been sending us clients and other business ever since.

"He must have mentioned I worked with partners."

"Yes. Something about a very beautiful and very leggy blond, and a very large Seminole Indian."

"That's them. The description fits."

Krift sat down in the chair across from my desk. Unlike most clients, he didn't fumble nervously for a cigarette. I assumed it wasn't because of all the No Smoking signs we had posted in various languages throughout the office, but his own concern with health and fitness.

"Let me tell you exactly what happened. I'm a professor of physiology at the Health Science Center at the university. I use domestic short-hairs in my government research project. Sunday night the CFAF broke into my lab and stole all my animals."

"And set them free?"

"Look at this. I found it Monday morning at the lab." He carefully unfolded a piece of white bond and passed it over the desk to me. I got up and examined it by the dim winter light coming through the window. It was a note made up of cut-out and pasted magazine letters and words. Just like on TV.

It read:

We have your cats, Professor Krift. How much are they worth to you? Do not tell the police, or they are dead pussies. You will be hearing from us. CFAF

"Nice phrasing that 'dead pussies' touch. You don't need a New Age crystal to tell you that a ransom demand is in your future. Have you heard from them yet?" I came up next to him and handed back the note, which he just as carefully refolded and put into the inside pocket of his suit jacket.

"No. That's why I decided to get help. I didn't want to wait any longer."

"Strange, coming from a group calling for animal freedom."

That pressed the right button to set him off. He lurched sideways at me, almost leaving his chair. "Animal freedom like hell. The animals don't mean anything to them. These groups are all alike. From the Animal Liberation Front to the Animal Rights Militia."

"I think I've heard of those two," I said.

"Of course. They're always in the newspapers or on TV claiming responsibility for one insane act or another. But they're nothing but terrorists and extortionists and arsonists. Look how they burned down the animal research facility on the UC Davis campus. They're criminals out to destroy research that could ultimately save human lives. Yet there are people on campus and in our society who idolize, or at least excuse these killers, and I mean the word 'killers' literally, because they are killing those who could have been helped with the research they are destroying."

I'd given animal rights some thought, and I had a general sense that if research on animals could prevent leukemia, cancer or whatever in humans, I tended to favor it. But then, I also got a lot of mail with graphic and disgusting pictures of tortured rabbits and dogs from animal rights groups fighting for the end of animal testing. Call me ambivalent.

"Why not call the cops? This is their kind of work," I ended up saying.

"You just read the note. They've threatened to kill the cats if I do." He was at the edge of his chair with his fingers locked on the arms. His face was flushed.

"What do you expect them to say? That's what they all threaten. They get it from TV and the movies." I sat back down behind my desk.

"I can't take that risk. My research would be compromised without the actual animals involved in the testing. As for the police, they've dealt with this kind of incident before at the Health Science Center with no success. I'm not about to let them try again."

"What about the campus police?"

"Might as well put in a call for the Keystone Cops."

"What kind of work are you doing?" I wanted to make sure that Krift wasn't running a miniature Auschwitz for non-master race felines at the Center.

"Not this kind." He got up and handed me a flyer that had a grainy black and white picture of a cat with its head bolted down in a vice to a steel table. "This is what the CFAF accused me of. Performing brain dissections on living cats. Horrible."

"But what exactly do you do with your cats?" This animal research business was suddenly making me very uncomfortable. I remembered vividly some of the gruesome pictures of rabbits blinded by cosmetics I had seen in my junk mail.

"My work deals with sleep. I study the breathing of cats during sleep."

"And I like to watch grass grow and paint dry. Why?"

"To get some answers about disorders like Sudden Infant Death Syndrome. I presume you have heard of that."

"Yes. Of course. I read the newspapers."

Things were slow over the holidays. With court out of session, even our juror profile business was off. As for case work, maybe people felt less inclined to cheat on their spouses or maybe everyone just got too depressed to do anything. Or maybe people were just too broke for vice.

With the fifteen grand in bonus money we got from a reluctant Reverend Starborn at the conclusion of the Gutman case, we added, at Mickey's insistence, more high-tech equipment for her, and, at mine, bars to the second floor of the Victorian. I didn't want a repeat of the break-in I had suffered earlier in the year. A ladder in the night had demonstrated that bars on the first floor were no better than the Maginot Line. That still left a good-size chunk of cash, and with both partners involved in cases, we didn't need the money all that bad. But I was seriously considering taking the case just to keep busy; I just needed a few more specifics.

"Exactly what do you want from me?" I asked.

"Help with the CFAF." Krift was pacing again.

"Like what?"

"Finding them."

"Finding them? And doing what?"

"Getting the cats back."

"Hold it right there. That's a good way to end up with, as they would say, a lot of dead pussies. Standard operating procedure in a human kidnapping is to pay the ransom, get the release, and then go after the kidnappers and the money. I'd suggest we do the same thing here."

"But suppose I don't hear from them?"

I took another look out of my window. Nothing much had changed. I said, "You will. That's their business. They're just making you sweat to soften you up for the payoff. They'll be making their ransom demand soon. They have to."

"I imagine you're right. It makes sense."

"Of course it does. How many animals were taken?"

"Eight. In eight cages. Each cat is tattooed inside the left ear with an ID number."

I also should have asked how many of the cats were black. That's what hindsight can do for you.

Instead I said, "Call the police."

"You said that already."

"Good advice bears repeating."

"I can't." He paused. "You've got to listen to me."

"I've been listening all along. I'll only listen to anything more if you sit back down."

He hesitated, but he did sit down. One small victory.

He cleared his throat. "All right. Here is the problem. My daughter, Claire, is one of my research assistants. If the police investigate they are sure to find out that my daughter engineered this catnapping to extort money from me. There. That's it. That's why Samaho sent me to you. That's why I want as few people involved as possible."

"Why didn't you tell me this before?"

"I didn't think you needed to know."

"Are we on a need to know basis here? You sound like the goddam CIA."

"Sorry."

I let it go. "Why would she do this? For the money?"

"No. For revenge. She hates me. I wasn't sure before, but now I'm certain. Yes. She hates me and this is her revenge." He was on the edge of his seat again.

"For a good reason? Or just normal everyday parent-child conflict?" I asked.

He slammed his fist into an open palm. "She has her reasons." He fell silent.

"That's it?"

"Yes."

"You mentioned revenge," I said.

"Her motives aren't important."

I didn't agree, but I didn't push him. "Do you have any actual proof that she's involved?"

"I just know."

"Could we talk hard evidence here?"

"We've had arguments. . . "

"What kind?"

"That's not pertinent."

"And that's not evidence. This is all pretty far-fetched."

"You'll have to take my word for it. Do you think I'm enjoying accusing my daughter of extortion?"

I started giving the situation some serious thought, when Krift made a few more comments.

"I want to protect her. She could be charged with a felony. That's why I can't have the police involved."

"Okay, okay."

"Will you try to find the cats?" he asked.

"Why not wait until we hear? That would give us some kind of lead."

"Then I would have to pay. I'm not going to be taken like that. I want to work it out with Claire. Without extortion. I want this stopped now. Will you help?"

This case was taking an interesting, if somewhat bizarre, twist. Which appealed to me. "When can I see the lab?"

"Then you'll take the case?"

"I'm thinking about it." I repeated my question about the lab.

"Now." He stood up. "Do you think you can pick up any clues there?"

"I doubt it. After all, this happened two days ago." I tried to map out a strategy. Compared to what a Police Crime Scene Unit could do, my investigation of the lab would be minimal and probably useless given the circumstances. But I could do one thing just as well. Interrogate. "You have other lab assistants?" I asked.

"One other besides Claire."

"When will he or she be there?"

"She. We plan to reopen tomorrow morning."

"That's when I'll go to the lab. I want to talk to them. Try not to disturb things too much, just in case there is some physical evidence."

Krift said, "We'll be careful."

"Good."

"What will you be looking for?"

"Mainly how they got in."

He nodded. "What are the chances of getting my animals back?"

I stood up and met his eyes. "Real good. If you're right about Claire, I just need to ask her a few questions. In private."

"No. I don't want her to know I even suspect."

"Now you're making it difficult."

"What are my chances otherwise?"

"Still pretty good, if you pay the ransom. Not so hot if I'm just out there trying to find eight cats who could be anywhere in the city."

"I don't want to pay a ransom."

"Then let me confront Claire."

"No."

I took the case without making any promises about results. I explained our fee structure for time and expenses and expected him to balk, but he didn't. He acted like he had picked up a bargain. I collected a five hundred dollar retainer and he signed our new contract form for service on the dotted line. Then he left me to my work.

I was now handling the Great Catnapping Caper. I wondered how my partners would react to it. Knowing their attitudes towards animals and the environment, I had a feeling they wouldn't quite agree with me on this one.

2

Early that evening, Michelle "Mickey" Farabaugh and Chief Moses Tamiami arrived bearing gifts in Union Square shopping bags, which they put down on the floor in my office. Both of my partners' faces and hands were red from the cold.

The Chief took off his extra-extra large brown suede jacket and tossed it on the chair that Krift had occupied on and off earlier. He was meticulously neat in his own office, but somewhat less so in mine.

Mickey took off her wool herringbone coat and hung it on the coatrack behind my desk. She looked great in a teal turtleneck sweater and short black skirt. While she rubbed her hands together to warm up, I admired the classic curves of her five-foot-eight figure. And warmed up myself.

Mickey joined the Chief and me in the agency after a stint in an Ohio city police department. When she posed nude in a *Playboy* "Women in Blue" pictorial, that job was over. Disgusted with her sexist treatment, she left Ohio and drove west until she ran out of highway. When she ran out of money as well, and needed a job, I got another partner. It worked out well for all of us. The only problem was that once in a while I was sure I was in love with her. A feeling left over from the brief affair she ended abruptly when she decided we weren't acting professionally. I wasn't convinced, but I lost my case with the lady. And continued to lose it after several more appeals, right up to the present.

Mickey and the Chief picked up their shopping bags, put them down on my desk, and sat together on my old leather couch. Mickey's redness began to fade, but not the Chief's, so that I could notice. Mickey put her head back and ran her long fingers through honey blond hair that had recently been cut into a short boyish style. It looked as if her fingers were searching for the hair that had hung to her shoulders just last week.

"How was the shopping?" I asked.

Mickey scowled. "Now I know what happened when the state cut funding for mental institutions. They dumped the inmates in department stores."

"Good thing you two didn't wait any longer," I said. "You should be more like me."

The Chief turned his fierce dark eyes on me and shook his mane of black hair. Even sitting down, Chief Moses, at six-foot-seven, and nearly three hundred pounds of dense muscle, was an intimidating specimen. And nice to have on your side.

"No way, White Man," he laughed. Even his redness had begun to fade some in the warm room.

The Chief was a mixture of bloodlines that he simplified to South Florida Seminole. He had wrestled 'gators at a tourist trap in the Everglades and unruly patrons as a bouncer in a Las Vegas casino. Before he came to the agency he had been a consultant to Indian tribes setting up reservation Bingo games. A lucrative occupation that he gradually got bored with.

For all of our joking around about our differences, we were like family to each other. We were even going to celebrate the Christmas holidays together. Not one of us had real family in the Bay Area, but we would have wanted to be together anyway. At least I thought so. But as my partners liked to tell me, I'm not always right.

I looked in the shopping bags and saw department store-wrapped gifts. "Come on and put these presents under the Christmas tree," I said. I led them upstairs to my rooms over the office. I had a kitchen, a bedroom, a bath, a small living room, a porch overhanging the backyard, and a personal gym, with weights, rowing machine, exercise bicycle, and my pride: a basketball court complete with parquet floor and an NBA-style glass backboard.

I put a plug in and the Christmas tree in the living room lit up in a spiral of frosted white lights. The glass ornaments glittered like colored ice, and the tinsel shimmered electric silver. I was a traditionalist when it came to Christmas trees. Right down to the tinsel.

Mickey looked at it and shook her head. "You should've bought a living Christmas tree so the forests wouldn't have to be cut."

"Come on," I said.

Chief Moses nodded in agreement with the lady. Mickey was my high-tech expert, and Chief Moses was my primal force, but when it came to nature and conservation they were like Greenpeace and the Sierra Club rolled into one. And since Mickey had started dating an environmental attorney named Mike Wesolski, who also happened to be a fanatical vegetarian, she had gotten even worse.

"Give me a break. They cut this noble fir at a tree farm in Oregon. They weren't cutting down a stand of virgin redwood in a national forest."

"Without trees there is no life," the Chief added. "Something the Great White Father in DC should learn."

I suspected he was putting me on, but I wasn't sure. I was never sure with the Chief. Not even when he threw in a reference to the Great Spirit, or Reagan and Bush.

"Please. Just put the damn presents under the tree," I said. "You can turn me over to the Sierra Club later for twenty lashes or whatever they do to Christmas Tree Criminals."

Under mild protest, and with some stifled laughter, Mickey and the Chief finally put their gifts under the freshly-cut sap-bleeding tree. I went into the kitchen and got us drinks. About that nobody protested at all. A Bud for the Chief, a glass of Sonoma County white wine for Mickey, and a Henry Weinhard's for me. All of the usuals for us creatures of habit. I put on a Christmas carol tape and told them I had an announcement to make.

"I've got a new client and a new case."

They applauded spontaneously.

"You'd better wait and hear about it first."

"At least you will be working," the Chief said.

"That's true." I went over the details of the case, but without mentioning the daughter's possible involvement.

My partners exchanged looks. No more applause. It was Mickey who spoke. She recited a detailed litany of the horrors of animal testing.

"That's not what Vernon Krift does," I insisted.

"How can you be sure?" she asked.

"This is not some noble act of liberation. This is extortion," I said.

"Then it is all yours," Chief Moses threw in.

"Fine. You already have a case, Chief." It was a Love Dick Special, a type of investigation increasingly in demand. Chief Moses was running checks on two men for a certain prosperous and divorced businesswoman named Shelly Detloff. Both had proposed to her, and she was considering marrying one or the other. The Chief was going into everything from finances to previous and current sexual partners. He had gotten all of the information he could from marriage licenses to credit history to civil judgments from the computer network we bought into, and now it was time to hit the streets for the rest of the more personal and sexual stories.

"Jeremiah, how can you do this? Don't you know that cosmetics are tested in the eyes of rabbits? To see how much of the product it takes to make them blind?" Mickey said, with much more emotion than reason.

"This is different. Besides, I'm not asking for your help. You have a case, too."

Mickey had just started to work on locating a runaway for a PI friend of mine, Jimart Arroyo. I had learned a lot from him during my days in the DA's office. He had since moved to San Diego for the warm climate, the Pacific beaches where you could actually swim, and the girls in skimpy bikinis or less.

and then lost. Mickey was working the mean streets on this one, hoping she wouldn't find that Vannessa was a teenage hooker or porno video star, or a crack addict, or dead.

If anyone could find her, Mickey could. We found that people in

The City were much more willing to unlock their doors and talk to a female PI than to a male investigator. Which is one reason women were increasingly going into the PI business with such success. Besides, women themselves claim to be better than men at the trade. Especially when it comes to finding something or someone. As proof they like to use the Refrigerator Test on us helpless males. How can a man, who can't find a bottle of ketchup behind the milk carton, ever find a missing person? They have a point. The Chief, the Great Tracker, as he calls himself in his lighter moments, is an exception, especially when it comes to kids.

I offered more drinks. They turned me down.

"How about dinner? My treat now that I have a case," I offered instead.

Mickey turned to me and said, "I don't feel like it." Then she asked, "Can you give me a ride home, Chief?"

"Mickey. You're kidding," I said, before Chief Moses could answer.

"I don't feel like watching you eat red meat," she said.

"I'll eat chicken. Well done. Okay?"

"You'll probably order veal."

"I haven't eaten veal in a year."

"After I twisted your arm," she insisted.

"It was after I read an article on how they were raised. Give me some credit. Besides, I'm into Chinese restaurants these days. My goal is to eat in a different one every week for the next two years."

"Well, maybe next week," Mickey said.

"How about telling me the truth? You just have another date with Wesolski, the Mad Polish Vegetarian," I charged.

"You're a hell of a perceptive detective," Mickey answered.

"I can give you a ride, lady," the Chief said.

That decided it. They put on their coats and got ready to leave.

"Stick to juror profiles," Mickey said, as she went out the door.

"We don't have any. Court's not in session," I reminded her.

It had no effect.

While I muttered a few curses to myself, they went down the stairs together to the Chief's King Cab pickup truck. He wasn't a great driver, and I hoped he'd make it to Mickey's apartment on the Embarcadero without running into a bus again. His truck was just out of the body shop after a collision with a city bus last month that damaged the truck bed and the chairs the Chief had put in the back. Now the back cover was off and the uncomfortable chairs gone. From Mickey's place, the Chief would have to drive himself over to the elegant bachelor-pad houseboat he lived on in Mission Creek. He had the good sense not to try to drive that floating glorified barge anywhere.

I called down after them from the porch as they started to walk away from the office into darkness. "Watch out for buses and cable cars. And wear your seat belts. It's the law. And don't run over any cats."

I didn't think they heard me. Or they just ignored me. I stood there for a few minutes in the cold, watching them walk down the street until they disappeared around a corner. Then I stared at the soft spun glow of a street lamp under a starless night. Over the lamp, clouds obscured the winter moon. A black and white cat wandered aimlessly along the sidewalk across the street. I started to shiver and went back inside. The carols played on. They didn't help my mood much.

I shut the music off, unplugged the tree, and tried to cheer myself up by putting on the Channel Five Evening News, hoping I would catch Wayne Walker covering the 49ers on the sports segment. No such luck, but I sat through the rest of the newscast anyway. It was worth it to see the lovely news anchor, Wendy Tokuda. If the news got too bad, I could always turn off the sound, and just watch her.

3

The Victorian we rented on Octavia Street in the Western Addition District was just a few blocks from California Street, where you could catch a cable car downtown. That saved you from losing your parking space and from paying the gouging parking garage rates. The only thing you had to battle were the tourists looking for Chinatown or Fisherman's Wharf.

But the Health Science Center was west across town in the other direction on the edge of the university campus. That meant taking the Muni No. 17 bus, or the "M" Light Rail vehicle. It was already ten o'clock and Krift was expecting me at ten thirty. Thinking it would be faster, I decided to drive. My first mistake of the day.

Mickey and the Chief were out on their respective cases, so I didn't expect them in this morning. I checked the tape in the video scanner that covered the porch and punched in the numerical sequence that set the digital alarm lock on the front door. With the office secured, I walked the four blocks south to where I had last managed to find a parking place for my black '56 Thunderbird coupe. It was the classic model, with the louvered air vent, the porthole windows, and the chrome spare tire cover. It ran well because of the Chief. Although he was a rotten driver, he was a hell of a mechanic.

I unlocked the car, got in, and abandoned my parking space to a woman double-parked behind me in a blue Honda Prelude with vanity plates that announced her car was PRLUD 10. At least without Mickey and the Chief with me I wouldn't have to listen to their usual gripes about the cramped quarters of the two-seater. Besides, as I liked to tell them, they were lucky that I had a bench front seat. In '56, Ford hadn't yet gone to bucket seats, which really would have been uncomfortable.

The mid-morning traffic was light and I got to the HSC with five minutes to spare. Then the real challenge began. I bought an overpriced parking permit from a vending machine by a campus entrance and started to hunt for a parking space. I might as well have been hunting for wild kangaroos in Palm Springs. As I made my way around the campus every lot was full, and the streets were jammed with double-parked cars. Hadn't anyone heard of public transportation? I finally took a chance on the parking garage on the extreme west edge of the campus. After trying each level, and finding even the illegal spots taken, I parked in a spot on the roof that was marked STATE CARS ONLY. Screw that. I was almost a half hour late already.

The brown stone buildings that filled the campus grounds were packed together, casting the faintest of cold shadows on each other. I imagined that if a major earthquake hit they would tumble into one another like giant broken dominoes. Overhead the silvery winter sky hung low and threatening. The blue blazer and camel crewneck sweater I wore were not enough to keep me warm. Driven by cold, my hands jammed into my pockets, I walked rapidly through the campus.

As I passed the library, I saw four Asian males in silver and black Raider jackets standing under the overhang by the entrance. It was clear to me that a drug deal of some kind was going down with a fifth male in a tan raincoat. That the transaction was out in the open didn't seem to bother any of them. It was like watching a gang do business on a street corner in East L.A. It took me another ten minutes to cross the rest of the campus. And I did it without noticing another illegal act.

The HSC building was about the darkest, bleakest, and probably the oldest, on campus. Architecturally I would describe it as a three-story shoe box. Only shoe boxes usually have a little more pizzazz.

When I opened its heavy main door, I was hit by a strange combination of odors. There was a smell that reminded me of the lion cage at the zoo on a hot summer day, commingled with the antiseptic odors of a hospital. Just the place you'd rather not be.

I got Krift's office number from the directory and followed an arrow to the 200 corridor. It was on the first floor in the east wing. I knocked on a solid wooden door that had 220 screwed in above the jam on the metal plate.

A voice I recognized as Krift's told me to come in.

I opened the door and stepped into an ice cold, cluttered office that didn't seem to go with his personality, or his style of dress. Books and papers were scattered about without any kind of apparent organization. On the walls were all kinds of anatomical charts of animals from cats to horses to whales to rats and mice. But no rabbits.

Krift and another man were sitting at a small table in the center of the office drinking coffee from mugs that had Save the Whales glazed on them. A nice touch for animal researchers.

"Nice of you to stop by," Krift said, as he shot his cuff and looked at his gold watch. He was wearing a wool turtleneck and a heavy ski sweater over that to fight off the cold.

"Had a problem parking," I explained.

"We all do. There are no spaces left after nine o'clock. I should have warned you."

"Obviously school isn't out for the holidays yet," I said.

"We're just finishing up finals. That brings out even more students than usual."

I shivered. "Is it always this damn cold in here?"

"Apparently this is part of the new campus energy conservation program. I've already filed a complaint about it."

I looked at the other man, who was holding the steaming cup of coffee to his lips.

"Want some coffee?" Krift asked.

"No thanks."

Then Krift remembered that there was someone else in the room and introduced us. The man's name was Dwight Snokes, and he was an associate professor of physiology. He had an office and a lab just down the hall, he told me, as he stood up and we shook hands.

I made Professor Snokes to be about fifty-five. He was around five-eight and must have weighed a solid one-eighty. His brown hair was cut in a brush style that was back in vogue these days, but I suspected he had worn it since the fifties. He only had on a light, out-of-style, sport jacket with leather elbow patches and a rumpled green shirt with a green and brown bow tie that looked clipped on. But he didn't seem cold. Overall he fit my image of a university professor much better than Krift did.

We all sat down. I waited for Krift to take the lead. After all, he was the one so concerned with keeping things quiet.

"We can talk about the cats," Krift said, with a hard stare at me. "Dwight knows that the cats are gone. He was with me when I found the note." I picked up on the meaning of his stare right away. Snokes didn't know that Claire might be involved. "I told him I've hired your agency to find the animals," he concluded.

Before I could say anything, Snokes took off his jacket and hung it over the back of his chair. He actually looked warm. I wondered what would go next. The man must have just moved here from above the Arctic Circle.

"Okay then. Did you hear from the CFAF?" I asked Krift, playing it straight.

"No. Not a word."

I looked around the office again. "Where's the lab?"

"Down the hall," Krift said. "Between my office and Dwight's."

"Take me there."

We stood up. As he picked up his coat, Snokes said, "Good luck. I hope you can help. This is a terrible thing to have happened, Mr. St. John."

"Just call me Jeremiah."

We all went to a more convenient first name basis before we stepped out into the hall. Snokes went to his own office, and Krift and I stopped in front of the door to Krift's lab.

"You didn't say anything about Claire to Snokes, I take it," I said.

"Of course not."

I looked at the lock.

"The lock and the door show no signs of forcible entry," I said. "Claire has a key?"

"Yes."

"Is Claire and the other lab assistant in there now?"

"Yes."

"I'd like to talk to them."

Inside the lab, two very attractive young women in white coats were sitting by a table that held a stack of metal slabs that looked like stainless steel cookie sheets. Beds for the cats, I figured.

I gave them a wave and they looked at me with curiosity.

"What are you planning to do?" Krift asked.

"I'm not in the fingerprint, hair, or fiber business. I'm mostly interested in how the CFAF got in. Now where were the cats kept?"

"In the back of the lab."

I looked at the now empty space. Just as I expected, there was nothing to go on. Except some traces of kitty litter on the floor that weren't going to help a bit. "Can I talk to your assistants?"

Krift signaled for them to come over. They got up from the table and came over together.

At six feet, Claire Krift had both the height and beauty of a model. She had her father's blond hair, but darker skin and dark velvet eyes. She had high cheekbones and a refined version of her father's nose. Even the lab coat couldn't hide a figure as good as Mickey's. I wished that Krift would let me interrogate her alone. I'd find out where the damn cats were.

On the other hand, Heather Clark was cute in a gamin way, rather than beautiful. She was five two, a little bit chubby, as if she had not lost all of her baby fat yet, with short reddish hair, green eyes, and a round and freckled pixie face.

With the preliminaries over, I asked them where they were Sunday night.

"We. . . I mean, *I* was at a party. Until almost three in the morning," Heather said. "With tons of people." She looked at Krift as if for confirmation, but he didn't offer any.

"Which gives you a great alibi."

"You don't suspect me, do you?" Heather asked, her tone full of indignation.

"Of course not."

Anyway, actually being present wasn't the point. Providing the key for access was. But I wanted to see what kind of reaction I got.

From Claire I got a cold unruffled stare, proving nothing at all. "I went to the movies with friends. Then out for pizza and beer."

"Until what time?"

"About one o'clock. I resent your implication, Mr. St. John."

"No implication intended. None at all." I smiled one of my best and most charming ones. It almost worked.

"Well, okay," Claire said, without enthusiasm.

I tried a few more questions, but I didn't get much more from them. I decided I needed someone willing to talk to me about Claire and Heather. To get a more objective reading of the two.

I walked with Krift to the door and shifted my ground. "Are there gangs on campus?" I asked.

"Why?"

"Something I saw on the way over here."

"Something that looked like gang activity?"

"Yes."

"The university reflects society. We can't escape into an ivory tower anymore. There's everything on campus. Including gangs."

"Asian gangs in Raider jackets?"

"A particularly vicious and clever group. Mostly students or former students. We recruited them from L.A. God knows why."

I walked with Krift to the door. "Call me as soon as you hear from the CFAF."

He nodded.

We were just about out of hearing range of the two women and I asked Krift softly about something I had been wondering about since his visit to my office, "If she hates you so much, why is Claire working as your assistant?" I had an answer, but I wanted to hear his.

"Infiltrate the enemy."

"That's what I thought. But why do you let her?"

"I'm hoping she'll forgive me."

"For what?"

"That's not relevant."

"We'll see."

With those final whispered words, I left Krift alone in his lab with Heather and Claire. I needed to know more about all three of them.

4

I wandered down the hall in search of Professor Snokes, and found him alone in an office that was cold as a meat locker. It made Krift's seem almost like a sauna. Aromatic Cherry Blend pipe smoke filled the space with a soft white fog that could have been cold breath. But Snokes had his sport jacket off again, and this time he had removed his bow tie and unbuttoned his collar. His feet were up on an old wooden desk. At least he wasn't wearing sandals. When I came in he didn't move a muscle except to point to a chair.

I took it and said, "For a moment there I thought you were having your body frozen in the interests of science."

"I suspect the university is attempting it. But I'm not ready for cryogenics yet."

"You're dressing for it."

"I believe in dressing the same in winter or summer, heat or cold. The body adjusts." He toyed with the brown and green bow tie he still had in his hands.

"Nice theory, probably works in Hawaii, but I think I'll stick to wool clothing in San Francisco."

The room was smaller than Krift's, but also much neater. The books were all shelved in the cases that lined most of the wall space and there were no papers cluttering a desk on which stood a framed picture of a beautiful Asian woman.

"My wife," he said, following my eyes.

A copy machine stood in one corner next to a pair of filing cabinets. I noticed scratches by the locks.

Snokes had put his personal stamp on the office beyond the orderliness and the picture of his wife. The empty wall space was covered with dozens of black and white pictures of wrestling teams and individual shots of a young man who had to be Snokes himself. Interspersed among the pictures were about a dozen plaques and awards.

I made a sweeping gesture towards the impressive collection. "You must have been quite a wrestler."

"At Cal in the fifties I was an NCAA champion in my weight class," he said, with obvious pride. "Put on some weight since then." He put down the bow tie and patted his stomach—which was not yet a gut, but was slowly getting there.

I looked at his memorabilia again. "You must have your trophies locked up."

Snokes swung his feet down from the desk and laughed. "There's no room in this little office for them all. Besides, this urban campus is not exactly what you would call the epitome of security."

"What do you do these days?" I asked, bringing us back to the present.

"What do you mean?"

"Instead of wrestling."

"Oh. Workouts in the university gym. Some swimming. I try to stay in shape at least. But it's a tough battle. I exercise and then I want to eat more." He tapped his pipe clean in a clear glass ashtray on his desk. He hung the pipe up on a small ceramic rack that held three others next to the ashtray.

"I take it you didn't come here to find out about my exercise routine, St. John. What do you want? I've got to get back to work." Although he did it with a smile, Snokes went cold and formal on me.

I just went cold. I blew on my hands and rubbed them together. "I'd like some information about Heather Clark and Claire Krift."

"Not much I can tell you. They're just two lab assistants, except that Claire happens to be Krift's daughter." He tried to give me an angelic smile. It was probably the same smile he gave before crushing a wrestling opponent in the fifties.

"That's not anything," I said.

He shrugged. "I warned you."

If he knew anything more, he wasn't about to tell me right now.

"Who can I talk to about them?"

"What are you trying to find out?"

"I'm not sure. I'm investigating possibilities." But I did have an angle I wanted to pursue. "I'd like to talk to your lab assistants." I figured these students would make up a tight-knit group with an effective grapevine, and a tendency towards gossip—as you find in most relatively homogenous groups. Nothing is more fascinating than what someone like you is doing. Or not doing.

"I don't want you interrupting their work."

"Wouldn't dream of it." I checked my watch. It was almost noon. "Do they break for lunch at twelve?"

"Yes."

"I'll buy them lunch. Struggling students should appreciate that."

"Have them back here at one."

"No problem. By the way, what kind of guy is Krift?" I thought Snokes wouldn't have much to say, but I was wrong.

"Professor Krift is a star. We recruited him away from UC San Diego."

"He didn't tell me that. But isn't that a strange way to go?" It was hard to imagine Krift, as a star, leaving the University of California for a less prestigious university since it has the vast majority of research funds in the state, unless Krift was trying to escape from some kind of intolerable situation. I got my answer quickly.

"There was a scandal down there. His wife committed suicide, and so he wanted out."

"Any other details?"

"It was over a coed."

"Interesting."

Snokes went silent and led me to his lab. I blocked out the animal smell and looked around. Nothing larger than laboratory mice in cages and a lot of expensive-looking equipment. The biggest piece looked like a futuristic chrome sewing machine. Besides seeing the white mice, I met Wayne Ness and Olivia Shimoda.

Wayne was tall, at least six four, and wiry. Under a head of thin brown hair, that he pulled back into a skimpy pony tail like an Indian, he had a sharp fox face with heavy brows, darting brown eyes, a struggling wisp of a mustache on his upper lip, and a few touches of the adolescent acne curse.

Olivia was short, dark, and beautiful with cascading black hair, dark Oriental eyes, and perfect unmadeup skin. She smiled at me with a flawless white crescent of teeth. Even under the lab coat I could tell that she would fill out any other outfit in all the right places. But she also looked very young. Maybe even still in her teens.

"Mr. St. John is a private investigator, and he's taking you two out to lunch," was all Snokes said before he left the room.

Wayne and Olivia looked at me.

"What do you want with us?" Wayne asked.

"I want to buy you lunch." Actually I wanted to buy one of them lunch, preferably the short pretty one. Alone with one of them I could find out much more, together they would be inhibited. At least that was my rationale. But I had both for starters. I'd do the best I could until I could lose Ness.

"There's a cafeteria in the basement," Wayne said. "We'd better eat there so we can get back by one."

Although this was not exactly my choice for a San Francisco restaurant, we went to dine in the basement. The first thing I saw as I came down the stairs was a huge No Smoking sign in six languages. The animal smell that permeated the rest of the building was present in the cafeteria as well. But at least there were the competing odors of institutional cooking. I wasn't sure if that was better or worse. On the other hand, Wayne and Olivia didn't seem to notice. We got trays and joined a slow-moving line that took us past warming pans of lunch entrees and assorted complementary vegetables. The two lab assistants piled up their trays with what passed for a meatless lasagna. But the smell in the place had put the kibosh on my appetite. The only thing I was willing to try was a previously-wrapped turkey sandwich on white. No beer to go along with the no smoking. I took a can of Pepsi instead.

The cafeteria was crowded and noisy, but we did find a small table in the corner by an atrium window that looked out on a small garden plot cut all the way down to basement level. So far, this was the most pleasant place I had seen in the entire building.

I let them get through most of their meal with nothing more than occasional small talk. Half of my sandwich was gone and I was through. I sipped my Pepsi and started on Olivia.

"Call me Ollie," she said.

"Sure. As long as you don't call me Jerry, instead of Jeremiah."

"Agreed."

"What are you working on with Snokes?"

"Transgenic animals."

"I need a little help on that one."

"Most people do," Wayne said. "We're working on the transfer of foreign genes into laboratory mice."

"For some good end?"

Ollie took it up. "A transgenic animal can be used to study how defective genes can cause hereditary diseases or lead to cancer. Such animals are invaluable for creating models for studying the tumor-growth process."

"And Snokes can do this?"

"Oh, a lot of researchers can," Ollie said. "But they have to work over a microscope, guiding a tiny needle into a fertilized egg, and then they inject that egg with a foreign gene to get their result. They use something like that chrome device we have in the lab."

"And Snokes is on to something better?" I asked.

Wayne took over. "Yes. Snokes is trying to develop a simple process using animal sperm to get the same result."

"Fascinating," I said.

"The old method is successful only about five percent of the time," Wayne said.

"And Snokes can do better?"

"He's projecting a thirty percent success rate," Ollie said.

"Projecting?"

"There's a lot of skepticism about Snokes' approach," Ollie said.

"But it can work. We have proof. We have the mice," Wayne insisted.

"What can you tell me about Claire Krift?" I asked, changing the subject. I felt as if I were injecting a foreign gene into the scientific conversation.

Before Ollie could get a word in, Wayne gave me his answer, "She's got a fantastic mind. She's one of the best students we have."

And a great body, I thought. Something that I was sure had not escaped Wayne's notice. I had a feeling this was not all objective information. I looked at Ollie, but she just smiled. She didn't look like she necessarily agreed, however. But she also wasn't going to contradict Wayne. This was the problem I feared would develop.

"What about Heather?"

Wayne again. "She's not one of our brighter students."

"But don't Krift and the others pick up the top students?"

They looked at me like I was a fool. And naive. I got it before Ness blurted it out. "Everyone says she's sleeping with the professor."

"Are they right?" I asked Ollie.

"Yes," she said reluctantly. She sounded sure. Like it was more than just the usual gossip. "That's why she came here from San Diego."

"Was she the student involved in Krift's scandal down there?" I asked.

Ollie and Wayne exchanged glances. They both shrugged at me. "I don't know for sure, but that's what we heard," Ollie said, and Wayne nodded.

I decided against pushing it right now. I was getting the idea of why Claire hated her father. It must be hell working with Heather.

I asked them if they wanted anything else to eat. They eagerly went back for dessert. Having checked out the selection before, I passed.

Over her dessert, I said to Ollie, "You look awfully young to be a lab assistant."

Wayne broke in. "She's the only undergrad doing it."

"Special treatment?" I asked.

Ollie blushed. It was a beautiful sight.

"I've been involved in the program since I was a freshman."

"And now?"

"I'm an eighteen-year-old junior."

I whistled. "That's precocious."

Ollie blushed again. It was a nice trait.

"Yes, it is," Wayne assured me. "She finished high school when she was fifteen."

"I'm impressed." In more ways than one, with this genius.

This time she just smiled without a blush.

At five to one we bussed our trays and the two lab assistants started to rush back to work.

"I don't think the mice will mind if you're late," I said.

"But Snokes will," they said in unison.

"What's his problem?" I asked.

"He's looking for promotion to full professor this year. And a lot depends on getting his grant renewed," Wayne said.

"And what will that take?"

"Some more successful gene transfers through sperm," Ollie said.

They started up the steps. I held my breath and followed.

They went back to the lab to work on transgenics and I got out of the building. Outside I was glad to breathe the city air, even if it was full of exhaust emissions. At least these days they were unleaded.

5

I was in a quandary. According to my client I couldn't pressure Claire for any information she may have, so my easiest route to the stolen cats was cut off. But Krift didn't stipulate that I couldn't tail her, so I decided to do just that, and see where she led me. If that didn't get me anywhere, I made preparations to implement a backup plan. When it came to plans, I had quantity, if not quality.

I parked my car on a street several blocks away from the HSC—at least that evening you could actually get a parking space near campus—so that in case there was any kind of problem the campus police or the city cops couldn't get to me through the plates.

I picked her up at six o'clock when she left the HSC, and followed her on foot to an apartment complex a few blocks from the campus. She disappeared into her second floor apartment, and I needed a cover. What I had was an empty briefcase and an outfit that consisted of a sweater and sports jacket. So I decided on my best cover and spent the next four hours acting like a pesky magazine salesman. One that was getting progressively colder. I even made a few pitches for authenticity and warmth, ignoring No Solicitors signs, trying to feel heat before a door was slammed in my face. Which happened every time, except for a drunk student who wanted to subscribe to *Penthouse* for those "pink shots." I had to disappoint him, telling him that since we were a Christian magazine outfit we didn't carry stuff like that. When he persisted, I slammed the door on *him* as I kept my eye on the landing in front of Claire's place. At ten o'clock I decided Claire was not coming out. Or she had climbed out through a rear second story window and lost me. In either case, it was time for a shift of tactics.

So I went to my backup plan. After a stop at my car to change clothes and to pick up some other supplies, I staked out the HSC building in what had become a bitter cold night. I was standing behind an eucalyptus tree, dressed in a navy blue pilot's jacket, trying not to freeze my butt off. I had on Nike running shoes in case I needed to do some quick moving, but they didn't do much to keep my feet warm. Under a canopy of high clouds and low fog, the HSC looked as attractive as San Quentin.

A parking lot stretched out between the building and me. At eleven o'clock there were still a half dozen cars in the lot. All with proper reserve parking decals on their bumpers. I shivered, wiggled my numb toes, and waited. When it got too cold, I took a swig of Korbel brandy for warmth from a flask I had taken from the T-Bird. By half past midnight the last car, driven by a young woman alone, had left the lot and disappeared into the fog like a train into a tunnel.

My second plan was simple. Krift had told me that there was custodial service every night because researchers worked in the labs weekdays, weekends, and holidays, and that a man named Hector Fernandez was there the Sunday night of the break-in. And he was also working tonight. Krift wanted to keep things as quiet as possible so he insisted that I wait until everyone else had left the building before I spoke to Hector. The reason I was out here freezing my butt off until now.

I hit the brandy. I hadn't seen a sign of the campus police so far. With everyone else gone I was ready to find Hector.

The lights went off in a lab, then a minute later went on in an adjacent one. It had to be the custodian at work. I looked over the layout of the building again. A large industrial dumpster was on the south end next to the loading dock. Any custodian who was doing his job would have to make several trips out to it during the night. With a chance of seeing a vehicle that could have been used to haul off the cats and cages. I figured it had to be a truck or a van. I was betting on a closed van. And I was betting on Hector Fernandez for my first real lead in the Great Catnapping Caper Case.

I crossed the empty parking lot and started checking doors. They were all locked. What a night to start taking care of security.

I should have waited until Hector came out to unload some garbage into the dumpster. But the threat of frostbite made me impatient. I went up to the one lighted first-floor room in the building. I could see Hector, a well-built man in his late twenties who was probably Mexican, at work. He wore earphones plugged into a radio in the back pocket of his jeans, and was mopping the floor to a rhythm that suggested a tango.

I pulled out my ID, and knocked on the window glass. Hector took off his earphones and stopped the dance. He stepped to the window and stared at the ID. He was close enough to see it, even through the glare of his own reflection. His first reaction was to tug violently at his mustache, then to run his fingers through his wavy black hair. Around his thick neck he wore a heavy gold cross on a gold chain. He suddenly gripped it in his hand. His color went from Mexican brown to sickly white. He slipped out of the room and closed the door.

He had taken me for an INS agent on the prowl for illegals. I chased him to two other rooms with no more success, despite my shouted assurances that I was only a private investigator with no power to deport him to anywhere. Hector pretended not to understand English. I shouted louder. I kicked myself for not waiting until he came out to the dumpster. Now there was no chance.

I wandered around the building looking for some way to get in. But no one had done me the favor of unlocking a door, and I couldn't find a window that could be opened. My lock picks were back at the office because I hadn't expected to need them tonight.

I realized I should have gotten a key to the building from Krift, and I considered calling him. Until someone called to me.

"Hold it!" It was an unpleasantly high male voice.

"Damn!" I muttered. It had to be the campus cops investigating some very suspicious behavior. Suddenly, in the window in front of me, I saw Hector's smiling face. The son of a bitch had called them. Smart move on his part.

I turned around and saw two cops, one male, one female, in a blue and white campus police car. As they started to get out of it I decided that I didn't want to answer any questions. Luckily, I was near the corner of the building and I quickly cut around it and out of their sight. I heard them get back into the car and start after me.

Only there was no road where I was going.

I took off through the darkness into a half acre of bushes and trees. I pushed the branches away that tried to slash at my face. The starless night would help me. Behind me, the two cops deserted the car, but it was too late. I cut through the grove and was out on the street and I hoped out of their jurisdiction. But I doubted it. They were coming along the sidewalk behind me with their guns out. I didn't realize the campus cops had weapons. This gave me a new respect for them; they could be harmful to your health. Fortunately, with my Nike running shoes, I easily put enough distance between us. Around a corner I cut back into the campus and lay down in high ground cover behind some thick juniper bushes. The cops walked past me, then finally turned around after they had gone another block.

"Well, at least he's off the campus," the woman said, as they came back past my hiding place. She holstered her gun.

"Yeah." The man still had his weapon out.

"You think he's a rapist?" she asked.

"Nah. He'd be hanging around the women's dorms."

"This guy hangs around the animal labs."

"So what does that tell ya about him?" he asked.

"Black Bart's girl," she said in reference to the old joke about a man and his jealous love for a certain sheep.

They both broke into giggles. Funny.

"He's probably just another harmless voyeur. But let's get over to the women's dorms. Just in case," he said. They dissolved into the dark campus.

I waited about ten minutes, brushed off dirt and leaves from my clothes, and went back to my car. I considered my options. Hector would be getting off at eight, and trying like hell to avoid me. I could go back to my place and get a few hours sleep in a bed. Or I could swig some more of the brandy right here and go to sleep in the car and let the dawn wake me. I wanted to be in a warm bed, but I didn't feel like driving back and then getting up to come back out there. I drank the brandy and lay down across the front seat, out of sight. I thought about Mickey, and thought about Olivia, or rather Ollie, Shimoda, who was a nice, if somewhat guilty addition to my fantasy life, and fell happily asleep.

I slept through what must have been a sunless dawn. When I woke up it was nearly eight o'clock and gray and overcast. I had a hangover headache that matched the miserable weather. Forgetting caution, I drove over to the HSC parking lot and got out. I figured Hector would try to get away by a rear entrance. I looked for my campus cop friends, but saw no one. I went to a corner of the building and waited. My main occupation for the last fourteen hours, if you included my futile time at the apartment complex.

At a minute after eight Hector came out of a basement door. When it closed behind him, I sprinted towards the man. He looked back at the apparently locked door, hesitated, then began to run. But I was on him before he could cover thirty yards. Hector was short and slow, but solid. When I hit him with a low hard tackle he almost didn't buckle at the knees. Almost. When he did go down he came up swinging. Until he saw the S&W .38. No more bullshit. This long shot was taking way too much time and energy.

"I'm not with Immigration," I shouted even louder than before, hoping to make him understand English. Either my shouting or the gun worked a miracle. Hector now spoke in tongues. Or rather the tongue of Barrio English.

"Wha' chou wan', man?"

"I want some information about Sunday night."

"I was workin' here Sunday night." He brushed his pants off. "I didn' do nothin'."

"I know. That's what I'm talking about. Did you see anything unusual that night?"

"I didn' see nothin'." He took out a comb and started to fix his thick hair.

I switched from my gun to my wallet. I held up a folded twenty, hoping to improve his eyesight, as well as his English.

"What about a truck or a van at the loading dock? Probably real late at night."

"Why didn' chou say so?" He finished with the comb and held out his hand for the twenty.

I gave it to him.

"I didn' know what chou was talkin' 'bout there. Sure. Wha's the big deal? There was this van pulled up to the dock 'bout three ayem Sunday mornin'."

"What was going on?"

"I don' know. Loadin' animals, I guess. Happens roun' here a lot."

"In the middle of the night?"

"We got some *loco* people workin' here." He pointed a forefinger at his head and made several circles with it. The international code to identify lunatics.

I did the same, then asked, "Did you get a license?"

"Wha' chou think, man? I didn' get no license. Wha' for? But I got somethin' else." He smiled broadly.

"If I'll pay."

"*Si, Senor.*"

I laid another twenty on him.

"This van had some kinda animal painted on it."

"What kind?"

"I didn' get a good look. Maybe it was two kinds. Or maybe not."

"Try to remember."

"Can', man."

"Anything else?"

Hector hesitated. "The van, it had. . . letters painted on it."

"What'd they say?" This was more like it.

Hector hesitated again. He rubbed his shoe along the ground like a nervous schoolboy who didn't have the right answer. "I don' know."

Missing the point, I reached for my wallet again.

"No, man. Ain' it. I can' read no English."

"Damn." I thought it over. There had to be another way. "What if you saw the van again? Would you recognize it?"

"Sure. I can do that. But wha' chou think? It's gonna come drivin' up here jus' this minute jus' for chou, man?"

I had a better idea. "You working tonight?"

"*Si.* Sunday through Thursday."

"I'll be back tonight with something for you to look at."

"Hokay. But man, donchou forget your wallet."

"I wouldn't do that, Hector," I promised.

6

After too much brandy during the night, I needed to absorb the alcohol into a solid breakfast. There wasn't much point in trying to find anything to eat on campus. There were only three days until Christmas, and if I remembered correctly, finals were over. In contrast to the overflowing parking lots of yesterday, the place was as shut down as a GM plant during model changeover time. Except for the dedicated researchers who were returning this morning like homing pigeons to the HSC labs. I wanted to see Krift, but not until I got some food into my stomach. I wondered for a moment if the basement cafeteria was open, but decided, even if it was, that I didn't want to handle those animal house odors while I ate.

Instead, I drove to the nearest McDonald's. With my appetite spurred on by its aromatic fast food smells, I went for a large orange juice, two classic egg McMuffins, double hash browns, a blueberry muffin, and a giant cup of black coffee. The meal revived me.

Krift was alone in his office at the HSC, sitting at his desk filling out some forms. Today it was actually so warm in the room that Krift didn't even have on a sweater.

"You have heat," I noted. "Quite a change."

"I told you, I filed a complaint."

"And you got results. Amazing."

He shrugged casually. Like it was nothing for a guy with clout like him. A star, like Snokes said.

I sat down across from him.

"Damn university paperwork," he muttered, as he pushed the forms away. He had not heard from the CFAF. I assured him that I had a lead that had nothing to do with his daughter, but that I needed a list of companies doing business with the Center. I was particularly interested in animal suppliers. He swiveled around in his chair and logged onto his computer, and printed out the information I requested in a matter of minutes. I was surprised to see several pet stores included.

"You think one of our suppliers is involved?" Krift asked, as he swiveled back to his desk.

"It's possible."

"I doubt it," he said, as he picked up his pen.

"Any of these companies have vans with some kind of animal logo painted on it?"

"What kind of animal?" He looked at his paperwork.

"I don't know. Maybe two animals," I said.

"Two?"

"I can't say for sure."

"And?"

"That's it so far."

"That is impressive detective work," he said and slammed down the pen.

"Are you going to help me or not?" I said, as I got up.

"Sorry. I'm getting impatient. Most of them have some kind of animal logo. But who pays attention?"

"That's what I figured. Why are these pet stores listed here?"

"They often have lucrative sidelines. Along with pets, they'll deal with lab animals as well."

"And in some cases an animal can either end up a pet or an experiment."

"Yes."

"So a sale is a sale," I said, as I folded up the green printout and started for the door.

"What are you going to do?" he asked.

"Take some pictures."

"This is your only lead?"

"So far."

"Did you talk to Hector Fernandez yet?"

"Where do you think I got this lead?"

"Good luck," he said. As a sharp PI, I picked up on the irony right away. I was tempted to start asking him some questions about Heather and San Diego. Let him know what a competent PI could find out. But I thought better of it and let it go. I left Krift to his work and went to mine.

I got my Polaroid and two packs of film out of the trunk of my T-Bird and started my tour of the city. By three I had pictures of every van associated with a business on the list even if I had to go out on delivery routes to get them. And I had to come up with a good story to get copies of those routes from the office. I imagined a few of the drivers would be quite surprised to learn that an attorney from Fresno who thought they might be due an inheritance was in looking for them. I hoped none of them quit because they thought they had struck it rich. But I had what I needed for tonight. My collection of animal logos ran from a white mouse to two giraffes to a lineup for Noah's Ark.

With my technically sophisticated photographic work done, I drove back to the office and found it empty. I assumed the Chief and Mickey were hard at work on their cases. The Love Dick and the Runaway. Like I was on mine.

At four o'clock, while I was doing some year-end paperwork at my desk, Krift called. Things were heating up feline-wise on his side of town.

"The CFAF has asked for ten thousand dollars."

I whistled. "Are you going to pay it?"

"I don't want to. That's why I hired you."

"Let me put a little pressure on Claire."

"No."

"Gentle pressure."

"It won't work. You'd have to beat it out of her."

"I have better ways than that, Krift."

"No. You don't question her."

I looked out my window. The sky was smoky and dark. "Okay. It's your money. And your cats. So stall."

"You're working on that lead from Hernandez?" he asked.

"Yeah." I could tell he wasn't expecting much from it.

"They've given me twenty-four hours to come up with the money."

"That should be enough time," I promised, and hoped I could deliver. I hung up the phone just as I heard my partners come in from the porch and settle in their adjoining offices.

I came out of mine to tell them about the ten thousand dollar twist in the case. At least that got them to go to dinner with me.

We ate at the Hyde Street Grille, a no-frills kind of place with whitewashed walls and plain storefront windows that happened to be one of our favorite restaurants. We talked over our cases while we consumed two hot and spicy Pakistani chicken dishes and a salad for the lady. After dinner, once again she turned me down. This time for a nightcap and a visit to the HSC. Instead she asked the Chief to drive her home.

"Don't you want to meet Hector?" I asked, as they got ready to leave and, I suspected, ready to stick me with the check. "Charming guy. Really."

"No," Mickey said.

"The CFAF is extorting ten grand. This is not a noble animal rights venture. This is a felony."

"No comment," Mickey and the Chief said in unison. I was tempted to tell them about Claire, but that would only support their argument. I could just hear the two of them. Even his own daughter is opposed to his work. So in frustration I shut up.

Almost. I went back to my other point. Ever persistent, and not ashamed to beg, I tried Mickey once more.

"Please," I said, giving her a soulful look.

"I've got a date with Mike," she said. "A Greenearth meeting. They're getting ready to go to sea."

"I hope you and Wesolski and the rest of them can save the planet."

"Actually, it's the whales, tonight."

To my pleasant surprise, Mickey picked up the check.

* * *

I got to the HSC just as Hector was arriving. We went inside the building and sat down in a lounge on uncomfortable orange plastic furniture. I showed Hector the picture collection. When he went through them and gave me a blank stare I showed him a fifty.

"This it, man." He selected a picture.

"You sure?"

"Didn' I say so?"

I was looking at a pet store truck with a dog and a cat painted on the side panel. Two animals. The name of the place was Dogg's Pets and Supplies. As Krift had said, pet stores sometimes had sidelines. With the fifty pocketed, Hector went to work, whistling to whatever he was hearing in the headphones he'd put on.

If I was going to liberate Krift's cats it would have to be tonight. I had come prepared. First, I changed in the restroom into black pants and a black turtleneck to play the part of a thief. It was the same outfit I'd worn when I'd attempted Hamlet as a college drama major years ago. Now I had a better use for it. But I needed an appropriate vehicle as well, one that could accommodate eight cat cages, which meant the T-Bird was out of the question. Unless I just took them out of the cages and put them in the front. Or in the trunk. Neither idea appealed to me. But I knew where to find the right kind of vehicle.

I drove over to Mission Creek where the Chief had his floating digs. I looked down the dock towards the line of houseboats and the dark waters beyond. Dim lights were on in the Chief's and it was rocking harder than could be accounted for by the light wave action. The decline in AIDS hysteria among heterosexuals had improved the Chief's sex life. He no longer went around complaining about the White Man's curse on casual sex. Instead, his favorite line was now, Lust Is Back. I assumed he would be occupied.

I found his King Cab pickup in the marina lot and parked next to it. I knew he wouldn't lend it to me to rescue the cats, so I did the next best thing. I left my classic T-Bird behind as security and hot-wired his truck in under five minutes, and took off with it. The houseboat, its chimney puffing gray smoke from the free-standing fireplace inside, rocked on.

I drove over to Dogg's Pets and parked in an unlighted spot next to the van behind the building. I took out a pocket flashlight and went up to the backdoor and windows. Everything was locked up, as I'd expected. I pulled out of my pocket an object that looked like a thin penknife. It held an assortment of metal sticks of various sizes and shapes. I selected a pick and worked on the back door lock while I held the flashlight in my mouth. After a couple of minutes of work the lock clicked and I opened the door. No alarm that I could hear, but that didn't mean it wasn't hooked up directly to a police station.

It was like walking into a combination monkey cage, tiger cage, and aviary. All of which came to life when I came in. I went past monkeys and parrots in the back room. The birds cursed at me or told me they loved me or what they wanted to eat. I went through the store, passing among rows of stationary cages that mostly held puppies and exotic-looking cats. No sign of my alley cats.

I tried a side door that had an Employees Only sign on it. In the room were the eight portable cages. I checked them and found the eight alley cats–half of which were black. Complete with tattoos. Easy enough so far.

Accompanied by a cacophony of animal noises, I loaded the relatively quiet cats, two cages at a time, into the truck. Just as I was finishing I heard a police siren heading my way. Time to get the hell out of there. On the street I passed by a police car heading towards the pet shop. I hoped no one had spotted the license plate. I wouldn't want to get the Chief in any deep shit.

I called Krift from a Chevron gas station phone booth and told him to meet me at the lab. I got there first and had Wayne and Ollie, who were working all night on Snokes' transgenes project, help me unload the cats. Hector had a key for the lab and, without asking for another tip, let us in.

"Merry Christmas," I said to Krift as he came in wearing jeans and a sweatshirt under a ski jacket that still had a lift pass hanging from it. A new look for the man.

He ignored Ollie and me and instead rushed to the cats and checked their ears. When he was done with all eight of them he announced, "It's them."

"I should have put bows on the cages," I said.

"Where did you find them?"

"Dogg's Pets and Supplies. The lead panned out."

"The bastard."

I left him to his precious alley cats and turned to Ollie. She looked tired.

"You're up too late for such a young kid."

"Oh yeah?" Then she smiled. "I am getting tired. I'd like to get out of here."

"Is that some kind of invitation?"

"What do you think?" She took off her lab coat and immediately looked great in a pink sweater and jeans.

Because of her somewhat tender age I was uncomfortable for a moment. But only for a moment. Then I figured what the hell. She was a beautiful girl. "I think I'll take you up on it."

"That's what you're supposed to do." She was flirting with me and I was enjoying it a lot. We went to Snokes' lab to tell Wayne we were leaving. I was surprised how he reacted. He seemed relieved, even happy to let her go.

We drove across town to Van Ness, the widest boulevard in the city. I was sure we could find some place open there. At this hour the traffic lights were all blinking amber. The best time to drive in the city.

We passed Harry's, the Hard Rock, and Tommy's Joynt. Then we found an all-night diner and went in. It was in the silver railroad car style of the fifties. We took seats across from each other in a red vinyl booth that had a rolodex of jukebox selections on the wall between the sugar and the ketchup. I put in quarters and she picked the music, which turned out to be heavy metal with unintelligible lyrics. Which was fine with me. For the first twenty minutes we were the only customers in the place.

After I told her a little about the cat rescue, Ollie told me a lot about herself, beginning with her Japanese ancestry. I knew she was too young, but I couldn't help but find her attractive in a tomboyish and yet exotic way. Did I see her as some stereotypical Cherry Blossom girl who would fulfill my Occidental geisha fantasies? Which made me feel damn uncomfortable again.

She told me how her grandparents had been interred in a camp during World War II. And from that somehow we got on to Snokes. She said, "He's okay. But he's a little too friendly at times."

"What do you mean?"

"Nothing really. Just too much patting and touching." Then she wanted out of the subject. Which was again fine with me.

We got safely into sports and I told her about my gym, basketball, and tennis, my current obsession.

"I play badminton," she countered over her piece of cherry pie and ice cream.

"Badminton?" I wouldn't have been more surprised if she'd said croquet. I put more cream into my hot coffee.

"It's a lot tougher than people think."

"Sure." I handed her another quarter for the jukebox.

"You sound skeptical. Ever play it?" She picked out a classic Righteous Brothers blue-eyed soul ballad this time.

"At picnics."

"I'm talking about the real sport. It's in the Olympics now." She made a few flicking motions with her wrists to demonstrate the strokes.

"I'm impressed." Though I wasn't quite sure I believed her.

"You ought to try it." She finished her pie and her glass of milk.

"My ceilings are too low."

She smiled. "There are other places to play, silly."

"Is that another invitation?"

"What do you think?" she said again.

"I think you're on," I said.

We shook hands. For quite a bit longer than it usually took for that ritual to be accomplished.

I thought to ask her if she had a boyfriend. I was still holding her hand when I decided I didn't want to know right now.

7

I left the Chief's pickup parked on Van Ness, then Ollie and I spent the rest of the starless night just walking along a quiet Broadway where the few remaining sleazy topless joints were dark, and through North Beach—which had actually been a beach back in the nineteenth century when the bay ran between Telegraph and Russian Hills—where the Italian restaurants had closed hours ago, talking, ignoring the cold, or at least not minding it. When we passed a wino sleeping with his bottle in a cardboard box she said she felt real safe and comfortable with me. No comment.

From Columbus Avenue we walked west on North Point, then turned back east on Beach Street at the bocce ball courts, a remnant of Little Italy, and past Aquatic Park and the Maritime Museum to the North Waterfront.

At dawn we were at the piers along the bay east of the *Balclutha*, a square-rigged ship that served as a floating museum, shivering, waiting for the sun to rise above the ridge of the Berkeley Hills and over the night outline of the Oakland Bay Bridge. We held hands comfortably and watched the dark sky lighten gradually to gray overcast. I put my arms around her and we looked into each other's eyes. Hers had become almost black. The wind was making mine tear. We kissed for a very long moment. Like it was the most natural thing on the planet to do.

Even through our coats I could feel her breasts pressing hard against my chest. "I'd better get you to your dorm," I said, pulling back from her. Although her parents lived in San Francisco, Ollie had preferred to stay in the one dorm kept open during the winter break. Closer to her work, she explained.

"Yes. You are right." Now she looked uneasy. "I should get back," she said softly.

We kissed again, our tongues hard at play.

"I don't want to stop," she said.

"We'd better, kid."

"Don't call me that."

After one more French kiss, we broke it off. I felt like a teenager with his high school girlfriend.

She took my hand and we began a hunt for a taxi on the Embarcadero. Luckily we spotted one in service and it actually stopped when I waved at it. More good luck. We took it to the Chief's King Cab back on Van Ness, making out in the back seat for most of the way.

I paid off the driver, who looked Iranian and bored, and gave him too big a tip because I felt foolish about our antics in the back seat. The tip got me a squinty leer from the guy as he took off.

I was glad to see the pickup had not been stolen or ripped off. All hubcaps present and accounted for, no key scratches on the paint, and no broken windows. As long as the cops didn't get the license plate, Chief Moses might never know.

I drove south on Van Ness until Army Street, which I took east to the Chief's marina and parked the pickup by my car. I wanted to reclaim it early so the Chief would still be asleep in his houseboat.

"What are you doing?" Ollie asked, as I went to work on removing my hot-wiring job from the King Cab.

"Some repair work. I'm trading in this pickup," I explained lamely.

"Wasn't that illegal?" she asked as she caught on to what I had done to the pickup.

"Only if you're caught," I said as I finished off the job. "Like new," I said, thinking the Chief would never be able to tell. I led her over to my car. "Now taking this T-Bird is very legal. I even have the keys."

"I like it," she said, as she looked over my beautiful T-Bird.

"Finally, someone with taste when it comes to cars."

With the switch completed I got on Interstate 280 until I could exit close to 19th Avenue and the campus. The whole time Ollie kept her head on my shoulder and her thigh pressed hard against mine. Neither one of us said a word. In the rearview mirror I could see that her eyes were closed, but she wasn't sleeping. I got her to her dorm, which was across a narrow street from the main campus.

I parked in a loading zone and we got out of the car. We stopped in front of the entrance to the gray high-rise that loomed like an over-sized piece of Stonehenge. She looked up at me and then we had another long moment of a soul kiss.

"I wish you could come upstairs with me, but we have such old-fashioned rules here and a resident director who actually enforces them," she said, as she tightened her arms around me and looked up the side of the building as if wishing alone would carry us up there. I wished I could too, I thought, after I got over my mild surprise at the explicit suggestion. And then I wondered what the hell I was doing. Making out in the back seat of a cab. Kissing a coed in front of her dorm. Talking about going up to her room. Grow up Jeremiah.

"Call me," Ollie said, as she gave me her number. She took out her key, unlocked the main door, and went inside. I watched her pass through the lobby, unlock an interior door, and disappear into an elevator. I wondered if I would call her. Growing up can be hard to do.

After two nights with little sleep, I spent most of Friday in bed. I did get up late in the afternoon and told the Chief and Mickey that the Great Catnapping Caper Case was wrapped up. I went over the details and put up with their snide comments. I refused to get into a discussion of animal rights when the case had nothing to do with rights of any kind. Except the right to extort money.

After they left I called Ollie and spent a half hour on the phone with her. The words came with ease, but right afterwards I had no recollection of what they were. It didn't matter. We were falling in love.

After reluctantly hanging up, I went out to do a little extra Christmas shopping—for Ollie, and for me. I knew exactly what I wanted to buy.

On Christmas Eve I had work to do. I concentrated on the food I had promised to prepare and put Ollie out of my head as much as that was possible to do. This was not my specialty, but every once in a while I don't mind trying some cooking. Tonight I was doing a Beef Wellington. I went at it, spreading paté over the top of the tenderloin of beef and then rolling out some pie dough to form a crust around it. The whole thing held together even when I put it into the oven and stabbed a meat thermometer into its red and bloody heart. Amazing.

A little after six in the evening I heard some noises on the second story back porch. When I opened the door I found a light-furred cat with darker tiger markings scratching at the jamb. It had a female face that looked part Siamese, and a round body that looked all alley cat. I had never seen it around before in the neighborhood. The cat looked at me like she was nearsighted and then slipped by to get into the warm house. She must have climbed up one of the wooden pillars to get to the upper porch.

The next thing I knew she was meowing in front of the refrigerator. I poured her some milk, which she snubbed.

"I don't have cat food."

She meowed.

"And you're not getting the Beef Wellington."

She meowed.

I brought out some deli turkey and tore it up on a plate for her. She ate it all greedily, furiously gave her fur a bath, and then curled up under the Christmas tree as if she had spent the last ten years living with me.

When my partners showed up for the festivities I pointed out the sleeping animal.

"So?" the Chief asked.

"Male or female?" Mickey asked.

"Female," I said.

"Have you taken it in?" Mickey asked, with a cold look.

"Of course." My safest response with these two.

Mickey went over and stroked her. "Are you sure she's female?"

"Her face looks female," I said.

Chief Moses took a more scientific approach that annoyed the hell out of the cat and came to the same conclusion.

"She scratched my hand," he complained.

"You'd scratch somebody's hand too if they were examining you like that after you'd been asleep."

To me he said, "The animal must have a name."

"How about 'Walks at Night Like Fat Cat'? That sounds like a good Indian name," I suggested.

"For a squaw," he said.

"Hey, guys, how about we name her for her color?" Mickey asked, getting us away from the squaw bit, which she hated.

"Okay with me. But what color is she, exactly? I studied her fur. "I guess she looks tan. Like taffy."

"Taffy? She's tiger-striped in cinnamon," Mickey said. "Cinnamon. That's it."

"So my stray has a name."

Mickey stroked the newly-christened Cinnamon's back. The cat tried to bite her hand. Maybe this cat would be okay.

"What are we having for dinner?" Mickey asked, as she pulled her hand away.

"Beef Wellington," I said.

The Chief smiled.

The cat curled up in a corner and went to sleep.

After some comments from Mickey about eating lower on the food chain, we put all of our separate tastes aside and had Korbel champagne before dinner. I had several bottles of rare Landmark cabernet open and breathing, ready to be drunk with the Wellington. The crust was perfect, the paté warm, and the beef rare. We ate, drank, and despite my original denial, shared some of it with the cat, who woke up while we were eating dinner. She ate the paté and the beef, but ignored the crust.

After dessert we opened presents. The presents were generally useful from Chanel for Mickey, to driving gloves for the Chief, to tickets for me to see the finals of the pro tennis tournament staged by Volvo each year in San Francisco, a videotape of tennis instruction by Jimmy Conners and a case of Wilson tennis balls.

"But nothing for the cat?" Mickey noted, as she looked at the unwrapped gifts we had gotten through so far.

"I've got something." I went and got her an old yellow tennis ball to play with.

Cinnamon eyed it suspiciously.

"There."

After two bats at it, Cinnamon lost interest.

"It's too big," Mickey said.

"She needs catnip," the Chief said.

"Anybody hot to go shopping for a cat that's going to ignore anything we get her?"

There were no takers and we went back to opening our gifts while Cinnamon took another strenuous bath.

"Thanks for the sweater, Jeremiah," Mickey said and gave me a warm kiss on the lips.

"Damn. I forgot the mistletoe," Chief Moses said.

"Who needs it?" Mickey gave Chief Moses his kiss for the perfume and a book of Native American Art.

"Glad you like the sweater, Mickey. I was going to get you a see-through Teddy, but. . . "

She gave me a wicked smile. "That would have been fine. Probably I wouldn't have tried it on for you, like I'm trying on this sweater though." She pulled the green sweater on and shook her short hair out. Green, since it matched her eyes, was one of her favorite colors. "Fits great. I'll keep it."

The last one I opened was the one I'd bought myself.

"A badminton racket? Who's it from?" Mickey asked after I unwrapped it.

"It's a Yonex graphite badminton racket. From me."

"What happened to tennis?" Chief Moses asked.

"The weather's too bad right now. Besides, badminton is the new sport of the decade. It's going to be in the next Olympics." The last statement was true. I had confirmed it myself with some basic research.

"You know what I think?" Mickey asked.

"No," I said.

"I think there's a woman involved."

"No," I said. Thinking there was a beautiful girl involved, and that Mickey was pretty damned perceptive.

"What I think is that your ceiling is too low for the game," the Chief concluded.

"I hear there are great courts nearby in Japantown," I responded.

The cat meowed and started scratching an ear.

"You need to get her a flea collar," Mickey said.

"First thing in the morning. A silver one. I promise."

Christmas morning brought enough snow to actually stick to the ground and accumulate in Northern California. The first such snowfall in a dozen years. After feeding the cat some more left over Beef Wellington, and letting it out the front door, I called Ollie and we drove over the Oakland Bay Bridge to the East Bay and Tilden Park, where the radio said the snowfall had been the heaviest. The skeletal trees glistened with ice and the evergreens looked like they were wrapped in white veils. The ground was thick with soft cotton-candy snow. On the larger hills, kids were riding saucers and garbage can tops down the slopes. At first we both felt adult and awkward, but after an exchange of a few well-aimed snowballs, we lost our inhibitions and played like children. We even found an abandoned garbage can cover and took turns sliding down the largest hill we could locate in the park. After that we actually spent over an hour building a snowman. Who sort of looked like an overweight Ollie, it turned out. A snowwoman.

"Good likeness," I said, as I added the dark Asian eyes.

She responded with a snowball to the snowwoman's head. I let her have it with a snowball of my own. She hit me with a snowball in the gut and the war was on.

A half an hour later we agreed on a truce and I drove Ollie back to her dorm. Our goodbye was the most intense we had shared yet.

When I got back, tired and still wet and cold, while warm with desire, to the Victorian, I found the cat waiting for me on the front porch. After a moment's hesitation, I let her in and then went to find an open store where I could get cat food, cat litter, and the flea collar I had promised to buy. Luckily, the Chews were not celebrating Christmas and their Vietnamese grocery was open. I found the unfamiliar aisle under the pet food sign and headed for the feline side. I passed on a Yuppie version of litter made from old currency shredded by the Treasury. I settled for what looked like a bag of old-fashioned sand. Only it contained green crystals to fight odors. Then I loaded up on little cans of wet cat food and a big box of dry fish-flavored cereal that some cat on TV advertised.

"So you have a pet cat now?" the Chew brother called Hank asked, as he rang up the items on his register.

"And don't try to make a meal out of her," I said.

"Hey, Mr. St. John, we in America now. We eat American. Hot dog and apple pie." Hank had a hurt look on his face that made me feel bad.

"Just a joke. Merry Christmas."

"Same to you. This year we have a tree at home."

"So why are you open, Hank?"

"Everybody else closed. Good business."

No wonder these guys did so well.

I also stopped at a drug store that was open and bought a dozen latex condoms.

Back at my place I put the litter and the food dish and the water dish out on the back porch and after a ten minute struggle the silver collar around the cat's neck.

Perfect. Until she cried during the cold night. I let her cry for about a half an hour and then relented. She ended up sleeping at the foot of my bed. In the morning I had a twenty minute sneezing fit that suggested to me that the cat needed to be outdoors. I went shopping again. This time for a warm and cozy two-story cat condo, one lined with green pile carpet. I put a bow on it and stuck it out on the porch. That she could take or leave. The cat moved in.

8

The rest of the week I took as vacation. More snow fell, temperatures dropped, and the roads turned into icy sheets. This was not at all normal for the Bay Area as all of the accidents on the highways indicated. But that didn't stop me from spending as much time as possible with Ollie.

Mickey tried to stay on her case, coming up with a possible lead on the runaway, but the bad weather had cleared the streets of snitches, and it was hard to follow anything up. The Chief continued to research the backgrounds of the real estate brokers' two men, but the going was slow once he had to leave the computer network.

I was looking forward to the weekend and the 49er-Viking game on Sunday, which was going to be revenge for last year's 36-24 defeat at the hands of these same Vikings who used to play tough out in the cold, but now had a nice domed stadium in Minnesota to keep them warm. We'd see how they liked it outdoors again.

And I was going to spend some more time with Ollie.

Krift called to tell me that things seemed to be working out with his daughter.

"Did you ask her if she was involved?" I asked.

"I didn't go that far."

"We didn't have any real evidence," I noted.

"I'm willing to let it go. I've sent you the check for your services."

"That will be appreciated."

Getting paid was good, but the best part of the vacation was the time I spent with Ollie, from just taking walks in the cold to playing badminton with her in a Japantown Community Center gym. I found out how hard the sport actually was when I met her there during the week. Ollie demolished me in straight games and I was left a panting, exhausted wreck, sitting on the gleaming wood of the court. I looked at all the court lines from that perspective and felt bewildered. Badminton over basketball over volleyball. White lines over blue lines over red lines. Give me tennis and save my life.

"I'm impressed," I told her when I caught my breath. "No more jokes about badminton and picnics."

"Good."

After the match and after showers, out on the street she started giving me the history of the sport, sounding like a sports encyclopedia.

"The game appeared in both England and India in the nineteenth century. English army officers played it in both countries. In India it was called 'Poona', and 'Badminton' in England after it was played at an estate of that name in eighteen seventy three."

"I should know so much about tennis." I hung the sports bag holding my racket over my shoulder.

"Actually, battledore shuttlecock, the forerunner of the modern game. . . "

To shut her up I kissed her right there on the street. I gave her the Christmas present I'd bought, a small gold badminton birdie on a gold chain. She reached up and kissed me. This kiss lingered and lingered.

After she hung the chain around her neck we walked on.

Japantown, which was only four blocks from my office, and boasts the Japantown Bowling Alley with its fully-automatic scoring system— a place I occasionally visited—runs along Post Street between Laguna and Fillmore. This section of Post is divided into two radically different parts: *wabi,* the new, on one side, *sabi,* the old, on the other. Twenty years or so after redevelopment most Japanese will admit that the area is finally getting *shibui,* the patina of age that marks survival with scars and grace.

I took Ollie to a Japanese restaurant I liked for lunch on the *sabi* side of the street. We got off to a great start, but halfway through the meal Ollie began to fidget nervously, mostly ignoring what remained of her food. And looking around and mostly ignoring me.

"What's wrong?" I asked.

She lowered her head and her voice. "Nothing is wrong."

"You don't want to be seen with me."

"No. That's not it."

"You just realized how much older I am than you."

She blushed and smiled. "I knew that right from the start."

After lunch we walked through the torii gate into a little street that represented a Japanese mountain village with a stream of stones running through it. The river ran around two metal sculptures, one an origami chrysanthemum bud, and one the flower in full bloom. There were benches all along the street beneath bare cherry and plum trees, which would be magnificent when in blossom.

"Do you want to sit?" I asked.

"Can we leave?"

"Of course. Whatever you want."

"Let's go." She looked around nervously.

"Where?" I asked, looking around to see if I could spot anyone who could be bothering her. Any one of a dozen young Japanese males was a possibility.

"Away from here. To your place."

"Who are you worried about?" I asked.

"Nobody."

I didn't push it. I just said, "I'm too old for you."

"Don't be silly. And if you're worried about it, I'm no virgin."

"That's a relief. Let's go," I said, half joking. But Ollie didn't laugh. We started back to the Victorian together before I got control of myself and the situation. For the moment.

"My partners will be back. This is a bad time," I explained.

"I don't believe you."

"Why not?"

"Your eyes. I can tell you are lying. Don't you want to go to bed with me?"

"Yes. I do. But I'm too old. . . "

"Don't be a dork. I told you. I'm not a virgin."

The situation was no longer in control. We started back to the Victorian. Quickly.

As we walked along Octavia Street I said, "You're too young. I'm too old. And we don't know enough about each other."

"Sounds like an old song. But I don't care about any of that. The only thing that matters is how we feel." She paused and blushed, then added, "But you better have latex condoms."

"That's putting it up front," I said.

My partners were out as I knew they would be and Ollie and I went upstairs. After a brief tour of the gym and the rest, we ended up in the bedroom. I took out my recently purchased proper protection. Lust was back, but AIDS hadn't gone away.

"I hope these are fresh," she said, as she looked at the box on my night table next to the king-sized bed. My one gesture towards the bachelor pad concept.

"I get a new supply every six months whether I need them or not."

After some additional mutual assurances about no high-risk behavior, Ollie disappeared into the bathroom.

I checked the porch. No sign of the cat. No chance that her meowing and scratching would disturb us. I got undressed and into bed. And waited naked under the covers in the chilly room.

Until Ollie slowly opened the bathroom door and emerged. I expected her to come out wrapped in a towel, but this was obviously no time for modesty. She moved naked across the room towards me. Her young firm flesh glowed golden in the natural light washing through the open curtains. Her dark hair was loose and tumbled wildly over her shoulders down to full breasts crowned with aureoles so light they almost looked white.

She stood in front of me and I just stared at her breasts, her softly rounded belly, and the dark pubic V between her slender thighs.

"I'm freezing," she suddenly complained. I saw her skin go to goose bumps and her nipples pucker.

"Well, get in here," I offered, "where it's hot."

"About time."

Our bodies came together under the blankets.

I showed her how the condom could be an erotic part of the sex act. Something I had learned from a former lover who was a nurse who learned it from a prostitute she was taking care of in a hospital. It added a nice touch to lovemaking these days.

Along with beauty, Ollie had the energy of youth and a few tricks of her own. And a request for something she called an iron butterfly which she had to teach me. It was an afternoon delight that kept us both warm and nearly depleted the condom supply.

No one blushed. No one felt guilty. It had to be love.

"I guess I'm not a dork," I said.

Ollie didn't answer.

It must have been exhaustion.

Now the best part of the vacation was making love to Ollie with the passion of fresh desire. We couldn't get enough of each other. Not just in bed, but in touch and feel and taste and talk. And a lot of bed. I was surprised at how little, if any, time she was spending at the HSC working with Snokes and Ness. But she told me they didn't mind that she was taking off all of this time, despite the fact that they were in the middle of their transgenic experiments.

The worst part of the vacation was when Ollie told me we couldn't go out together on New Year's Eve. I wanted to know why, and Ollie told me it was a family thing, but she wouldn't answer any more questions. She just asked me to understand. So I did.

After some minor soul-searching I asked Mickey if she wanted to go out as a friend. That made her suspicious and she turned me down for New Year's Eve for a date with Wesolski, who was soon to sail off on some crusade. I could tell Mickey was getting serious about her environmental attorney, not because she was going out with him on New Year's Eve, but because she was now talking about becoming a vegetarian.

I called Rita Silverman, a friend from my first big case, and finally got lucky. I took her out to a comedy about an incestuous affair between a teenaged brother and sister at the Magic Theatre at Fort

Mason, and a late dinner, avoiding the crowds of revelers by going to the Lyala restaurant down by the Civic Center. The place was Ethiopian, with what I understood was traditional fare, mostly stews served with *injera*, a spongy pancake used instead of a fork to scoop and sop up the food. In contrast to the ethnic cuisine and the wild African music and dance videos flashing over the bar, the surroundings were high-tech modern and cold with steel beams across the ceiling and steel banisters around the upper levels.

There were no hats or noisemakers, just *alicha wet*, a lamb curry that we both had. And an African beer I had never had before and never will again. After two sips I changed back to Henry's.

It was a pleasant evening and I didn't get a hangover or anything else. Which was fine with both of us. Mostly we talked about her son, Richard, and how he was doing in school and with the tennis team and about her new career as a returning college student. We didn't go over the past, which included the murder of my client and her ex-husband, Richard Silverman. Overall things worked out well enough for a New Year's Eve, usually one of the worst nights for dating for me. Maybe everyone is trying too hard to have the required good time and everyone comes up short. Including my date.

Despite the pleasant time with Rita, I still couldn't get Ollie out of my head. Which was understandable since she was coming over to my place the next morning.

Ollie had already left after our morning lovemaking and I had the playoff game on TV Sunday afternoon, when Krift called and announced, "I heard from the CFAF again."

"What do you mean?"

He took a deep breath. "They claim they've got my daughter this time."

"Goddam," I muttered. At least the 49ers had opened up a big lead on the Vikes. That was some consolation. "So much for cats."

"This time I'm out of patience."

"Then you think your daughter is behind this too?" I asked the question, but I knew the answer.

"I'm sure of it. She's angry about her failure to get the ten grand with the cats. What else can it be?"

"What do you want to do?"

"Spank her."

"Too late. And maybe that's not the problem."

"What is?"

"I'm not sure." I didn't mention keeping his paws off the coeds. I wasn't exactly one to toss stones in that area.

"Can you come over?" he asked.

I was worn out from this morning, but said, "If you have the Niner game on."

He didn't take it as a joke. "I own a TV, if that's your goddam concern."

"Just kidding, Krift. Trying to ease the tension. I'm on my way."

He hung up before I did.

9

I drove over to the Bernal Heights address Krift had given me when he filled out our contract, with the game on the radio. The district had a brief gold rush in 1876 when a Frenchman claimed to have found a couple of nuggets there. They must have been imported like him, because the rock crushers who claimed the heights after that only found red clay, iron, and feldspar.

The area, just south of Mission, was a pastoral slice of the city with narrow, leafy streets and renovated pre-earthquake cottages set among quiet gardens and impressive views. This was the kind of place I'd like to retire to someday, if I survived that long in my PI occupation. At least, unlike my partners, I hadn't been shot yet.

I passed gingerbread-trimmed cottages on Lundy's Lane, surrounded by white picket fences and postage-stamp gardens. I saw everything from delicate triple flowering Yesterday, Today and Tomorrow shrubs to the lush greenery of carob trees to enormous and ancient Canary Island date palms. The district had to have a mild micro-climate banana belt for these plants to have survived the recent cold spell.

In contrast to the older homes, Krift's was an impressive ultramodern residence of redwood and glass. Also impressive was the almost-new red Porsche parked in front of it. I checked it out carefully before I went in. It was one of the top of the line models.

Inside Krift was pacing in his living room on a plush white rug beneath an enormous two-story window. Filtered light came in through a pair of evergreen elm trees.

I wished him Happy New Year, then added, "Nice area. Nice house. Nice car. You must do pretty well."

He ignored my comments and handed me another note made up of letters and words cut from a magazine.

It read:

> *How much is your daughter worth? CFAF*

"Is this it?" I asked, as I sat down on a modern piece of chrome furniture that looked great, but was uncomfortable as hell. I put the note down on a matching chrome and glass coffee table. I spotted a giant screen TV next to a stereo across the room.

"Yes," he said, without stopping his pacing.

"Are you sure they have her?"

"I'm sure she's gone with them. They're her accomplices."

"Did you check around?"

"Of course. I tried her apartment. Her roommate. Anyone I could think of. She's disappeared. That is, she's playing this game with me."

I looked at the original oil paintings on the walls. I recognized some of the names. All abstract artists. All very in and all very expensive. "I know. No cops again."

"Right."

"You're making this difficult," I said.

"This is serious trouble for her. As angry as I am at her involvement. . ." He broke off the sentence and went over to a bar by the TV and opened it. "Want a drink?"

"I think I'll keep my head clear."

"I'll have a scotch." He poured himself a triple Chivas on the rocks. To take the edge off his anger.

"If she was involved in the catnapping, and her accomplices turned on her when it failed, she could be in real danger now," I said.

"I don't believe that. Not with her personality. She's domineering.

Just like her mother. She's giving the orders; I'm sure of it."

"But there had to be more people than just Claire planning to split up ten grand. Then there was nothing. Somebody's unhappy."

"Claire. Who else? Anyway, she's obviously promised them another shot at it. And she'll ask for more if I know her at all. She's not in danger from whatever the hell the CFAF is." He took a long swallow of the scotch.

"How did this message get here?" I asked.

"I found it slipped under the front door."

"It doesn't give us much to go on."

"What do you suggest we do?" he asked.

"That we wait to hear from them again."

Krift collapsed on a chrome-framed couch. It looked more comfortable than my chair. "I'm not a patient man," he said.

"It's the best virtue to have right now. Mind if I turn on the game?" I asked.

"Go ahead." He tossed me the remote control.

It was a challenge. It took me about fifteen seconds to get the game up on the big screen TV. They were in the fourth quarter when I finally got it on.

"Nice TV," I said. "Nice red Porsche out in front."

Krift was staring at his redwood tongue-and-groove cathedral ceiling. I suspected that he had lapsed into something like a coma.

I tried again. "You're not living on a professor's salary."

He snapped out of it. An Awakening. "It's none of your business, but I collected quite a bit of insurance money when my wife died."

I played dumb. "Recently?"

"A few years ago. She committed suicide."

"And the policies paid off?"

"Certainly. They had been in force long enough for the suicide clause to no longer be in effect."

"Did Claire receive any money?"

"No. I was the sole beneficiary."

"Maybe this is her way of collecting her share."

"I've offered her money. That's not it."

"Then what is it? I don't get it."

"I was having an affair with a student. I was divorcing my wife when she killed herself. Claire blames me, and calls the insurance money blood money."

"But you think she's trying to extort it from you? I'm not sure that makes sense. Not if she sees it as blood money."

"She's trying to purify it. She's cleansing it. At least that's what she thinks she doing. Making it acceptable to take."

"A version of moral laundering," I said.

"Yes. You might say that."

"And then she could spend it without a qualm," I said.

"Yes, that would be her plan. Cheat her father to honor her mother."

I paused. "And Heather was the student?"

He did a double take. "How did you know that?"

"I'm a detective. Remember?" I turned back to the action on TV. The 49ers won 34 to 9 over Minnesota. The Bears, who had defeated the Eagles yesterday, were next. Less than a minute after the game was over the phone rang. Krift grabbed it and signaled that it was them. I took it as a good sign that they were football fans. Or it had been a lucky coincidence.

"What! You're joking!" Krift yelled into the phone.

He listened.

"I'm not–" he began.

He listened. I picked up an extension in the other room just in time to hear a voice say that Claire would be a real dead pussy.

Krift regained his composure and played along. "Yes. Okay."

"Got that amount straight?" the voice of the CFAF asked.

"Fifty thousand dollars. . ." I head him say on the line. He continued, "But the banks are closed this Monday. I can't get the money until Tuesday."

Today was actually New Year's Day, but on Monday the holiday would be observed with bowl games on TV and closed banks and no garbage pickup. My tree would have to last an extra day.

Krift was left holding the phone. I put down the extension.

"Did I miss anything?" I asked.

"They want fifty grand for her." He laughed, and then cursed.

"I heard. She has to be worth more than eight cats. Do you have the money?"

"Yes."

"What else did they say before I got on the line?"

"They said not to call the cops, and to wait for instructions. And they want the guy who screwed up the cat deal to be the one to handle the payoff."

"Sounds like they resent being outwitted."

"And now they're trying to get revenge."

"Do you still think your daughter is behind this?"

"This is her style. And she knew about you."

"Good point."

"Your advice?" he asked.

"We wait. It's going to be a while. But we have to see where they lead us."

"No. I want you to find her before I have to pay." Once more he offered me a drink and once more I turned it down. He poured himself a double scotch this time and gulped half of it. "Find her."

"She could be vacationing in Mexico while I tear up the streets of San Francisco looking for her."

"I don't care. I'm paying you."

"There are no leads," I said.

"I won't be robbed. Not even by my own daughter."

"All right. I'll see what I can do. But don't get your hopes up."

"Just find her and get her back here."

"Call me as soon as you hear anything more," I said. "These people are our best lead."

"Of course," he promised, as he swallowed the other half of his drink. Goodbye clear head.

I abandoned him to his problems and his Chivas and went outside to admire his Porsche before I left the warm pastoral setting of Bernal Heights. And everything it hid.

Back at the office I called Mickey and Chief Moses and told them to come over. Mickey, traveling by California Street cable car, arrived first. I was glad to see that she was wearing the sweater I had bought her for Christmas.

"Nice sweater," I said.

"I'm also wearing the Chief's perfume," she said. "Smell." She offered me her wrist and I sniffed.

"Chanel. Wearing anything from Wesolski?" I asked.

"That I'm not going to show you," she said, with a mischievous grin and a slight lift of her hem.

The Chief arrived a few minutes later in the famous King Cab he hadn't realized I'd borrowed to free the cats. I planned to keep it that way. When he came in he was wearing a Warrior warmup jacket and baseball cap.

We all got comfortable in my office and had a very serious discussion about the kidnapping. My partners had a change of heart about the CFAF. However, I still did not tell them that Claire herself might be behind it. Despite Krift's certainty, I had my doubts. Not strong ones, but doubts nevertheless. Too many times I had seen partners, not us of course, turn on each other when it came to cash. Never forget the moral of *The Treasure of the Sierra Madra*. Or Humphrey Bogart, for that matter.

"What is your strategy?" the Chief asked.

"Krift wants me to find her."

"Like the cats?" Mickey asked.

"Exactly."

"That could endanger the woman," Chief Moses said.

"Also exactly. So I'm not in a big rush to go on this womanhunt."

Chief Moses asked, "What about the police?"

I ignored that question. Instead I offered, "Since I'm in no hurry, how about if we go out to dinner? My treat."

I got agreement again. This was my good day. I put up with the complaints about the front seat of my classic Thunderbird and took them to a new Brazilian restaurant Mickey wanted to try.

We got a parking spot on the street, which amazed us all.

"With some forty two hundred restaurants in San Francisco, which comes to ninety per square mile, I'll get you out of your Hyde Street

Grill rut," Mickey said, as she got out of the car.

"I told you. I'm taking your advice. Like I always do. And I plan to do every Chinese restaurant in the city. But the Grille's still one of my favorite restaurants," I said, as I locked up the T-Bird.

The restaurant was just off Market. It had a festive atmosphere with walls covered with vibrant Brazilian Indian paintings and sequined masks and Carnival-style confetti hanging down from the ceiling.

"I'll have the vegetable plate," Mickey said to a waitress who was dressed, or rather undressed, for the year 'round Mardi Gras, in a yellow Brazilian bikini.

"She's gone vegetarian," I muttered.

"As I've been saying, you ought to eat lower on the food chain," she insisted.

I looked at the Chief. "I think she ought to date higher up on the evolutionary chain."

"Go to hell, Jeremiah."

"Except for his head, your Mike is a hairy ape."

"I like the way he looks, and what he stands for."

"No accounting for taste." Since they didn't know about Ollie, I didn't have to take any cheap shots about robbing the cradle.

I ordered *feijoada completa*, the national dish of Brazil: a black bean stew containing chicken, sausage, and several other kinds of meat, just to torment her.

The Chief compromised and ordered *camarao ao molho*, prawns sautéed in onions and garlic.

"I wouldn't count on dating tonight, Chief," I said.

He picked up a sprig of parsley. "Old Indian trick. I will chew on this."

"Good luck," Mickey said, as she attacked her vegetables.

I noticed that every once in a while she gave my meat stew a longing glance. There was hope for the woman yet.

"Is Wesolski sailing away soon to save the whales, I hope?" I asked.

I didn't get an answer. Just a Medusa look from the lady.

But with Ollie on my mind it was all teasing now. Somehow what

Mickey was doing in her personal life didn't seem all that important anymore.

Although I had promised to pay, in a nice gesture Chief Moses picked up the check.

"What brings on this generosity?" I asked.

"It's Native American New Year," he said with a straight face. "The Year of the White Rat."

"Does that mean what I think it means?" I asked, with a glance at Mickey.

The Chief gave us a grin that was hardly inscrutable.

10

The CFAF called Krift on Monday during the early bowl games televised from the eastern and central time zones, and told him to get the money out of the bank Tuesday morning. Then he was to wait at home for a call with directions for me, the PI who was about to be properly humbled for interfering in a catnapping.

"Anything else?" I asked over the phone.

"No. Any leads?" he countered.

"No."

"What should I do?"

I said, "You should try to take it easy until tomorrow. Then go get the money out of the bank."

"I don't want to pay."

"Then call the cops and tell them everything. Especially Claire's involvement."

"No. I can't do that to her."

Or to himself. I was sure he didn't want another scandal dogging his life. "Then you don't have any other choice. Watch some football," I advised him. "Take your mind off your problems."

"I don't like football."

"Then read Herb Caen. Or go to the zoo. Maybe they still have those pandas from China there. I've always been partial to pandas, myself."

"Don't be absurd. Can't you do anything?" he pleaded.

So much for the San Francisco Zoo. "This isn't like finding some missing felines. I don't have a lead. But I do have a plan for how to handle the payoff."

"What is it?"

"Just get the money. We'll talk about it tomorrow."

"Are you giving up on finding her?"

"We're going to let the money lead us to her. It's the only way."

I hung up and called the Chief to let him know the situation and that I would need help. I explained what I wanted him to do and he agreed.

"This plan makes sense," he said.

"Unlike some others?" I asked.

"No comment. I will be ready tomorrow," Chief Moses said, as he hung up.

Then I called Mickey. I would have preferred for her to be out of this deal, but I needed her. Mickey had been shot during a similar payoff earlier in the year, and I was concerned about involving her in this one.

"We'll have to use you on the double tail. But be careful."

"Jeremiah, don't worry. I was a cop. Remember?"

"You took a bullet for me. I remember that too."

"So you owe me. You get the next bullet."

"Funny lady. Okay. Go rent a car. The Chief is getting a Chevy station wagon. Get a sedan."

"What color?"

"What's your favorite?"

"Brothel Red."

"Red's fine. The Chief is going for white. Good luck."

"No sweat," she said.

"How about a bulletproof vest?"

Mickey hung up.

With that more or less settled, I took some of my own advice and took it easy and watched the Fiesta Bowl and the Rose Bowl, and tried not to think of Mickey bleeding in my arms in Golden Gate Park, or lying wounded in a hospital bed. After a while I had some success. At the Orange Bowl halftime show I went brain dead from football over-load and couldn't tell you who finally won the game.

Tuesday morning Mickey, Chief Moses, and I were waiting with Krift in his Bernal Heights home. The ransom money was in the standard leather briefcase on his glass-and-chrome coffee table. Not that I didn't trust the bank, but I counted the money while Mickey walked around, openly admiring the house, the furnishings, and especially the art. She had already admired the Porsche outside. The Chief just took it all in from the couch where he sat like he owned the place.

Fifty thousand in hundred dollar bills was my confirming count.

Krift didn't like having my partners involved and he let me know it.

"Tough," I said, and then I explained the double tail. "One partner will tail me. But that's easy for the kidnappers to pick up. So we have a second car switching off with the first one. It looks like the first car is gone, but it's really tailing the second car. If necessary, we pull another switch and so on. That should keep them confused."

"So what does this game get me, besides car rental charges added to my bill?" Krift asked.

I was getting annoyed, and so was the Chief, I could tell. Mickey was too busy with her self-guided tour.

"Without it we could lose your money."

That shut him up.

Of course we could lose his money anyway, but I didn't mention that possibility. Let the glass be half full for now.

The CFAF call came at precisely eleven o'clock.

"They want to talk to the prick who stole the cats," Krift said.

"Prick? Is that any way to talk about a distinguished PI who single-handedly rescued some stolen cats?"

"Take the phone, White Man," Chief Moses said.

Krift stared at him and the Chief smiled back. Mickey reluctantly left the painting she was admiring from a variety of angles and came over.

I took the phone. A male voice asked me to identify myself. I did.

I said, "I'm your favorite prick." He told me to shut the fuck up and listen. He instructed me to take the money right now to a telephone booth on Pine in front of a certain drugstore and wait there for a call.

"Hold on. I want an assurance that Claire's okay before I go anywhere." I was playing this for real.

I was told to fuck off. But instead, I insisted. "I'm a prick, remember?"

I got Claire on the phone and had Krift confirm that it was indeed his daughter. Then Krift handed me the phone back.

The voice told me, "There better be no cops. And nobody tailing you. And nobody tracing this call. Now move your ass." He hung up.

"Mickey and Chief Moses, be careful. They warned me off about a tail."

"They will not pick it up with two of us," the Chief said.

"I'll be safe in the red Buick I rented," Mickey added.

We went outside and got into the three cars.

"Then lady and gentleman, start your engines," I shouted, as I turned the ignition key on my T-Bird.

The caravan snaked out of the residential hills and spread out for the ride to Pine.

We started at the booth on Pine, with the Chief as the lead tail. Then we moved across to Grant and Chinatown, where I had to double park to get to the designated booth in the allotted fifteen minutes. I was given a little more time to get to a booth in the Castro, which was occupied by a gay couple. I waited impatiently until they were done.

The call came through. I had to head back downtown to Union Square. After that it was on to the Tenderloin, where I took a call on a pay phone inside of a Cambodian grocery store. Through all of this goose chase either Mickey or the Chief was in the lead car behind me.

The last call brought me to Columbus and instructions to leave the cash in a dumpster behind a North Beach restaurant a block away, and then to proceed to a telephone booth on Lombard. Mickey was behind me now after numerous switches. I dropped the money and I left her to pick up the kidnapper and went on to the next telephone booth on Lombard. I didn't see the Chief's wagon, and that worried me. At the Lombard booth the caller told me the name of the motel and the room in which I would find Claire.

I drove over to the place and knocked hard on the thin wooden door to two-fourteen. I waited and knocked again. No answer. I was at the right room at the right cheap motel, doing what I was told to do. I tried to see into the room, but the drapes were drawn. With my Smith and Wesson out, I turned the doorknob. I wasn't expecting a violent reception, but why take a chance? The door swung open.

Two steps inside I saw her. The beautiful woman on the bed was either very unconscious, or very dead. This was not going down as planned. I went over to her and felt for a pulse. There was none. Very dead was the diagnosis.

Her fully-clothed body was lying spread-eagled, bound by the wrists and ankles to the four posts of the bed with heavy silver duct tape.

I'd just dropped fifty thousand dollars in ransom in a garbage dumpster for a kidnapping that my client was certain was a phony. Only now his daughter was dead. Which wasn't phony at all. This would be tough to break to Krift. Not to mention the cops. They weren't going to be happy with my involvement in a kidnapping that turned into a homicide. They would be particularly pissed off that we had kept the police out of it. But at least, when they were through with me, I'd be out of it. Private investigators don't do homicide investigations. Just ask the cops.

On the positive side, if there could be one now for Krift, I hoped Mickey had kept the money and the kidnapper in sight.

There was a phone in the room, but I didn't want to disturb any possible evidence. I had learned about leaving my prints around at a crime scene the hard way. I went out to use the phone in the manager's office.

The manager turned out to be a heavyset middle-aged bald guy with a marine tattoo on his left forearm. When I asked to use the phone he told me there was a pay phone across the street.

"A woman's been murdered in two-fourteen. I'm calling the cops."

"Shit," he said. "Business is bad enough as it is." But he backed off.

First I called Krift. He was incredulous.

"But this was her scheme," he cried.

"It doesn't look that way right now."

He broke down.

When he pulled himself together I told him to stay at his home until he heard from me again. There was a long silence and I half expected him to ask about the money.

"Where are you?" he demanded instead.

"I'm at the motel where they must have been holding her."

"Which motel?"

"I'm calling the police. There's nothing you can do here."

"Look, St. John. . . I can't just. . ."

"Stay where you are. Have a Chivas. Have a double for me."

I hung up. Even if it was going to cost me my last check from the man, I didn't want him down there disturbing anything. The cops would be angry enough as it was.

I made the call to the police and while I waited for all hell to break loose I asked the manager some questions. I didn't get any answers until I showed him my ID, and some hard currency. In these hard times money always seems to work.

"I seen some guys comin' an' goin', but no broad. What is she, some kinda hooker?"

"A college girl."

"Shit. That's even worse than a whore."

"Who checked into two-fourteen?"

He got out the card for the room. Someone had spilled coffee on it. I looked at it. "At least the rates are cheap," I said.

He grunted.

"Mr. and Mrs. John Smith. Come on. How many of these you get a day?"

"Hey, somebody out there's gotta be named Smith. Just look in the goddam phone book."

"How'd he pay?"

"In cash for three nights."

"What'd he look like?"

"Young guy. Medium height. Maybe five ten. Blond hair. Kinda skinny. Had the fag look, if you know what I mean. Even dressed in leather like one of 'em."

"I can guess. See anybody else?"

"Maybe an older guy. Maybe not. That was today. I thought he went into two-fourteen, but I ain't sure. It coulda been another room. Anyways, I didn't get hardly a good look at him."

I tried for something specific in the description, but got nowhere. And the manager didn't notice him coming in by car. Not much of a lead. "What about the young guy? Ever see him after he checked in?"

"Couple times."

"What was he doing?"

"Going out somewhere."

"Often?"

"Couple of times a day."

Given the outcome, that seemed strange to me. Unless Claire's death took some accomplices by surprise too. I looked at the card again. John Smith had left the space for vehicle description and license plate blank.

"When was the last time you saw him go out?"

"This morning."

"About the time the older guy arrived?" I asked.

"Guess so. A little before. Maybe."

"So this second man could have been alone with the victim?" I pressed.

"I told ya. I can't even say what room he went into. It coulda been nothin'."

"Did you see the car the young guy was driving?"

"Some kinda old red Chevy. But sharp. Kept real clean. A fifty-five, I think."

"Nice car. Those were usually two-tone."

"Yeah. This was red n white."

"You get the plates?"

"They're supposed to be on the card."

"Sure," I said, as I pointed to the empty line.

"Hey, you're gettin' your money's worth. An' more."

Maybe I was, but I also wanted some time to think this over. But no chance. The door behind us flew open. The boys from Homicide had arrived, and then more or less all hell broke out.

11

Detectives Johnny D and Oscar Chang of Homicide were not real glad to see me. A PI who had discovered a corpse made them nervous, irritable, and generally suspicious. And unfortunately I had discovered a few in my time. Which intensified all of the above unpleasant cop attitudes.

We were standing in the tiny lobby space in front of the manager's desk. Oscar Chang, as usual, asked the first questions.

"Who is the victim?"

"A woman named Claire Krift."

"A client?"

"Daughter of a client."

"What were you doing here?"

I explained about the ransom.

Chang's face went ashen. "Don't move. We'll be back." To make his point, he shoved me back into a creaky wooden chair. "Sit right there," he said furiously.

"Wouldn't think of moving. Might provoke some more police brutality. I'll just sit here and read one of these three-year-old magazines."

"Do that," Chang said.

I figured that after a visit to the murder scene the Homicide pair would question the manager. That gave me plenty of time to put a call in to Mickey. Without having to even get out of the chair.

"How'd it go?" I asked.

"Don't ask."

"Come on, Mickey."

"Not good," she said.

"What do you mean?"

"This guy in a ski mask picked up the briefcase on foot. I got out of the Buick and chased him down an alley and through two back yards. Until I got attacked by a goddam Doberman and almost had to shoot it."

"Did you?"

"No. Actually, I missed. But I scared the animal off."

"Good. I know how you feel about cruelty to animals."

"Screw you."

"Where was the Chief?"

"He was the second tail and got caught in traffic. By the time he got there it was too late. The guy was long gone."

"What's the bottom line?" I asked, using one of Mickey's favorite phrases.

"The bottom line is that the bastard got away with the money."

"Damn."

"All right. I feel shitty. I blew it. How did you do with Claire?" she asked. "Go ahead and gloat."

"Gloat? Like hell. Don't feel bad. I did even worse."

"How could you do worse than me?"

"Easy. Claire Krift is dead."

After a stunned silence, she said, "Some deal we worked out here."

I didn't have an answer.

I spent the rest of the time waiting and trying to figure out what could have gone wrong. The possible visitor to the room when Claire was alone preyed on my mind. If it had been Claire's plot, this would be someone outside of it. Somehow taking advantage. But as for a motive, I was at a dead end. I picked up an ancient *Time* and thumbed through it, looking at the pictures.

When Johnny and Chang were done with the manager, they came

back for me.

"Nice to see you improving you mind," Chang said.

"Did you know that back in eighty-five. . ."

"Can it," Johnny said.

"It's canned."

The pair did an hour Q&A on me in the back room behind the motel desk. It was where the manager cooked, slept, smoked cheap cigars, and drank cheaper booze. It smelled about as good as a public toilet in a downtown bus station.

At the conclusion of the session, Chang fixed me with those anthracite eyes and said, "This is what happens when you do not involve the police in a kidnapping case." After all the questioning, Chang still looked sharp and pressed in his dark gray three-piece suit. Not even his red-and-black-striped tie was loose. And his black hair was slicked perfectly in place. But that was how he always was.

"Yeah," Johnny D added for emphasis. In case I missed the point. Johnny Dajewski was very different from the immaculate Chang with his tousled crayon-yellow hair, sleepy blue eyes, and broad Polish good looks. And his wrinkled suits, shirts, invariably loosened tie and unbuttoned collar.

Together they made a good before-and-after team.

Chang started to repeat his comment about kidnapping in his precise flat tone, pinning me like an insect specimen with those dark eyes again.

"Sometimes," I interrupted.

"They removed the only witness after they had the money. It is very logical," Chang said. "And all too common in these cases."

"Yeah. It's a possible motive. I don't think this was how they were getting their revenge for the cats." I slipped that in intentionally. Chang had to know what was going on.

"Cats? What are you talking about?" Chang demanded.

"Here goes." I told them about the CFAF's Great Catnapping Caper on campus. Something I had skipped during the Q&A.

"And that wasn't reported?" Johnny asked.

"No."

"Why not?"

"Client request. And not exactly a major crime."

"You walk on thin ice," Chang said.

"And sometimes you try to walk on goddam water," Johnny D said, trying to go his partner one better. Without much success.

"With the expected results," I admitted. "But I do appreciate the pithy sayings from you boys. You keep my wits honed sharp."

"Bullshit," Johnny said.

"That's even better. Let me write that one down."

But with a new arrival, Chang's attention turned away from me.

While Chang talked to the young, husky, and handsome ME who was, as usual, casually dressed and oddly bespectacled—with small gold-rimmed round glasses that got lost on his large pink baby face—Johnny and I went outside. I was surprised to find cars with headlights on and evening falling. I wasn't surprised to see a city ambulance in the parking lot. I looked at my watch. I hadn't been paying attention to the time.

Police barricades were up and yellow police line tape was strung across the front of the motel. Behind it reporters and photographers and a TV live camera crew with a yellow van from a local station were all vying for good positions in the parking lot. They started shouting questions at us, but Johnny waved them off.

To get away from them we went around to the back of the building where they couldn't reach us.

Even though we were downtown in a pretty ratty area and standing in a patch of high weeds, the cold air was clear and clean and we were free of the reporters, for now. Compared to the room we had just left, a coal mine would have seemed clean and clear. We got a little personal and informal in this new and improved atmosphere.

"How's the wife?" I asked.

"Fine."

The wife was a Mexican lady who had finally learned English. Now she and Johnny could fight it out in the same language. I had always predicted their marriage wouldn't last once she knew English, but so far I was wrong. The fighting was just better when Johnny could understand it.

"What'd you get from the manager?"

"What do you mean?"

"He told us you questioned him. Didn't see why the fuck he had to answer ours for free."

I told Johnny D what the man had said about Claire's apparent kidnappers, especially the part about the Chevy coming and going. And the unidentified possible older visitor that he couldn't describe.

"That's what we got. Some curious shit in there. Something don't seem right. But I don't have it pinned down."

"I know what you mean." But I didn't tell him about how Krift had assumed his daughter was masterminding the entire deal. Which made sense of the comings and goings at will. I was mildly surprised that Claire herself had not gone out for a stroll.

"This cat stuff. That was pretty weird."

"Yes. But understandable. An animal rights thing. They're nuts that way."

"We better go back in. Chang'll miss me," Johnny said.

I was interested in what the ME had to say as well. We went back in with waves to the frustrated members of the media who insisted on shouting questions at us.

As we were going into the motel, Claire was hauled away in a body bag, on a gurney. After that the boyish ME gave us a summary.

It wasn't much more than what we had noticed. Some apparent violence to subdue the woman. Bruises on the arms, legs and face. The contusions on the face indicated someone wearing a ring, most likely on the left hand, and most likely a wedding ring. And she was an apparent victim of strangulation. For anything more we would have to wait for the autopsy. Which Chang had put a rush on, because he knew the media waiting outside would jump on the story of a university coed murdered in a sleazy motel room while taped spread-eagled to a bed. It was their kind of story.

After Johnny and I cleared out, the Crime Scene Unit descended on the room with empty evidence bags and a fiendish attention to detail.

While they searched with vacuums for fibers or hairs or mud or any kind of physical evidence that could tie the crime to a perpetrator, Chang joined us outside of the motel. As we looked out over the crowded parking lot, Chang just shook his head. We got through the press gamut with a series of "No comments" that got us to Chang's car. We all got into it and he started it up. He wedged it slowly through the crowd that was at our windows, leaving a wake of reporters behind us.

Chang and Johnny wanted to talk to Krift and I rode along with them to provide directions in a stripped-down green Plymouth that anyone who had anything to do with any kind of larceny knew was an unmarked police car.

As usual, even though it was quite dark outside, Bernal Heights was an oasis of lit tranquillity. But when we got to Krift's place he had more bad news for us in a message attached to the front door.

Johnny pulled out a small flashlight to read it: *"Arson at the lab."*

"What lab?" Chang asked.

"At the Health Science Center at the university," I assumed.

Johnny D turned on the siren and stuck a pulsing police light on the roof and called in on the police radio to try to get some information about the fire at the HSC.

12

The floodlights of the HSC building were shining on a yellow city fire truck parked by a white hydrant. We pulled up as close as we could get to the scene and parked on a patch of grass behind a row of wooden barricades. The firemen in boots and slickers were already pulling out long black hoses from the building and flattening them like snakeskins as they rewound them on large brass wheels.

Chang, Johnny D, and I sat in the car for a few moments looking the scene over.

"Not much of a fire," Chang said.

Apparently the media agreed. Compared to the scene at the motel, there was a distinct lack of coverage here. A single TV cameraman was packing up his video gear. A few photographers were drifting away with their equipment.

We got out of the car and Chang used his badge to get us past the fire department line and into the building. The smell of smoke was strong in the hall, but there didn't seem to be much damage visible.

"At least it doesn't smell like a zoo anymore," I said to nobody in particular.

To our surprise, Krift was in his office, which was untouched by the fire. He was in a state of near collapse, which condition was reflected in his disheveled appearance. We expressed our condolences for the death of his daughter. He barely nodded in response. I didn't mention the missing ransom. Instead I asked, "How'd you get in here?"

He shrugged. "I just walked past the barricades. Nobody stopped me."

"So much for security," I noted. Maybe if you looked frantic enough they wouldn't stop you.

Between the death of his daughter and the fire, Krift was in no condition to talk about much. The most he could tell us was that his lab had also been spared any damage.

Chang tried some questions about Claire's murder, but got nowhere with Krift, who lapsed into incoherence.

"We'll be back," Chang said. "Pull yourself together."

Krift nodded.

"So don't leave," Johnny added, just in case Krift had missed the point.

Krift gave a second puppet nod.

We left Krift in suspended animation and went down the hall. Following the main line of activity led us to Snokes' office. Apparently it was Snokes who had the immediate and major problem with the fire.

The campus police were there along with several firemen in yellow slickers and an arson investigator in a suit and a fireman's hard hat. Which didn't leave much room for anyone else.

From the hall we could see that Snokes' office had been torched in an apparent act of arson. CFAF was spray-painted across one wall in bright red enamel paint. STOP ANIMAL TORTURE NOW was sprayed across the opposite wall.

"Kidnapping. Murder. Arson. The CFAF has been busy as hell," Johnny D noted.

The firemen stalked out of the office in their rubber slickers and boots, definitely overdressed for the job. The wet smoldering heap in the middle of the floor indicated that their work was done. After a few words with Chang in the doorway, the campus cops left too. There was finally room for us in the office.

I looked around while Chang and Johnny spoke to the arson investigator, a black man with a short beard, coffee skin, and piercing dark eyes. Damage was slight. The rubber tile floor was charred and flames had reached the old desk—but left the wife's picture untouched—and the books in one wall unit, but that was about it, except for the burnt papers in the middle of the floor, which were a total loss. I noticed the filing cabinet drawers were pulled out and that there were scratches on the metal around the locks. But they looked like the scratches I'd seen before.

While they were talking, Snokes came in and stood by the door. He was dressed in a shirt and loosened tie and looked upset as hell. I took my opportunity while Johnny D and Chang were otherwise occupied to get in my own questions.

"What's the effect on your work?" I asked Snokes as I walked over to him.

"A year of research destroyed. All of my records. I won't be able to prove the success I had with my transgene process. I won't be able to apply to renew my current grant."

"They stopped your research."

"For now. The sons of bitches. But there will be another grant cycle."

"They knew what to look for," I noted, as I pointed to the remains of what had been a small bonfire.

"Yes, they did. They knew exactly what to destroy. But I don't understand why. I'm not torturing animals. I'm transplanting genes."

"Was your research stored in the filing cabinets?" I asked.

"Yes. The goddam CFAF got them open somehow. They used all of my papers to start the fire."

I looked around at the walls again and realized I had missed something. The memorabilia was gone.

"What happened to the wrestling pictures?" I asked.

"I decided to take them home after Krift's animals were stolen. I was afraid of something like this. Luckily, I finally got around to doing it."

"Wasn't there anybody here?"

"School is on a break."

"I thought there were always researchers working in this place," I said.

"There were a few people down the other wing."

"And they didn't hear anything?"

"I guess not."

"Where were you?"

"I just happened to come by to pick up some papers to work on at home. When I got here there was smoke coming out from under my office door."

"Did you see anybody?"

"No."

"Did you call the fire department?"

"Of course."

I looked around the office. "One thing at least about this fire," I said.

"What's that?" Snokes asked.

"It's warmed up your office."

Snokes almost cracked a smile. And that surprised me.

Johnny D and Chang left the arson man to his investigative work and joined us.

"Who's this?" Chang asked as they maneuvered me out of their way.

I introduced Snokes and they asked him some of the same questions I had just asked. Snokes handled them with polite patience.

"Any attempt on the lab?" I asked when Chang and Johnny D seemed through.

"No."

"They didn't even try to free the captive mice," I said to Chang with obvious irony.

"So?" Chang asked, missing the irony.

"So they're an animal rights group. That's what they do. Free animals," I said.

Chang just shook his head. "Do they free rats too?"

"White ones," I said, and smiled.

"Let's see this lab," Chang said, weary of our exchange.

Snokes took us down the hall and let us into the lab. There was only a faint odor of smoke in it. The mice were agitated in their cages, but not harmed. There wasn't much to see. After a few questions from

Chang about the equipment, we left Snokes and got out of there.

"How did they get the filing cabinets open?" I asked Chang as we stood outside in the hallway.

"It looks like a crude lock pick of some sort. There were scratches around the lock, but no actual damage to the lock mechanism itself. They're not hard to get open."

True, but there were marks on the cabinets before. I didn't bother to mention that to Chang.

"What about the office itself?" I asked.

"A cleaner job. Or the door was open," Johnny said.

"Hmmm," I noted. "Or someone had a key."

"Of course. Do you know something we don't?" Chang asked.

"Do I ever know anything you don't?"

"Right. Sorry I asked."

"And keep it that way," Johnny threw in.

"Let's get back to Krift and the murder business," Detective Chang said to Johnny D, and the two of them started to leave to question Krift again about his daughter's death.

"What? No invitation?" I asked. "To the man who found the body?"

"Kiss off, civilian," Johnny D said.

I didn't kiss off. I just wandered around, acting like I belonged there. I saw the arson man going through the dumpster and pulling out a spray can of red paint.

"The weapon. Any chance of fingerprints?" I asked.

"Probably been wiped clean." He looked at me. "Who are you anyway?"

I told him the truth.

He returned the favor. "You don't belong here."

"I'm with Oscar Chang."

"Then go bug him."

"Whatever you say." I got out of his sight.

I waited around until Chang and Johnny D were done, then went in to see Krift myself. With the case a homicide and the police in on it now, I figured my work was done. It would be up to them to recover the fifty grand and find the murderer.

"What went wrong?" Krift asked.

"Everything." I told him about the money without going into details. I also told him that the agency had to be out of it now.

Krift, who had pulled himself together emotionally, but still looked like he had come here from sleeping under a bridge somewhere, didn't see it that way. "I don't want to leave it all just up to the police," he said.

"I don't do murders."

Krift struggled to form the words. "The murder's one thing. There's also the matter of the fifty thousand dollars. What exactly happened to it?"

I explained the screwup as best I could. I felt responsible for both Claire's death, and the missing ransom. "Maybe you ought to try another agency to find the money."

"The thought did occur to me. But no. I'd rather stick with the devil I know."

"All right. I can't just cut you loose. I feel a certain responsibility here," I admitted.

"Good. What are you going to do?" he asked.

"Find out who is behind the CFAF. That should give us some answers and the money. Maybe we'll even find out who started the bonfire in Snokes' office."

"Before they burn down mine," Krift said.

"I'll be treading pretty close to the murder investigation."

"Do you care?"

"Usually. And I'll have to try to stay out of Chang's way. Which isn't always easy to do. But I'll do what I can. I owe you that much. And no fee. This is on the agency."

"Find out who's behind this. . ." he began.

"I will."

"And recover the money and the ten grand is yours. I would have gladly given it to Claire, but not through extortion."

"I understand."

I needed to talk to Johnny D to get whatever information he was willing to put on the table. Johnny, paying off some old debts, often came through. And Oscar Chang, despite how he acted towards me in public, owed me a lot for rescuing him from possible criminal prosecution in a cover-up case. So he was usually willing to look the other way. It's nice to have friends on your local police force, especially if they're in your debt. They may not like it, but they respect the reality of it. Only catch was that they had to know something before they could let you in on it. And I didn't think Johnny and Chang knew very much about anything right now.

I sat down with Krift and we went over all of the circumstances of the case once more.

"You have a plan?" he asked, when we were finally through.

"Of course," I more or less lied. I had a half-formed idea, but that was it.

"Good."

I thought of all the people who had keys to offices and labs. And all the people who, like me, could be good with a lock pick. Or not so good, from the scratches left on the cabinets.

"Was I so wrong? Was Claire not a part of this?"

"We don't know. Her accomplices may have turned on her. They may have decided they wanted all the money. Why split it with her? Or maybe you were wrong all along. But I don't think so."

"Why not?"

"Just a hunch." I told him about how Claire was apparently left unguarded and about the '55 Chevy seen coming and going.

He didn't know who owned such a car, but he did say, "She could have been left bound and gagged."

"It's possible, but that would be risky in a real kidnapping. Also, all of the bruises were fresh, indicating that the only struggle was with her murderer. At least apparently."

"Being right doesn't make me feel much better," he said very slowly.

"You did what they asked. You played the game like it was for real."

"It did turn out to be real."

"They were the ones who broke the rules," I assured him.

When I got up to leave, Krift began filling out a stack of university forms. Just like last time.

"Mindless work, but it keeps you going," he said, then added, "I'm going to identify the body tomorrow at the morgue. I couldn't face it tonight."

As I went out the door I realized I had left my car at the scene of the murder. I raced out to the parking lot hoping Johnny and Chang had spent more time in the building. I got lucky. I caught up to Johnny as he was backing the green Plymouth out of the parking lot.

"How about a ride back to the motel?" I asked.

"What is this, a goddam taxi?" he asked.

"I can give you my thinking on the case," I offered.

"Pearls of wisdom," Chang said. Then added, "Get in."

I got in the back seat and told them what they already knew about the case.

"Pearls of bullshit," Johnny concluded in disgust.

"One more pearl," I said. "I wouldn't drop Snokes as a suspect in the arson."

"I don't plan to. Or anybody else in the building. And we'll be checking murder alibis too. Everybody's. Including Snokes' and Krift's."

"Police efficiency. I love it."

"The way the SFPD is running out of money it won't last long."

"More budget cuts?" I asked.

"What else these days, in San Francisco?" Chang responded.

"Do you miss Dianne?" I asked, referring to our lovely former mayor.

"Sometimes I actually do," Chang said.

Johnny grunted, which was just as good a political comment.

13

On Wednesday, the city began to warm up considerably. Instead of freezing weather, the prediction was for mild mid-fifties and sunny skies.

The agency triumvirate, dressed less warmly than usual, met in the morning in my office over coffee I had made in the Mr. Coffee machine, to discuss strategy. With the machine even I don't screw up coffee.

First we got through Mickey's apologies for losing the fifty grand.

"It could happen to anyone," I said.

"It *would* have happened to Jeremiah," Chief Moses threw in.

"Remember, Great Tracker, you lost sight of *her*. . ." I began.

"I remember," the Chief admitted, preferring not to be reminded.

"I still feel like shit," Mickey said. "I was the one in the lead car. It was my goddam responsibility."

This was not how she usually talked. "We'll get the money back. In fact, if we do, Krift promised us ten thousand dollars for the recovery."

That made everyone feel better.

"Besides, nobody died on your side of the operation."

The Chief as Love Dick Investigator had enough to hold his client for a while, but Mickey had some hot leads she had to follow up on the missing girl. She apologized for not being able to help with the money she lost.

"You'll get your chance," I said. "You need to work on your case."

Sitting at my desk, I went over all of the facts I had.

"Something bothers me about this kidnapping," Mickey said, as she sipped black coffee on my couch.

"If the manager is telling the truth," the Chief, who was sitting next to her, drinking his coffee with cream and two sugars, noted, "it almost seems that Claire was left alone."

"Let me tell you all about it." I went into Krift's assumption that his daughter was behind the extortion.

"Then something went very wrong," Mickey said.

"If Krift was right."

"Why didn't you tell us before?" Mickey asked.

"I wasn't sure he had it straight. I wanted everyone to treat it like it was for real."

"It became real quick enough," the Chief noted.

"How did that happen? Assuming Krift was correct?" Mickey asked.

"That's what we'll have to find out. All of it."

We decided that a logical place to begin would be at Dogg's Pet Shop. If we could find out who kidnapped the cats, we'd have a hell of a lead in the case.

Mickey left for downtown with what she swore was her last apology for the lost money, and the Chief and I went to pay a visit to Mr. Ken Dogg at his pet shop. Over my objection, the Chief drove the King Cab. And lived up to my expectations—or fears. He did make it, but there were quite a few close calls. Chief Moses just doesn't have the patience for city driving. Or maybe he has trouble fitting behind the steering wheel. He pulled in and parked behind the building in a cloud of dust. Right where I had parked the night of the rescue. I wondered if the Chief or Mickey would ever ask how I got eight cat cages into my T-Bird. Would the Chief figure out that I had ripped off his pickup for the job? That was one secret I hoped to keep forever.

I remembered the place well. It looked, smelled, and sounded exactly the same. I even recognized some of the dogs and birds. No takers yet. And the puppies were growing.

When we identified ourselves, Ken Dogg, a short, bald, timid man in blue overalls and work shirt, made it very clear that he was not glad to see us. At first he denied everything, blinking at us with brown eyes that were tearing constantly. Which meant the Chief gave him a threatening look. And a menacing step towards him. Which meant Ken Dogg spilled everything without anyone touching him.

"They told me to keep my mouth shut," he whined.

"Stop whining like one of your mutts. Who did?" I expected him to say the CFAF.

"The gang behind this," was his less-than-precise answer.

"Gang?" Chief Moses asked. "Do you mean that literally?"

"Yeah. Some kind of Asian gang."

"How do you know it was a gang?" I asked.

"They were dressed like it. In silver and black Raider jackets and black bandannas around their foreheads. That means gang to me."

"Exactly what happened? From the beginning," I demanded.

He looked at the Chief. There was no way out. He pulled out a chair from behind the counter and sat down. "I was delivering some animals to the HSC labs three weeks ago. On a Wednesday. I was parked at the loading ramp at about two in the afternoon. As I was leaving, suddenly these two Asian guys jump into the cab of the van. They tell me they want my van that Sunday night and that they're going to have some animals for me to take care of. They offered me fifty bucks. I said that I wasn't interested. They said that if I didn't go along with them my store would be burned to the ground. I lent them the van. They brought some cats."

"Did they pay you the fifty dollars?" Chief Moses asked.

"You've got to be kidding."

While the Chief looked around the store, I ran off the next questions.

"What happened to the cats?"

"Somebody broke in and stole them."

"What did these guys think about that?"

"See these scars by my lip and chin? From stitches. You should've seen what I looked like Christmas Eve. Some present. At least they didn't burn the place down."

"I wonder what they'd do to the guy who stole the cats?" I asked. Dogg shivered.

"Cut off his balls," Chief Moses shouted, "and feed them to wild boars."

"Thanks Chief. Now I can sleep nights."

"What are you talking about?" Dogg asked in a petulant tone.

"Take it easy. Do you have a name for this gang?" I asked.

"No. I mean they didn't have any name except Raiders on their jackets."

"And they were all Asian?"

"Yes."

"Could you recognize them?"

"I've been trying real hard to forget them. That's the advice they gave me. I'm taking it."

"Were they Vietnamese?" Cambodian? Japanese? Korean? Chinese?"

"I don't know for sure."

"Try."

"Maybe Chinese. Maybe Japanese. I can't always tell."

"What do you think, Chief?" I asked.

The Chief wandered back over from a white and gray Alaskan Husky pup he was admiring. "I think he is telling the truth." He glared at Dogg. "Am I correct?"

"Yes, sir."

"You had better be," the Chief concluded.

After one last look at the Husky pup, we left Mr. Dogg to his pet and laboratory animal business.

"No forked tongue there. Just fear," Chief Moses said.

"Good call."

I wasn't sure where this was getting us, but a connection between an Asian gang and the CFAF was interesting, and possibly useful, information. Now where to find out about this gang? And was it related to the university? And how was it involved in Claire's kidnapping?

"The logical place to go is to the campus cops," the Chief said.

Maybe logical, but not very friendly. We sat in the Public Safety Office getting nowhere with the Chief of Campus Security, a tough old buzzard who used to be a cop in New York City, a fact he mentioned several times to impress us, until I remembered the man with clout. Professor Vernon Krift. If he could get heat in his office he could help us here. I didn't bother to ask to use a phone, but instead went outside. I gave him a call from a pay phone in front of the police building and told him our problem.

"I'll make a call. Give me a few minutes."

Ten minutes later we went back inside to see if he'd had any effect.

The atmosphere had changed. Chief Maxwell Richwine, formerly of New York City, brought in Officer Dixie Wynne, a young and attractive black woman with a sculptured dark Afro, who would help us out inside the office, and Officer Barry Kobida, who would be our contact on the outside. Kobida looked part-Chinese. He had glossy black hair with sixties-style sideburns and black eyes that reminded me of Chang's. He was at least six feet tall and well-built. He had to have spent a lot of time in a health club lifting weights.

I could tell the Chief was taken with Dixie Wynne. Which was hardly unusual. I could also tell that Barry Kobida was not too thrilled about working as our liaison. And one other thing. He kept staring at me as if he recognized me. I wondered if he was the cop who had rousted me that night at the HSC, but I didn't think so. I stared back and smiled. He didn't smile back. So much for charm.

We went to a file room in the back of the building with Kobida and Dixie. Without hesitation she went to a cabinet, pulled out a drawer, and came up with a file. She handed it to Kobida.

He looked it over, grunted, then said, "The gang you're talking about is the Co Gang. They're the Asian gang that wears the Raider jackets and black bandannas. William Co, a Chinese from L.A., runs it like a junior Mafia. Only no one gets anything on them. We got leads on stolen property, mostly VCRs and camcorders, and some grass and coke, and maybe even the production of amateur blue videos. But nothing we could pin on them good enough to make stick."

"And they're students?"

Dixie commented, "Oh yeah. On financial aid with the best grades money can buy. Or if that doesn't work, the best grades threats and intimidation can get. Which we can't prove either. Though one faculty member who defied them had his car blown up. He doesn't defy them anymore. Nobody does."

"Nice guys. Any other names besides Co?" I asked.

Kobida handed me a list from the file. I looked it over and Dixie made a copy for us.

"You must have addresses?" I asked.

Kobida forced a laugh. "We're supposed to. They all turn out to be phony."

"This is all hard to believe," I said.

"Gangs are never hard to believe. It's like we imported the whole bunch of them up from L.A. Damn. Some job of minority recruiting." The black woman laughed sardonically. "Here's a student directory. Maybe it'll help, but I doubt it."

We had names and bad addresses, but it was something.

"Thanks for the cooperation," I said to both of them.

Dixie looked around, then smiled for real for the first time. "Anytime. Barry and I are into sharing, unlike some other people around here."

I wondered about that.

"Sure. Anything you need, give me a call," Barry said without much enthusiasm. Only that same stare at me.

"Same here," Officer Wynne said, but sounded like she meant it.

Before we left, Chief Moses got her home phone number. Nice share.

"I would like to have her over to my houseboat," he said on the way out.

"It's good to see that lust is back."

"This is love, Jeremiah."

"Oh? No comment."

"Good. White Man. By the way, speaking of love, Kobida has his eye on you."

"Yeah. But I don't think it's love," I said, as I got in the pickup.

"Lust is not so bad." The Chief buckled up and drove off. Then added, "You should have taken his phone number."

"Next chance I get." I fastened my seatbelt.

First we checked the address for Co. 2020 Geek Street.

"Geek Street?" I asked.

"That may be a bunny," Chief Moses said.

"What are you talking about?" I asked.

"It may not be there."

"It's on the map. Right here at L dash two."

The Chief repeated his bunny line. And smiled enigmatically. I was baffled, but I wasn't going to ask about a bunny on the map.

"Is this some old Indian map trick?" I asked instead.

No answer.

No Geek Street either. We drove along Sansome to where the map showed it intersected with Geek. Nothing.

"A bunny," Chief Moses said.

"Okay. I give up. What the hell is a bunny?"

"It is a false street."

"If it's a fake, what's it doing on the Official San Francisco Street and Transit Map?"

"The map maker is protecting his copyright. If another company comes out with a map that has a Geek Street in the same spot it is easy to prove plagiarism."

"How many of these on a city map?"

"At least half a dozen I know of. Geek is a new one for me."

"Why bunnies?"

"After the children's puzzle. Find the hidden bunny."

"I should have guessed. Very clever."

"Also clever is this Co."

"I got that impression before."

"But we will get our man eventually."

"That's the agency spirit. Just like the Mounties."

"Mounties? White men in funny hats and silly red suits visible from miles away?"

"Sorry. I meant just like the Great Tracker of the Everglades."

"Better. Much better."

"Tell me. How did you track anything in a river of grass?"

"In an airboat."

Back at the office I got behind my desk. Johnny D had left a message on the answering machine. I called back just as Mickey walked in. I gestured for her to sit down on the couch next to Chief Moses while Johnny gave me the autopsy results. I turned on the speaker so my partners could hear.

"Like we thought, the bruises were fresh. There were no old bruises, suggesting there was no other earlier struggle than the one on Tuesday. The facial contusions indicate a ring on the left hand–probably a wedding ring. The actual cause of death was strangulation. There was no evidence of sexual abuse. No evidence of any recent sexual activity."

"Any idea what the killer used to strangle her?" I asked.

"Some kind of silk cord."

"Did it seem professional?"

"No. A clumsy job. An amateur. But a strong one."

"What about the time of death?" I asked.

"Sometime late Tuesday morning or early afternoon."

"While I was running from phone booth to phone booth. Anything else?"

"Two very interesting items. First, there was metabolized cocaine in her brain."

"Metabolized?"

"She'd probably been using it over the past few days."

"That's interesting," I said.

"Pretty good treatment from your kidnappers."

"And the second thing?" I asked.

"She had been injected with sodium pentothal, truth serum."

"Sounds like something out of the CIA," I said.

"Or worse," from the Chief.

"Yeah. But that cocaine. That bothers me. Was this for real?" Johnny asked.

"What?" I asked.

"The kidnapping."

"What do you think? She's dead, isn't she? This wasn't any trip to Disneyland."

"I don't know."

I had one more big question, but Johnny D didn't have any more answers. So I hung up and tried it out on my partners.

"What information did someone want from her so bad that they resorted to sodium pentothal?"

"And did they get it?" Chief Moses asked.

Mickey had another one. "Did she have a secret life?"

"Seems like it, Mickey, but who doesn't?" I said.

"A cocaine habit would be a motive for extortion," the Chief said, as he adjusted himself on the couch.

"Sure would be," I said. "Could explain why she wanted her old man's money so desperately."

"Speaking of money, what did you two find out today?" Mickey asked. "Any leads on the ransom money?" She crossed her legs under her short shirt, a sign that she was uptight.

I went over our visit to Dogg's Pet Store and to the campus police. The Asian gang got her going.

She moved to the edge of the couch. "In my search for this Vannessa kid, I've heard talk about a campus Asian gang. May not be anything, but. . ."

"Go for it. There may be something there. But be careful."

"Don't worry about that on either count. I'll go for it. You know how I feel about that missing money. But I'm worried about finding Vannessa."

"I'd like to keep Jimart happy, if possible," I said.

"I'm trying," Mickey said.

"That's good enough for me."

"I want that money back," she said.

"You're obsessed," I said.

"So what? That's how I get things done," she said, as she got up and walked out of my office.

14

Thursday, January fifth. Interrogation day. The weather continued to improve as I prepared to set out to question a few key people. I hoped that I wouldn't bump into Johnny or Chang, but I figured I'd be running behind them at this point. I'd be surprised if I got to any of the individuals on my list before the police. But first I remembered to feed the cat and put out fresh water.

I began with a telephone call to Ollie. She was still in shock from learning about Claire's murder. And somewhat cold to me because I hadn't called her for days. Beautiful women, no matter what their age, aren't used to being ignored.

"You've been reading the newspapers," I said.

"Yes. And watching TV. It's ghoulish."

"What about the cops?"

"They've been by. I didn't have much to tell them." Then she caught her breath. "Why haven't you called me?"

"I'm sorry. I just got buried in the case."

"Some excuse. I called you, but you were never in."

"Didn't you leave a message?" I asked.

"I hate those machines."

"I thought the younger generation were all high-tech," I said.

"I'm just an old-fashioned girl."

"Right."

After that exchange she somewhat reluctantly agreed to meet me for badminton at the Japantown courts.

"I miss you," I said.

"Me too," Ollie offered. The reluctance was gone. "Is this just going to be badminton?" she asked.

"I hope not. That's up to you."

"I forgive you for not calling, Jeremiah."

"Then let all the games begin."

We set up a time and I went upstairs to get ready.

Ollie was waiting for me on the courts dressed in silky black shorts, a tank top, white socks, and white court shoes. Her long hair was pulled back in a pony tail. She looked like a kid. A very beautiful one.

We started warming up. It was hard for me to concentrate. I was in love with the girl across the net. I needed help. I needed a little more resistance. I needed to get the damn shuttlecock over the net more often.

I lost the match in straight games to the relentless Ollie. Not as bad as last time, since I did get a few more points on overhead smashes, but bad enough. I collapsed, out of breath, against the gym wall.

She sat down beside me, breathing easily.

After I recovered, I asked her, "With the weather improving, do you do tennis?"

"No. The stroke is different. Tennis would ruin my badminton."

"I don't believe that. A racket is a racket."

"Don't be silly. My instructor said the two sports are not complementary. It is wrist versus arm."

"A pro speaks. What can I say to that?"

"Nothing."

After showers in our respective locker rooms, we met by the soda machine outside the gym doors. I bought her a diet Pepsi and I went for an A&W root beer.

"I've got to ask some questions," I said.

"About what?"

"Claire."

"Is that why you finally called?" she asked, her voice moving towards anger again.

"That. But mostly I wanted to see you."

That seemed to mollify her.

"Can't we just go over to your place?" she asked. "I really missed you."

"I've got to ask you some questions about Claire," I repeated.

"We can talk about it in bed."

"Oh sure. Why don't we just get this over with? Then we can discuss other activities."

"I told you. I was questioned by the police."

"Now it's my turn."

She sighed in resignation. "Let's sit down."

We took our sodas over to a bench by a candy machine. I offered to buy her something.

"Whatever you like," she said.

We each had a Reese's Peanut Butter Cup.

"What do you really know about her?" I asked.

"I wish I knew more. But I don't think she liked me. She certainly wasn't a friend." She took a bite of candy.

"Why do you think she didn't like you?"

"I don't know. The way she acted towards me. But as far as I could tell she didn't like a lot of people. Especially if her father paid attention to you and you happened to be female."

"Did Krift?"

"Yes. But nothing serious. The usual flirting."

"So, no friends, no acquaintances you can name?"

"Not really. Nobody you don't know."

"Who would she talk to?" I ate half my candy.

"Certainly not Heather. She'd talk to Wayne Ness. Who had a monumental crush on her. He is totally devastated by all this." Her candy was gone.

I didn't have much faith that Wayne Ness knew a lot, but it would be worth a try. "Anybody else? What about her roommate? Misty Finch. Were they close?"

"I don't know. They lived together."

"Did she ever mention the CFAF?"

"Sometimes she would talk about how cruel some animal experiments were. I had the feeling she didn't much like what she was doing. But she never mentioned any specific animal rights organization."

"Then exactly why was she there?" I finished my piece.

"That doesn't take a lot of thought. It was to torment her father for her mother's suicide."

I nodded and changed the subject. "What about Asian gangs? Could she have been involved with one?"

"Not that I know of."

"What about her use of cocaine?"

"I'd heard rumors. That's all."

"That she had a habit?"

"More of a social user. But who knows?"

We walked out together through the *torii* gate into that little street that represented a Japanese mountain village.

This time we sat down on a varnished wooden bench under a bare cherry tree.

We looked at each other and knew it was time to find my bedroom again.

Without saying a word we got up and walked hand-in-hand to the Victorian. I knew my partners would be out again.

Our lovemaking was a reprise of that first time. It was like discovering each other and our bodies all over again. It was a delight to see once more her full breasts, the light aureoles of her nipples, her softly rounded belly, and the dark inviting V between her slim thighs.

After the second time, both of us dipped into our separate repertoire and came up with a few new games to get up a third and fourth time.

Once again we came close to depleting the condom supply.

"You ought to put in a bigger supply, lover," she whispered in my ear as she bit it.

"I'll order a case. Any preference for color?"

"Whatever turns you on," she said.

"You do."

And she did.

As we came apart one last time, I said, "I love you, Ollie."

"I love you, Jeremiah."

Then we just held each other. It was a moment of higher love. Or another moment of exhaustion.

I finally thought about my partners and checked my watch. It was late enough so that they might show up at any time.

"We'd better get dressed." I sat up in bed.

"Why?" She pulled the covers over her head.

"I do have a business to run downstairs."

She pretended not to hear me, but finally gave it up. We got up and got dressed with our backs to each other. Some people smoke after sex. Some people get modest. We were the latter.

Properly dressed, we went downstairs. It was supposed to look like a Q&A was in progress. Except that we couldn't stop looking at each other. Or keep our hands off each other. Ollie ended up sitting on my lap.

I made her get up and sit down in the client's chair to get a little distance between us.

"No getting up now. This has to look right," I insisted.

I sat down behind my desk. I started checking the student directory I'd gotten from Officer Dixie Wynne. I found the address for Wayne Ness. It was in the same apartment complex close to the campus where Misty and Claire had shared an apartment. No "bunny" here.

The timing was perfect. Mickey and the Chief arrived and I introduced them. They were both still working on their own cases. The Chief had more work to do in the Love Dick area for his client. Mickey was still hunting for Vannessa. With her eye out for the fifty grand and the Asian gang.

"How's it going, Jeremiah?" the Chief asked.

"I'm going to see a man who had a crush on Claire."

15

We left my partners. I dropped Ollie off at the dorm, with a passionate kiss, and descended on Wayne. With school out of session, Wayne was in his living room, reading. The place looked like the typical graduate student's apartment. The shelves and tables were bricks and boards and the furniture would have been rejected by street people. The bottom half of each window was painted black, which saved on shades and curtains. Wayne didn't seem real happy to see me again. He told me that the cops had been by already. That was good. I was bringing up the rear and staying out of their way. I sat down on the couch. That was a mistake. A cloud of dust rose up around me. Wayne sat down on an ancient leather recliner.

"You ever hear of a vacuum cleaner?"

"It broke."

"You ever hear of maid service?"

"I'm broke."

"You have a roommate?"

"He moved out."

"I wonder why."

"I'm advertising for a new one. I need the money to keep this place."

"Good luck."

"Can we cut the crap?" he asked.

"Sure."

"I understand Claire's funeral is Saturday," he said morosely.

"I didn't know."

"Who could have done this to her?"

"It's not my job to find out. But I may just bump into it along the way. I'd like to ask you some questions."

I could see that he was thinking it over. Finally he said, "What the hell?" He dropped the recliner back slightly. He looked like he was ready to be barbered. Which wasn't a bad idea.

"Good attitude. Did you have a crush on her?"

"Crush? I was in love with her, if that's what you mean."

"Did you know she did coke?"

He sat up straight. "No. I don't believe it."

"It's in the autopsy report. Metabolized cocaine."

"The people who kidnapped her forced her."

"Maybe. But I doubt it. How did she feel about you?"

"She. . . liked me." He was on the edge of the recliner now.

"How?"

"As a friend."

"Did you date?"

"Yes. No. Not really. We went to some lectures together. And coffee afterwards."

Pathetic, I thought.

"Did she ever say anything about a William Co?" I asked.

"The Co Gang? No way."

"You know about them?"

"Everybody does. They're terrorists on the campus."

"If she thought of you as a friend, who was the guy in her romantic life?"

"She didn't have one." He settled back.

"Why don't I believe that?"

"She never talked about anybody."

"Maybe not to you. What'd she have against Ollie?"

"Nothing really. Except that she was another pretty coed around her father."

"How about Heather?"

"She hated Heather. It was her father's affair with Heather Clark that drove her mother to suicide."

"Any idea what kind of information she could've had that someone would use sodium pentothal on her?"

He jumped out of the recliner. "Christ. Did they do that?"

"Yes. They must have wanted to learn something awful bad."

"And when she talked, they killed her," Wayne said.

"Very good. You'd make an okay detective. That's the way I read it," I said, bringing him along.

"What could she have known?" he asked.

"That's what I asked you."

"Something she shouldn't have," Wayne tried.

"That doesn't help."

But that was all I got from Wayne.

I walked over to the B Building to what had been Claire's apartment and found the charmingly named Misty Finch at home. She was a short, freckled redhead with a pug nose, sensuous red lips, light green eyes, and a very full figure—Rubenesque in another age—that she packed into faded designer jeans. Ironically, she looked like she could have been Heather's sister. Maybe Claire liked to torment herself.

This apartment was neat, with cheap, but decent, Danish Modern furniture, white window shades, and green curtains that matched the green rug. I was sure they owned a vacuum cleaner.

Ms. Finch was clearly upset and at first reluctant to let me sit down, much less talk, telling me that the police had already questioned her. Funny how everybody says that.

"But I'm a private eye working for her father."

That didn't cut it.

But after some more friendly persuasion, Misty Finch invited me to take a chair. She herself stayed standing. She told me what a private person Claire was, but confirmed what Wayne said concerning Heather Clark, Krift, and her mother. "That's why she wouldn't live with him in that big house he owns."

I understood.

"Weren't you surprised when she didn't show up last Sunday and Monday?" I asked.

"No. She told me she was going out of town with some friends. She expected to be back Tuesday night."

Just when the kidnapping was scheduled to come to an end. "Did you see who she left with on Sunday?"

"She packed her bags and went out to the lot."

"Did you see a car?" I was hoping for a red and white '55 Chevy.

"No."

"Did she ever talk about Wayne Ness?" I asked.

"Yeah."

"What'd she say?"

"That he was a jerk."

"He was in love with her."

"She didn't care. She still thought he was a jerk."

"She have a boyfriend? Wayne said no."

"Oh what does he know?" She finally sat down.

But for me to know took a while. I got up. I had to get pushy. I went into the bedroom and started going through what remained of Claire's things. And making a mess.

"Stop that. You can't do that," Misty shouted from the door. "Some of that is my stuff."

"Too bad."

"Please."

"I can stop if you help me." I could tell I wasn't coming up with much of anything myself.

"The police have been through everything."

That didn't stop me. I started tossing bras and panties on the bed.

"Stop! What do you want?"

"A lead. A name. A boyfriend."

"All right." Misty came up with a little black telephone book.

"Is her boyfriend in there?"

"Yes," she said, as she waved it in front of me.

I moved closer to her. Threatening. Even though I knew I wouldn't touch her. But she didn't know that. I put out my hand for the book.

Misty looked at me. She backed away and sat down on the bed and opened the book. She pointed to a name and a phone number and said, "Cody Zering." She didn't have an address.

"Thank you. Did you give his name to the police?"

"No. I didn't tell them about Cody."

"What could she have known that someone would use truth serum on her?"

"God. Did they do that?"

"Yes."

"I haven't got the faintest."

"If you have any idea, for your own protection tell me, or tell the police."

"I don't know anything. I swear."

"I'm not the one you have to convince. One last thing. Did she do coke?"

She gave that a second's consideration. "Sometimes she did. But not much."

"Where did she get it?"

"I don't know."

"What about her boyfriend?"

"I've seen them snorting coke together here."

"Was he the supplier?"

"I guess so. I really don't know."

I had a lead. I left Misty and went out to my car. I checked my directory and got an address for Cody Zering that was out by Ocean Beach along the Pacific Coast Highway. I drove out to the western edge of the city—and out of the continent. The Beach, as the area is known, is different from the rest of San Francisco. It is colder, foggier, and more clannish, as if the shifting windblown sands initiated residents into an oddball fraternity.

The address turned out to be real. I found a rundown wooden duplex that at least had a nice location. The Pacific was pounding the coast less than a hundred yards away across the Great Highway and the salt air had weathered the redwood siding of the building to dull driftwood gray. No one was home when I tried the doorbell. I wondered if Misty had given him a call to warn him.

I drove along the highway until I spotted a pay phone in a parking area by the beach. I gave Johnny a call to see if he had come up with anything.

"What the hell are you doin', Jeremiah?"

"Trying to protect Krift's cats from the CFAF." That seemed like the best approach to take with the police. "And don't forget his fifty grand."

"And interfering in a murder investigation."

"Speaking of that, what's your take on it?"

"Shit, I shouldn't be talkin' to you."

"If I come across anything, I'll let you in on it," I promised.

"Bullshit."

"Look, with all the budget cuts you're taking you can use all the help you can get."

"Goddam politicians. They'll bankrupt this city yet." Then he went on about how gays were trying to get health benefits for their domestic partners while police were being laid off. "This city is ass-backwards."

"It's the San Francisco tradition. Like Rice-A-Roni."

"Great." He started again.

I interrupted him with a question about the case. It put him back on track.

"Okay. We're treating it just like we said. Kidnappers disposing of the victim to protect themselves."

"What if Claire was involved herself? To get revenge on her father?"

"For what?"

I explained.

"That's pretty good, but it doesn't change the scenario. Maybe she went along with it. What her roommate told us would substantiate that take on it. But they decided to wax her anyway to keep all the money. Still makes sense. Only the victim is not so blameless here."

"Only these would be people she knew. People she trusted. That changes the mix of possible suspects."

"Friends who got greedy," Johnny noted. "We're following that angle too."

"It's a real possibility. What about the sodium pentothal?"

"Someone wanted information."

"Brilliant."

"Could you do better?"

"If I do, I'll let you know."

"Stay out of it, Jeremiah."

"I've got a job to do too. I'll keep in touch."

"Oh Christ, thank you." Johnny hung up.

But I knew he appreciated what I had given him about Claire. Sure.

I drove over to a grocery store on 48th and bought some supplies. I went back to Cody's place and set up a stakeout in my car. I watched strands of fog break off, and mist dampen the windows of my car. I opened up some brandy to fight the cold and hoped I had put out enough cat food this morning. I settled in for a long stay.

16

While I had no luck with my stakeout of Zering's apartment, finally leaving the beach at one in the morning, I started Friday with a nice surprise. I was having coffee with Mickey in my office when the Chief brought in a huge check from his client, who had decided to run off to Las Vegas to get married to a third gentleman, one that the Chief had not investigated. So much for the Love Dick job.

"What happened?" I asked.

"She said she did not want to marry either one, after what I uncovered about their unsavory sexual activities. And she does not want to find out the same kinds of things about this one."

"You've put the mystery of romance back into her life," Mickey said.

"She did not wish to discover any warts."

"So she didn't look," Mickey said.

"Let us hope she does not catch the genital variety from this adventure," Chief Moses said.

I looked at Mickey, then asked the Chief, "Now that you're free, can you run a check on this Mike Wesolski we keep hearing about? Maybe check out his warts?"

"Which kind?" the Chief asked.

"Both."

"Kiss off, you guys," Mickey said. "He and I have had open and honest discussions. About everything."

"Very mature and very contemporary," I said.

"Enough, Jeremiah," Mickey said. Her face was unnaturally flushed. "He's sailing soon with Greenearth."

I backed off. The teasing was wearing thin. I turned to Chief Moses again, "At least the lady paid. But now you don't have a case."

Which meant the man was free to help in mine. Mickey, on the other hand, had dropped the word on the street that she was interested in the Co Gang, and was waiting for some kind of response. It was our best lead to the fifty grand and most everything else.

"What do you want me to do?" the Chief asked. "Now that I am no longer gainfully employed as a Love Dick."

"Go to college."

"Can I date coeds?"

"If they'll have you."

"How about campus police?"

"Named Dixie Wynne?"

"You have it."

"No. You'll be undercover. She knows you. Stick to coeds."

Chief Moses grinned. "I have my shirts." The shirts were Florida State football jerseys that he gave out as party favors. The numbers on the back were different and helped him keep the ladies straight. The Indian logo on the front looked like him, which kept him in the minds of the ladies. The jerseys went back to the days when Chief Moses briefly played on the Seminole offensive line in Tallahassee.

I called our regular ID forger, but he was on a skiing vacation in Aspen. We would have to wait until he got back on Sunday to get Chief Moses the right student cards for identification. Unless we shopped around for another practitioner of the art.

"Can you wait for our man?" I asked the now anxious Chief.

"I will go hang around the campus. Get used to the college scene. Suck up some atmosphere."

"I'm not sending you to a fraternity party."

"Then what is my cover?"

"This better be good, Jeremiah," Mickey threw in.

"You'll be an animal rights activist from the Everglades trying to hook up with the CFAF. You ought to be comfortable with that."

"A fraternity party will not hurt while I fight to protect the white ibis and the alligator. Besides, it is Friday."

"Oh, let him have some fun," Mickey said.

"When doesn't he have fun? The bad news is that school is not in session yet. That could cut down on the fun quotient significantly."

"When does it start?" he asked.

"Registration is next week. All of the groups, from the Mormons to the atheists and from the Students for Vivisection to the Humane Society will be out recruiting at tables outside of the gym."

"You expect the CFAF to be signing people up at a table under their banner? Someone there is wanted for murder and kidnapping. Join the CFAF and Go to Jail," Mickey pointed out.

"There will be other animal rights groups. One of them could be a front for the CFAF."

"Which one?" Chief Moses asked.

"That's your job. You've got to do something on your own."

"One last question?" he asked.

"Yes?" I wasn't sure what to expect from the Chief.

"Will I have to go to class?"

"Did you go to class when you played football at FSU?"

"Not often."

"Maybe that's why you didn't last too long."

"It was my knee. But I did study *Macbeth* and *Hamlet*."

"Sit in on some big classes. Play the role. Maybe you'll learn something new."

"I will take a course in Native American Studies. I am interested in the reburial rights issue."

That Chief Moses was concerned about the bones of his ancestors being returned to their burial ground didn't surprise me. The Chief likes everything in its proper place.

"I didn't know you were interested in that issue," Mickey said.

"What if Indians went around digging up the graves of white people to study their bones?" he asked rhetorically.

Actually, I thought that had been going on for hundreds of years, or what was the point of an Anthropology degree? But I didn't say anything.

"I get the point," Mickey said.

"You may enjoy going back to college, Chief," I said.

"I might even get more out of it this time."

On Saturday I went to the funeral. The day was warm, continuing the recent weather trend. I wore the only dark suit I had, a woolen three-piece dark gray pinstripe left over from my lawyer days. It still fit pretty good, though the cut of the lapels was out of fashion. I didn't think anyone would notice or care.

The funeral was in a non-denominational chapel near the campus. I parked in a lot behind the building, facing a stained glass window depicting a fifteen-foot-high Christ with a lamb in his arms. Christ as Shepherd. Not much work for shepherds of any kind these days in The City. Maybe that was what was wrong with modern life. Not enough shepherding jobs for teenagers and too many at Mickey D's or Domino's.

I signed the mourner book and took a seat in a polished wooden pew. Unlike the Catholic churches I was used to in childhood, there was nothing to kneel on. So like everyone else, I sat and looked around. I knew a few people in the chapel, but not many. I wondered if Cody Zering was there.

Claire's coffin was at the front of the chapel, surrounded by flowers. The scent was sickly sweet, cloying like the smell of a woman wearing too much floral perfume. The bronze coffin was open, but I didn't plan to go up to see Claire's body. I knew what she looked like in death already from the motel scene. Once was enough when it came to dead bodies.

Until I saw Misty Finch go up to the coffin. She was dressed in a dark blue suit and a light blue blouse and black hose and heels. I got out of my seat and moved up next to her. She didn't seem real happy to see me, but I was used to that. I looked at Claire's face resting on a pillow of white satin. It was beautiful.

"She looks at peace," Misty said.

"She's not. Not until her killer is found."

"Nice thought."

"Is Cody Zering here?" I asked.

"I didn't see him."

"Look around."

"From up here?"

"Be subtle. You can do it."

She turned around and looked quickly at the people in the chapel. "No." She moved away from me and took a seat before I could ask her to give it a second chance. I went back to mine to wait for the service.

After the minister finished with his reassuring platitudes, his quotes from the Psalms of David, his retelling of one of the parables of Christ in contemporary non-sexist English that had none of the effectiveness of the King James' version, and his mispronunciation of Claire's name as "Kraft," we heard the expected tributes from her friends and relatives. Wayne Ness had his say, as did Heather Clark—which surprised me. Vernon Krift was too emotionally drained to say much more than that he would miss his daughter. I didn't much like speaking at these services and I doubted that anyone wanted to hear from the PI who had discovered her body. I had the good sense, which I wished some of the other speakers had possessed, who seemed hardly to have known Claire at all, to keep quiet. They reminded me of the old Italian professional mourners you could hire in North Beach if you needed some moaners to swell a funeral crowd.

I drove through the city out to the suburban cemetery with my lights on, despite the sunny day, following symbolic tradition and the funeral procession. I noticed several press cars were with us. At the place of burial there were more reporters and TV cameras. I took a folding chair next to Misty's and asked her about Cody Zering again.

"I don't see him. Now leave me alone."

"You're not looking."

"I did look. I swear."

"Did you tell him I was looking for him?"

"No. Now please leave me alone."

I didn't believe her, but I did leave her alone.

After the words at the grave, after the rite of the flowers, before the casket was lowered hydraulically into the fresh grave, I had a chance to talk to Krift when I rescued him from several annoying reporters who had him cornered.

We stood under a eucalyptus tree, whose leaves had been frostbitten to a dull brown by the cold. The leaves were curled up like the fingers of dead men, but none of them had dropped yet. Suspended. Refusing to let go.

The weather had warmed quite a bit even since the morning. I was sure it was in the sixties this afternoon. I was getting uncomfortable in my woolen suit.

After the condolences, I got down to basics with Krift.

"You still believe she was involved in her own kidnapping?"

"I do. Damn it."

"Did you see the autopsy report?"

"No."

"She was using cocaine."

"I'm not surprised. She would do anything to hurt me."

"During her kidnapping."

"That proves she was in on it."

"Probably. Any idea where she got it?"

"How am I supposed to know that?"

"Think about it. Who deals on campus?"

"Who doesn't?"

"Do you know a Cody Zering?"

"No. Who is he?"

"Supposedly Claire's boyfriend."

"Was he at the funeral today?" Krift asked.

"Not as far as I know."

"She never mentioned him. Was he involved in the kidnapping?"

Before I could try for an answer I noticed Oscar Chang and Johnny D slowly heading our way, walking with their heads down.

"We need to talk to you," Johnny D called to me in a mournful voice.

I watched their slow march towards us.

I didn't want to talk to them. I didn't want to hear what they had to say. I didn't like the way they were looking at me. I had seen looks like that before and the news was always bad.

But I knew I would have to face their reality. The two of them acknowledged Krift and then took me to the base of a small rise that overlooked a green valley of simple white crosses.

I looked into Johnny D's blue eyes and then into the anthracite of Chang's. Something was very wrong. My first fear was that something had happened to Mickey or the Chief.

"What's wrong?" I asked. "What's happened?"

Chang, cool and pressed as ever, did the talking. "There's been another murder of a coed. This time on campus."

"Today?" I almost felt relieved. Not Mickey or the Chief.

"Actually, early this morning. The body was discovered in the bushes near the HSC by the campus police."

I didn't understand. "So what are you doing here talking to me?" I started to worry again. It couldn't be. . . The HSC. . . *No.*

"I hear that you knew the victim pretty well."

No. It couldn't be. "What's her name?" I asked.

"She's been identified as Olivia Shimoda."

My jaw dropped. My knees buckled. I wanted to howl out my anguish. I looked towards the fresh earth dug up for Claire. Its ripe smell filled the warm air. If this was true, if this just wasn't some nightmare, I would be going to another funeral. For a child. For a child I loved furiously.

"Are you sure it's her?" I tried in desperation.

"Her father identified the body at the morgue."

At the morgue. "No. No." Then I got hold of myself and tried to be professional. "How did she die?"

"Strangled to death."

I let that sink in. I was trying to hold on. "Any possible connection to Claire Krift's death?" I asked.

"Only the means of murder seem similar," Chang said.

"How?" I asked.

"We've had a preliminary report. The fibers from her neck indicate a silk cord."

"The same silk cord?" I asked.

"Forensics can't be sure. The fiber sample was inadequate," Chang said.

"There wasn't anything about a silk cord in the newspapers," I said.

"We decided to withhold that information."

"That increases the chances of the same killer."

"And cuts way down on the chance of a copycat."

"But there is still coincidence," I said. "Were there any differences?"

"Facial bruises were similar. We don't have a toxicology report yet on truth serum," Chang said.

"Two young women who worked in the same building murdered in identical ways. I say we have one killer," Johnny said.

It struck me again like a sucker punch. Ollie dead. I had to get objective. "Any suspects? Any leads? Any witnesses?" I knew the answers I was going to get, but I had to go through the drill for my own sanity.

"*Nada*," Johnny D said.

"What was your relationship with Miss Shimoda?" Chang asked.

"We. . . played badminton together."

"Come on," Johnny put in.

"I think we were a little bit in love with each other. That's as far as it went." I started to walk away.

"What the hell does that mean?" Johnny asked.

"Nothing."

"Were you sleeping with her?" Chang asked.

"None of your business."

"She's talked about you. We know you were lovers."

That surprised me. "Does that make me a suspect?"

"You have an alibi?" Johnny asked.

"Go fuck yourself."

"That won't substitute for a good alibi," Johnny let me know.

"This relationship with the girl does not change anything, Jeremiah," Chang said. "You stay out of this."

"This makes it personal. Very personal. Now go talk to Krift. He knew her too." I tried to escape.

"If you two were in love, we got a possible motive," Johnny said. "One that cuts two ways."

I stopped. "What're you talking about?"

"This Olivia was engaged to be married."

"No."

"Her father told us," Chang said.

"He's lying."

I couldn't take any more. Before they could say anything else I was over a small green hill, through rows of tombstones, and gone to my car. I drove back like a lunatic–I always wondered how I managed to avoid getting a ticket for reckless driving–to the office, and then rushed over on foot to the nearest bar, which I got to by heading up Octavia through Lafayette Park at the top of the hill and then down to a small place behind the lobby of a hotel on Lombard. I liked the bar because it was usually pretty empty and the people there didn't go in much for idle bullshit. Even the bartender was the silent type.

I bought the evening *Examiner* and read what they had to say about the murder. They were connecting it to Claire's death and talking about a serial killer stalking and killing coeds on the San Francisco campus. That was it. Not much for details. Not much to inspire a copycat. I read the headline story over and over as I spent the next three hours with two new partners, Jim Beam and Henry Weinhard, trying to figure it all out. And trying to dull the pain so I wouldn't visualize what my beautiful Ollie had suffered.

Ollie murdered. I moved from that fact to other painful ones that I had to come to terms with. Ollie engaged. What else was happening in her life? Maybe like Claire, she had other secrets? Maybe she knew much more about Claire than she had told me? What if she had the same information that Claire was killed for? Was the motive for her murder to keep Ollie quiet? And who had told Chang about Ollie and me?

I downed another boilermaker. Trying to feel better. But after those three hours I only felt worse. But at least I didn't have a car to drive. The last thing I needed was a DUI.

To this day I'm still not sure how I made it back. I do remember going down to the sunken tennis courts in the park and trying some shadow tennis in the dark. And I remember rushing off the courts to throw up in some convenient bushes. The highlight of the evening.

17

Sunday was supposed to be fun. I was badly hung over, sad, and angry. And I needed some food to feed all the fires raging inside me.

Mickey and the Chief came over to celebrate the Chief's birthday, which happened to be January 8th, the same birthdate as Elvis.

I came downstairs looking like shit.

"You look like shit," my partners echoed each other.

"It's my new contemporary look."

"I will sing 'You Ain't Nothin' But A Hound Dog'," the Chief, who had combed his hair into a parody of the Las Vegas Elvis hair style, and was wearing some kind of strange striped jump suit, offered.

They hadn't heard about Ollie. I turned the Elvis imitator down with a comment on his look and his musical selection.

"You do not like the hair? Or maybe you do not like the outfit? I found it in a Goodwill previously-worn clothing store. How about 'Love Me Tender'? Or 'Blue Moon'? Or 'Heartbreak Hotel'?"

"Please. My head is killing me. Didn't you read the goddam papers? Or watch the news?"

"What did we miss?" Mickey asked, concern written across her face.

Chief Moses grew solemn.

We had been through things like this before.

"Another murder."

"I was just too busy to see a newspaper or a TV," Mickey said in apology.

"I decided not to read any. Part of my disguise as a college student," the Chief explained.

I told them what had happened to Ollie. The word "murdered" stuck in my throat like a bone.

They had only met her once. The Chief asked, "This is the badminton girl?"

"Yes."

"And you cared for her, didn't you?" Mickey asked.

"Very much."

"She was beautiful. And young," the Chief said.

Although it was hard for me, we talked about whether her death was related to Claire's murder. There were similarities, such as the silk cord. And then there was the truth serum, or lack of it.

After that discussion I tried to get things back to normal. We all ate sandwiches and my partners drank beer and wine while I drank cream-flavored New York Seltzer and watched the 49er game against the Bears. At halftime we had a chocolate birthday cake Mickey had brought over. It was in the shape of a guitar and it had Elvis' face on it. And forty candles, which the Chief laughed at. No one knew exactly how old the man was, not even the Chief himself. We got up a pretty sorry version of "Happy Birthday" while he blew out the candles. We ate the cake and gave him our gifts during the third quarter. I gave him a plastic Jesus.

"Put it on your dashboard. You need all the help you can get." And then I gave him three tickets to a Warrior game.

"Glad you had a real present, White Man."

"And three. In case you have some friends you want to take along."

"No one I can think of. I will scalp them at the Oakland Arena before the game. I like that. Ticket scalping. It seems appropriate for an Indian."

We watched the end of the game. The Niners annihilated the Bears, 28 to 3. It was on to the Super Bowl against Cincinnati in two weeks.

And on to another funeral on Wednesday as I read in the obit column. I put it out of my mind.

When the game was over, I called our vacationing forger. The man was back from Aspen. He told me what a great time he had. I told him we needed his services.

"I am now open for business."

We got the Chief over to the ID man, whose operation was in a large back room behind a legitimate photocopying business downtown. The man, a prematurely bald, recent Stanford graduate, who had gone into this lucrative sideline after two legal ventures had failed, kept talking about his skiing vacation, and the one warm day when he had seen two women skiing topless on his run, while he worked on the Chief's IDs. In less than two hours he set the Chief up with just what he needed to pass for a student.

"Next time you're out of town, leave someone to cover for you," I suggested.

"Plan ahead better," he recommended, as he locked up behind us.

On Monday I forced myself to get back to work and drove out to the Beach once again. This time I located Cody Zering at his Pacific Highway address. He wasn't happy about opening the door for me, but I told him it was me or the cops.

"They don't know about you yet. But they will," I promised.

He let me in. The decor was different. Everything was nautical, including the cheap unframed prints on the wall, and the Maine lobster trap that had been converted into a coffee table.

He noticed me looking around and said, "It came furnished."

I shrugged.

Cody was tall and handsome, with blue eyes, dark hair, and a lean body. He was dressed in a white fisherman's sweater that matched the decor, faded jeans, and worn running shoes.

We sat down on Salvation Army Modern chairs that had nothing to do with the nautical theme.

I went through a lot of the same questions. Who were her friends? Who could have been involved? Did Claire set this all up herself? What was the killer after with the truth serum? And some new ones: Why wasn't he at the funeral? Where did he get his cocaine? What did he know about the Co Gang? What did he know about Ollie Shimoda's death?

I didn't have much success with the old or the new. He claimed to know very little. And he denied a lot. Like the cocaine. I let him off for now, but I knew I would be back. I knew he had better answers to give me. I could be patient.

Students were beginning to return to the college and fear was starting to spread across the campus. Two murders of coeds during the break did not inspire a sense of security. And an unfounded rumor spread about other attacks on women. Claire's name and Ollie's name were put in black letters on the side of the Student Union building. The newly created mourning wall. Flowers were strewn all about at its base. Some coeds just turned right around and went back home. Others agreed to share rooms in the dorms, or to sleep in the dorm lounges, rather than alone in apartments. Whistles were given out to everyone on campus. An escort service was established to walk women home at night.

The women I was worried about were those who knew what Claire had known. And maybe what Ollie had known. Or what a killer might think they knew. Knowledge by association was a very real assumption the killer could make.

I spent an hour with Officer Barry Kobida walking around campus. As it turned out, he was the one who had discovered the body. I tried to get a sense of what he knew, but it was very little. He had heard nothing. No screams. No struggle. He just happened to stumble over the body. I didn't feel like I was getting anywhere.

On Wednesday the Chief went to register for classes at the university. Or at least to pretend that was what he was doing. He already had all of the documentation that he needed, including a phony permit to register, marked "paid", and his student ID card.

On Wednesday I went to Ollie's funeral dressed in the same woolen suit I had worn to Claire's. It was in the same chapel. For the first time I realized that Ollie was a Christian. It had never come up. Wayne, Heather, Snokes, and Krift were all there. And a lot of Japanese family members, some of whom were giving me hostile looks. I tried to pick out Ollie's fiancé, but there were too many young men who were possibles. And then I noticed that Barry Kobida had come to the funeral with Dixie Wynne. That was a nice touch.

It was a moving service with a different, much younger minister who got the name right and did a reasonable job with the eulogy. I stayed after most of the people had left, praying Catholic prayers I dredged up from a long time ago. After that, I walked out into a warm and sunny afternoon. The rain we needed was keeping away and drought conditions were not far off. The temperature was nearly seventy. The earth had changed.

It was time to drive to the cemetery again.

As I got near my car, I heard a shot and felt a burning sensation along my left biceps, like a whip had been snapped across it. I hit the ground as several more bullets tore over me into the metal of my T-Bird. I scrambled around the front end of the car and got into a fairly safe position. Instinctively, I felt for my S&W, but I had left it at the office, having seen no need to bring it to a funeral.

The gunman, a young Asian dressed in a black suit, certainly one of the mourners, and making no attempt to hide, was standing across the street from the lot, in the open. The crowds of people who were on the street a moment ago had disappeared like people in a western town during a high noon gunfight. He fired three more bullets that hit the concrete wall behind me and ricocheted harmlessly away. I had counted six shots so far.

When I saw that he was trying to reload I took off after him. He fumbled with the revolver and then decided he couldn't get it loaded in time to get off a shot and took off. He was fast. I finally ran the guy down in an alley behind a Chinese grocery store, and dropped him to the ground. I pinned his arms, forced him to drop the gun, and looked at his face. He was worse than young, he was just a kid.

I was out of breath. When I recovered I let him up and asked, "Why'd you shoot at me?"

"Because you were Olivia's lover." He brushed himself off.

"Who are you?" I had a pretty good idea.

"The man who was to marry her until you stole her from me."

"I didn't know she was engaged."

"You've been seeing her behind my back for months."

"What are you talking about? I only met her last month."

"Liar. You've been sneaking around with her all summer and autumn."

"You have a problem with jealousy."

"An Asian woman who has a white lover deserves to die." He looked at the gun on the ground and spat at me. The spittle landed on my arm.

"And maybe you did the killing?"

His anger turned to sorrow. "No. Never. I loved her."

"What's your problem with me?"

"She said she did not wish to marry me."

I didn't answer that one. I repeated: "Did you kill her?"

"No. No."

I believed him. "Do you know who killed her?"

"No."

"How old are you?"

"Seventeen."

"I thought so. Younger than Ollie."

He started crying.

"And this was an arranged marriage?"

"Yes. Our families were to be united." Tears were running down his face. Blood was running down my arm. It wasn't a pleasant feeling.

I didn't ask how Ollie felt about their arranged marriage. "Why did you accuse me of seeing her as long ago as the summer?"

"Because I know she has been seeing someone. I followed you in Japantown. I saw you together. It had to be you."

"We played badminton. I'm talking about the summer when I didn't know she existed."

"Lying dog." He made a move to get the gun on the ground. I did some minor damage to his wrist with my foot. I picked up his gun and tried to get some more out of him. It was no use. And I didn't have the stomach to use any more force. Besides, I expected the police to be arriving any moment. I checked his wallet to get his name and address for later reference and for the police. No matter what he said, he was a suspect. Then I left him crying in the alley behind the Chinese grocery. It was pretty bad shit all the way around. I checked my arm and saw that blood had completely covered my jacket sleeve. It was dripping down onto my hand. I went into a chain drugstore a block away to get some bandages to stop the bleeding.

I took off the suit jacket. It was ruined, but the cut was out of style and I hoped to hell I wouldn't have any more funerals to attend.

The pharmacist, an elegant looking man of about sixty, with a full head of white hair and an aquiline nose, went into a panic and put on rubber gloves to go with his white lab coat when he saw me bleeding all over the center aisle of the store. I didn't blame him. I would have done the same thing. I took my bloody shirt off and put it in a plastic bag. The pharmacist looked at my arm and got out a first aid kit and patched me up quickly.

"It looked a lot worse than it was. You won't even need a stitch," he said.

"Thanks," I said.

"What happened?"

"An accident," I said. "How much do I owe you?"

"No charge. Just get that jacket out of here." Then he gave me advice about cleaning the wound and changing the bandage.

I thanked him again, bought a bottle of aspirin, some bandages, an antibiotic cream, and a cheap white shirt that I put on in the aisle, and tried to leave the suit jacket behind, but he noticed and insisted that I remove it. I dumped it in a garbage can on the street, along with the plastic bag that held my shirt.

I drove back to my office.

On the good news front, the Chief had made contact with various student groups during registration. He was an all around activist specializing in animal rights and the environment, with a record of constructive destruction in Florida. Where it was too hot for him.

He had dates with several female animal rights coeds to look forward to.

"They will talk."

"How is it there?" I asked.

"Fear is the word. Here is a whistle they gave me in case of trouble." He pulled it out from under his shirt.

"You planning on using it?"

"If necessary."

When Mickey came in I told them both about the shots that Ollie's fiancé had taken at me, and the motive he suggested for Ollie's murder.

"The motive he proposed is interesting, but it leads right back to him," the Chief said.

I called Johnny D and went over what happened.

"Do we tell these Asian broads to stay away from white guys?" he asked, after I gave him a possible motive. "That's unconstitutional."

"I'm saying we might be looking for a bitter Asian male in this case." I gave him the name of Ollie's fiancé.

"We've talked to the family already. But we'll pick him up for the shooting."

"Don't. I won't testify. There's no case."

"We'll talk to the boy again. Check his alibi."

"Glad to help whenever you need it," I said.

"This is too personal for you. Stay the fuck out."

"Thanks for the sensitive advice."

"Any time."

"Don't hang up. Anything new from Ollie's autopsy?"

He hesitated. "Strangled with a silk cord. No sexual abuse. No cocaine. No sodium pentothal. Facial bruises. Some inflicted after death. Again the killer was probably wearing a wedding ring." He hung up.

"So you're not going to let them press charges," Mickey said.

"No."

"Let's hope he doesn't try again," Mickey said.

"I know. He might get my blue blazer next time. Then I *would* sic the DA on him." I tried to be funny but it fell flat.

I told them about Ollie and that truth serum wasn't used on her.

"Then it wasn't for information?" Mickey asked.

"There are other ways of getting information," the Chief noted.

"Is this one really different?" Mickey asked.

"No. The MO seems the same," I said. To my surprise I felt tears well up in my eyes.

18

I spent Thursday and Friday in mourning. And in a deep depression that was going to last a lot longer. I missed Ollie; I felt sorry for her fiancé; I felt sorry for myself. And I felt guilty. What business did I have falling in love with an eighteen-year-old? One who was engaged to be married. And why hadn't she told me? I knew the answer to that one. And I was bothered by her fiancé's accusation of an affair that went back to last summer, even if I did write that one off to his raging jealousy.

I wondered if there was something different I could have done, something to keep her alive. And I was sure there was. But not sure what.

I also believed that she was probably killed for the same reason that Claire was killed—even though no sodium pentothal was involved. Either for information or to bury information with her body.

I was particularly annoyed and depressed that the weather was beautiful and had reached the mid-seventies in the middle of January and I was miserable. I wanted winter fog and rain to match my dismal mood.

I kept annoying Johnny D with my calls. I persisted in trying to get whatever information I could from the detective even though I had been warned off the case.

"What about alibis?" I asked on my latest call.

"All the possible suspects we identified have iron-clad alibis for both crimes."

"That's a lot of territory. Who are we talking about?"

"Just about anyone who knew either one. Krift, Snokes, Ness, the fiancé, his family, all their friends."

"Would you run through them?" I asked.

He cursed me out handily, but he did go through everyone's alibi in each case from the fiancé's visit with relatives in Los Angeles the night of Ollie's murder to Ness' whereabouts at the time of Claire's, to Mrs. Snokes' statement that she was with her husband all day Tuesday, January 3rd, the day of Claire's murder.

He finished with a warning that I was not to badger these people. If the police were satisfied, I had to be.

"I'm working other angles," I said and hung up.

My first angle was to fight the bad feelings. Taking care to favor my left arm, I started to work out in my gym, but gave it up. I turned down a one-on-one basketball game with the Chief on my upstairs court. Instead, I sat in the park at the top of the hill above Octavia and looked down at the Bay. I took walks through Japantown, looking in at the badminton courts, following the way I had walked with Ollie, through the replica of the mountain village, back to the Victorian, remembering the days we made love. Sometimes I just cried.

On Saturday I couldn't stand it anymore. I had to do something else. I bandaged my left arm, went up to the courts at Lafayette Park, and played tennis with a guy from the USF tennis team for three hours. I felt sore, but better, even though I lost two of the three sets we played. Then I put things into focus. Ollie was beautiful. Ollie was gone. I had loved her both innocently and passionately. But could I have been responsible for her death? Did her fiancé know something? Did any of those people Johnny mentioned? I had to focus. Which was still damn hard for me to do through the pain of loss. But I was going to do it. For Ollie. And for me.

I had three cases now. I put the one about the CFAF in front. That was legitimate. Who were these people? Were they a threat to Krift?

And where was the fifty grand? The money made me nervous because it could have been spent or split up or out of the country already. And then the cases I should have nothing to do with. Who killed Claire Krift? Who killed Ollie Shimoda?

Sunday wasn't too good. No football diversion as we waited for the Super Bowl next week in Miami. The cable sports channel was running a preview of the big game program, but it wasn't holding my interest any more than the Sunday newspaper with more sensational stories on the murders and the fear on campus had. I changed the channel.

I was staring at the six o'clock news, watching scenes of the terrorized campus, trying to think about dinner when the phone rang. It was Mickey on my private line.

"How're you feeling?" she asked.

"Don't ask."

"I'll take you out to dinner," she offered. "One of the Chinese places you've wanted to try."

It was hard to get motivated. Even for Mickey. I finally decided I had better try to revive myself. "The Canton Vegetarian. For you," I said, trying to reciprocate.

"Not tonight."

"I'm willing. No problem."

"I said not tonight."

I could tell that she meant it. Something wasn't right with my female partner. I began to revive.

We met at a restaurant called the Lucky Court on Clay Street. We took a table on the second floor where they served the Dim Sum and you had a view of the street below.

She ordered a Russian vodka on the rocks and I joined her. No messing around with white wine tonight. Then she ordered another and belted it down. I switched to beer for self-preservation.

"Something you want to tell me?" I asked.

"Let's order first."

I went for the shrimp dumplings and Mickey ordered the pork dumplings with black mushrooms. We would share, of course.

After the waitress left, Mickey asked, "Remember Mike's whaling crusade? I just got a radio telegram from him at sea." She passed it to me.

It was a Dear Mickey. Wesolski had fallen in love with a Korean woman on the Greenearth boat and they had been married at sea in between protests against whaling by the Japanese.

"I'm sorry," I said.

"Don't be."

"Okay. I won't. But I had to get off the cliché."

She laughed in spite of herself. And so did I. For the first time since Johnny D had told me about Ollie over a week ago.

Then we tried to get away from our lost lovers and talk about our cases until the food arrived. Without that much success.

"Down with vegetarians," I said, as I spooned out mounds of steamed rice for both of us.

"Especially those who get married at sea. Screw them. I mean that figuratively, of course."

She tore into her pork dumplings. Next I expected her to order rare steak.

"You know what? I hope their goddam boat sinks. Rammed by one of their beloved whales," she said.

"I don't think I'll drink to that."

"I don't mean it, Jeremiah." She raised a glass of ice water. "To their long and happy marriage."

We toasted Mike and his Korean bride.

After dinner I drove her home along the Embarcadero. The night was cold after the warm day and I had the heat on in the T-Bird. Mickey was close to me in the car. Her breath was warm and tangible and mixed with her familiar Chanel perfume. It brought back memories.

A miracle. I found a parking space in front of her apartment.

Holding hands, we walked to her door.

I brought her inside to the elevator. When it arrived she kissed me on the cheek. "Goodnight," she said.

It still wasn't.

I watched the elevator doors close on a woman who had just become very vulnerable.

Monday, ironically Martin Luther King Junior Day, turned out to be one of tragedy. While I watched Miami's Overtown burn in the riots over the shooting of an unarmed black man on a motorcycle by Miami police, Chief Moses came in. In a gray sweatshirt and jeans he was in perfect disguise as a student.

A spokesman for the NFL came on the screen to assure everyone that Miami was perfectly safe for the Super Bowl, despite the riots.

"I believe the man. He reeks of sincerity," I said to the Chief. "Now you on the other hand just plain reek."

"Student facilities are not the best. I had to crash in some pad that lacked running water last night."

"All this suffering is to some good end I hope."

"These people were very willing to talk. Especially after I bought the cases of Bud."

"I hope they were all of age."

"I checked their ID's." The Chief grinned. "Right after they passed out."

"Who were they?" I asked.

"Another animal rights group. ARP, I believe. They were delighted to have an actual aboriginal type, as they called me, living among them."   "Did you do aboriginal things?"

"I bought the Budweiser Water of Darkness, as we aborigines call it."

"Water of Darkness. Very aboriginal. Anything else?"

"A little war dance in Seminole style. Actually, I borrowed it from the Florida State mascot."

"What do the letters ARP stand for?" I asked.

"Animal Rights Posse."

"Find out anything specific?"

The Chief grinned. "I think I have your leader."

"That was quick."

"Water of Darkness can be like truth serum. You know him," he said. "Cody Zering."

"Son of a bitch."

It was time to visit Cody again. I called ahead and found him at home on the Beach. I suggested that he be there for our visit or face some very pissed off people when we did find him. He agreed to stick around.

This time I was bringing the Chief.

We drove out in the T-Bird to the duplex off the Great Pacific Highway. The road was empty because of the King holiday. Today it was clear to the edge of the Pacific and I took one long look over the breakers towards Japan and Ollie's ancestors and gave a little bow. It was awfully hard to get her out of my mind even for a little while.

"Watch the road. Old Indian saying," Chief Moses said.

"Like fasten your seat belt?"

"That is the White Man's way. Better to watch the road. That is the Indian way."

"Put on your seat belt," I said. "It's the law."

The Chief complied. "Watch the road anyway."

Before we went into Cody's place we got our roles straight. I asked the questions; he provided the unspoken threat.

When we walked in Cody recognized the Chief as that crazy activist from Florida.

"That was in another life," Chief Moses explained.

We went into our number. It seemed to work at first. We put some heat on the man and it all poured out. Even without beer.

"Claire was part of the CFAF. She hated her father's work. She was an animal rights fanatic infiltrating the HSC. The cat snatching was her plot. The kidnapping was her idea too, after the cat scheme failed. She wanted revenge on her father. And some of that blood money he owed her."

Was this far-fetched? Children do strange things to their parents. And was she really a CFAF fanatic? Who knows? There was a terrible logic to it all if you go back to Krift and Claire's mother.

"Who killed her?" I asked Cody.

"I don't know."

"You could be a hot suspect."

"Not me. No way. I was in love with her."

"Who were you working with?"

"Wayne Ness knew about it, and so did Boas."

"Who is this Boas?" This was a new name for me.

"Bruce Boas. A professional student and activist. He was the one who set it up at the motel. He was supposed to be with her."

"What happened?"

"He went out to make the calls so they couldn't be traced and never went back after he got the money."

"How do you know that?"

"That's what he said. I have no reason not to believe him."

"What kind of car does he drive?"

"An old two-tone Chevy. Red and white."

"A fifty-five?"

"Could be." He shrugged. Not a classic American car fan.

"About the fifty grand. Where is it?"

He hesitated. He pursed his lips.

"The money," I insisted.

"I don't know where it is."

I looked at the Chief, who had been silent so far. Playing his part. Then I looked at Cody.

"Boas has it," he said.

"Why don't I believe that? Since the Chief doesn't ask questions, you might wonder what his function is during a Q and A. Want to find out?"

"I've studied karate," Cody warned.

Chief Moses laughed and moved towards him. Apparently Cody forgot whatever it was he had learned at all of his karate lessons. The Chief picked him up by the throat, lifted him from the floor, and let him hang.

After a few seconds of that he cried, "I've got the money. Call him off. I'm choking." He started to cough violently.

"Get it," I said.

The Chief let Cody down and then accompanied him into the

bedroom. We didn't want any unpleasant surprises. Like Cody coming out firing an Uzi or a Fat Mac at us. Chief Moses came out carrying the same old leather briefcase I had put in the dumpster. Cody came out massaging his neck. We opened the briefcase and counted the money. It was all there. This would make Mickey very happy.

We took the money. "For safekeeping," I explained.

"Sure. Anything else you want?" he asked ironically, a hand still soothing his throat.

I checked the student directory. "Is this where I can find Boas?"

"Yes."

"What about the Co Gang?"

"What about them? They're the gang of Asians on campus."

I nodded to the Chief, who took a step towards Cody. This time Cody didn't mention his karate training. Instead he said, "Claire used them to get the cats."

"Why? You didn't need a gang to pull off a simple stunt like that."

"Claire figured they would be more intimidating. Word would get out that the Co Gang was behind it, and that was supposed to shake her father up."

"Didn't exactly work," I noted.

Cody shrugged.

"Were they involved with Claire's kidnapping?"

"No. They didn't know anything about it. We decided we didn't need them. More trouble than they were worth. And they screwed up with the cats anyway."

"Claire use the Co Gang for anything else?"

"For coke."

"And you?"

"Same as Claire. Recreational use. At parties. That kind of thing."

"What are you studying at the university?" I asked.

"I'm a grad student in philosophy. I'm interested in Critical Thinking."

"You should apply it," the Chief said.

"This doesn't look too good for you, Cody," I noted.

"No shit."

"Is that your Critical Thinking appraisal?"

"Yeah. It's the best I can do."

"One more thing. I wouldn't blow the Chief's cover if I were you," I warned. "You've seen what he can do."

Chief Moses took a step forward.

"Okay. Okay. I get the message."

"Good. You didn't waste your college education."

We left Cody to think critically through his problems. Which were myriad right now.

We drove back to the office along the same Great Highway. Salt spray was getting on the windshield and I used the washers and wipers to try to clear it off. The result was a smear that I had to squint to see through. It was like trying to look through a jellyfish.

The Chief wore his seat belt without my saying anything.

At the office I called Krift and let him know what I had learned. And to tell him about his money. Considering his daughter's death, he was about as relieved as you could expect. But then his voice turned angry at the mention of Boas' name.

"Do you know this Bruce Boas?" I asked.

"Oh yes," he said. "He was a student of mine."

In retrospect I should have picked up on the significance of his tone of voice. But I didn't then.

"We should call in the police," Chief Moses said after I hung up.

"Not yet. I want to talk to these guys."

But first I locked the money in our new safe. "Wouldn't want anyone to take off with our twenty percent."

Chief Moses finally smiled.

19

"Before we go anywhere, we eat lunch," the Chief announced.

I wasn't feeling hungry, but I agreed to keep the Chief happy and functioning efficiently. At least that's what I thought. When I got the food out, I got as hungry as the Chief.

While we were upstairs eating sandwiches of corned beef, Swiss cheese, and sauerkraut on toasted rye with fresh kosher pickles and cold beers, Mickey came into the office and called out our names.

"We're up here, Mickey," I called back.

She came up the stairs, and when she stepped into the kitchen and saw us eating, she said, "Some job you guys have got."

"Join us." Chief Moses waved his Reuben sandwich like a little flag at her.

"I ate at a Burger King salad bar. I'll pass on the calories and the cholesterol."

"Sounds like a great lunch. Anything on Vannessa?" I asked.

"I think I've got her picture in the hands of the right people. Uh, heard anything about the money?" She was embarrassed to ask the question. It was charming.

I was tempted to torment her just a little longer but the Chief warned, "No forked tongue, White Man."

"Not me, Chief."

"What is going on?" Mickey asked impatiently.

I finished my sandwich and got up. "Come downstairs." My bottle of Henry's in one hand and her right hand in my other, I took the woman to my office while the Chief made another sandwich for himself.

I opened the safe, dramatically took out the briefcase, and showed her the money. Dramatically.

"Oh Jeremiah, thank you." She hugged and kissed me with enthusiasm that from a distance could have been mistaken for passion.

"Your thanks are gratefully accepted."

We broke our clinch. I went over the story of how we recovered the money, which led to another affectionate display of hugs and kisses.

Just in time for the Chief to come down and see us at it.

"I do not think the late Olivia and the living Mike Wesolski would approve," he said, with a mock leer at Mickey.

Mickey let go of me. "You didn't tell him?" she asked me.

"I left that up to you."

"Tell me what?" the Chief asked.

"Wesolski got married to a Korean woman at sea," Mickey said, her voice a little huskier than usual.

"The Indian is always the last to know. My regrets."

Mickey sent a loud and wet raspberry at the Chief.

"And now she eats red meat," I noted.

"And now I can tell Polish jokes again," the Chief said.

"All you want," Mickey concluded.

Mickey wanted to help us out with the CFAF and the murders, but I had a feeling it would be better to keep her away from the people involved for now.

"We may need you later. Undercover," I said.

"What should I do now? I'm just waiting for someone to bite on the picture bait."

"Be patient. Keep checking. Something will come through."

She thought it over. "I'll take the afternoon off. I could use a break."

"Me too," Chief Moses announced.

I looked at the two of them. "Okay. Get the hell out of here," I said.

They did, and I went back to work, which was the best way I had of taking my mind off Ollie.

Because of the King holiday the university was closed, so Ness wasn't in his apartment when I called. I took a chance and drove over to the HSC. As usual, it was open for research. Despite the fire, Ness was at work in Snokes' lab on the transgenic experiments. He wasn't glad to see me, but since when was that a surprise?

After he put the white mouse he was working with back in its cage, the first thing he talked about was Ollie's murder, which was hard for me to take, but I hoped it would lead somewhere. That hope was dashed immediately.

"But what do you actually know about it?" I asked, after listening to a string of eulogistic clichés.

"Nothing." He wiped his hands on his dirty white smock and gave me a blank look.

"What about Claire's murder?"

"What is this?"

"Rehearsal for the cops and their Q&A. You've been implicated in her death."

He was starting to sweat nervously. I could see the beads forming at his hairline and above his upper lip. He wiped his hands again.

"By whom?" he asked.

"Your friend Cody Zering."

"Shit." Ness slammed his fist against a lab table, rattling the mice cages with a miniature earthquake.

I explained to Ness, nicely, about his vulnerable position. He tried to hang tough. But when I told him what Cody had admitted, and how I now had the money and the names of those involved, he broke down completely. He asked if he could plea bargain and I reminded him that I wasn't the DA.

"But keep talking. I can put in a good word for you with my many friends in Homicide."

He did, admitting enough to make him an accomplice. But he swore he didn't know anything about the murder, which, he claimed, had shocked all the conspirators.

He confirmed that Bruce Boas had been with Claire and had picked up the money and turned it over to Zering. But it was all supposed to be a neat sting to get the money from Krift that was rightfully Claire's. There was no reason to kill her.

"Not everyone would agree. Someone obviously came up with a pretty good reason."

That shut him up. I switched back to Ollie and he swore that he knew nothing about her murder. Then he started talking again about how tragic it all was.

"Those were the two most important women in my life," he said, right before he broke down in tears. He did such a good job of feeling sorry for himself I didn't have to waste any sympathy on him or any time telling him what they really thought of him.

I left him bawling like an infant over the two beautiful and dead young women, and went in search of Boas. His address gave me a clue to a number of things, including his sexual predilection. I drove across town, and parked at Market and Castro, near Harvey Milk Plaza, one of many memorials erected in the city to the San Francisco gay martyr after his murder.

As I got out of my car, I bumped into a young muscular man with his brown hair in a crew cut wearing a T-shirt that proclaimed: It's MISTER Faggot To You. It was warm for January, but not that warm. Sometimes making a point can be more important than being cold. The young man passed me without a word and swayed on.

I was in the Castro, cruising land for Harvey Milk when he was alive and still the Mecca of the gay world. I passed the Twin Peaks bar, the first gay bar in America to have clear plate-glass windows, bringing light to the once dark and secret meeting places of the third sex.

I walked for a couple of blocks and found the address on a side street. A red and white '55 Chevy was parked outside the two story duplex. I went up on the porch and found Boas' name under the second story doorbell. I pushed it, but it was obviously broken. I knocked on one of the two solid wooden doors. No answer. I knocked again. Same result. I tried the doorknob and it turned. The lock above it was unbolted, indicating that someone had left in a hurry. Or didn't have a key to lock it.

I went up an elegantly wallpapered staircase to the second story interior landing of the duplex.

"Boas?"

No answer. But it didn't seem like no one was home. An ironing board stood in the middle of the living room, a hot iron tilted back over an oxford blue shirt. Behind it hung his finished work. Under the ironing board there was a basket of laundry waiting to be pressed. Past the living room I could see a dirty dish, a knife and fork, and a cup on the kitchen table. Someone should be home. But something was very wrong.

I found a small bedroom off the living room. From the doorway I could see a young man who fit the vague description the motel manager had given me. He was lying on his back on the floor next to a double bed with a flowery print bedspread that matched the curtains and went with the wallpaper. The walls were covered with framed pictures of male body builders. Above the bed was a poster showing two males in erect states with a caption that read: Love Your Condom.

Boas wouldn't be getting a rise from the pictures, and he wouldn't be needing a condom anymore. Boas was beyond fear of AIDS or anything else mortal.

A knife, actually it looked more like a letter opener, was sticking up out of the center of his chest. Just to make sure, I felt for a pulse. Dead.

The first thing I did was to shut off the iron. Maybe that was tampering with evidence, but if the place burned down there wouldn't be any evidence at all to worry about, so I took my chances. Holding the phone with a handkerchief, I called my friends in Homicide.

I got through to Chang and said, "I promised to let you in on whatever I came up with."

"I wish you would promise to go away."

That was the routine. I waited for the questions.

"All right. What did you come up with?"

"The man who was with Claire at the motel."

"Where is he?"

"He's right here with me."

"And where are you?"

I gave him the address in the Castro.

"Don't let him get away."

"No problem. He's pinned to the floor. With a knife." It was an exaggeration, but I got my point across.

"Cute, St. John. He's dead." Chang said.

"Brilliant deduction. So there's no need to hurry."

They did anyway. Chang and Johnny D arrived in Riverside 500 time. I watched from the porch as they pulled up, tires squealing, parking the green Plymouth half on the sidewalk and nearly scraping my T-Bird with its bumper.

"Watch my car," I complained. "What is it with you cops and driving?"

"Watch your ass," Johnny D said. "This body collection stuff is getting to be a bad habit."

"It's one I'd like to kick real bad."

I went over with the two of them exactly what I had done before I found Boas. As the three of us stood in the bedroom looking at the body, we heard the ME arrive downstairs with the meat wagon.

The ME was the same large and youngish man who had been there for Claire. Today he was dressed in a red ski sweater, jeans, and black boots. He looked like he had been interrupted on his way to the slopes.

He looked at me over those round granny glasses and said, "You again? What do we do? Pay you a finder's fee?"

"I'll put in a claim, but I didn't get anything for the last one."

"Good. Now the three of you get out. I've got some work to do and there's not much room in here." He put his large black bag down next to the body.

We went into the living room and stood around the ironing board on a bare hardwood floor that looked recently refinished.

Johnny looked at the ironing draped on hangers hung over a curtain rod. "One thing about gays, they do nice work. Better than my wife."

"No comment," I said.

At the bottom of the stairs we could hear the Crime Scene Unit making their preparations to photograph, vacuum, and scrape the rooms.

"How about giving us the rest of this one straight, just for a refreshing change?" Chang asked.

"You got it."

I gave them everything and everyone I knew, including Ness, Cody, and the money. With those pieces in place, it made sense to them. Cody killed Claire for the money, and then had to kill Boas to cover it up, or to keep it all for himself. They figured Ness would make a good material witness with immunity if the DA would buy it. That was even better than what I had promised Ness for his cooperation.

It was one way of reading the tea leaves, but it didn't necessarily satisfy me.

"There is the matter of Ollie Shimoda's murder."

"Olivia Shimoda's death will fall into place. She worked with Ness. She may have known too much," Chang said. He was feeling pretty good with all the evidence and suspects I had turned up for him.

"Now stay out of this," Johnny said.

I said, "Ollie."

"I explained. . ." Chang began.

Johnny D tried to play rough. "You fucked with the evidence," he said. "We're overlooking that."

"What evidence? I only shut off an iron and made a call."

"The money," Chang said.

"The money? I was holding it for you. I didn't want Cody taking off with it."

"This Cody will probably take off without it," Chang said.

"If he does, the Great Tracker and I will help you."

"Kiss off," Johnny said.

I made my way out through the CSU team which was now at work on the staircase. Out on the street I found a pay phone and called Krift to tell him about Boas. He didn't sound surprised enough. Maybe murder didn't surprise anyone much anymore.

20

It turned out that Cody did run. But he didn't get far. True to my word, I helped the boys from Homicide. They themselves couldn't get anything out of Wayne Ness, but a little violation of rights pressure on the lab assistant and I easily had Cody's most likely hideout, a place he had discussed with Ness, Boas, and Claire as the place to go if things went wrong. It was up in the wine country some seventy-five miles north of the Golden Gate.

I passed on the information to Johnny, and that same day Cody was arrested without incident at his grandmother's vineyard in the Dry Creek Valley in Sonoma County. They owed me one more.

Instead of calling a lawyer, Cody blew his call on me. I got in touch with Forsander and Samaho and it was Forsander who came down to the Hall of Justice.

We met at the elevators. Scott Forsander shook my hand warmly. He is a six-foot-six WASP, a former city league basketball teammate of mine who was almost as tall as the Chief, but a hundred pounds lighter. As usual, he was dressed like a model out of *GQ*. He had on a pink shirt, a pink-and-gray diamond-checked tie, and a gray camel jacket that looked like cashmere. His blondish hair was still Beach Boy long, but healthy and clean as hair in a TV shampoo commercial. It was good to see him again.

I briefed him on the case, and then we took the elevator up to the prison floors to talk to Cody.

All three of us were put in a small conference room that was painted a seasick green that matched the prison coveralls that Cody was wearing. Cody needed a shave and his hair washed. I introduced them to each other.

After the preliminaries, Scott, with his easy going manner, got Cody to relax and talk some more.

"I stopped by the motel that morning. Everything was going fine. She was alive and joking about sharing a motel room with Boas. They both thought it was hilarious."

"This refers to his sexual orientation?" Scott asked.

"What else? Boas was openly–flamboyantly–gay; the kind of gay to march in gay freedom demonstrations or AIDS protests where they try to close down the Golden Gate Bridge or to get dressed up like a hooker or a nun for a Gay Pride Parade in the Castro."

"After I found you and talked to you about Claire's death, who did you call?" I asked. "Who did you warn?"

"Ness and Boas."

"That's all?" I asked.

"Yes."

"Are you sure?"

"Positive."

"Could they have called anyone else?"

"It's possible. But who?" He folded his hands on the table in front of him and looked vaguely angelic.

"That's what I'm asking." I turned to Scott. "You want me to stop with the questions?"

He leaned back. "Not yet. You're doing fine. I'm taking notes on your technique."

"What could Claire have known that someone used truth serum on her to get her to talk?"

"I don't know. She did a lot of things on her own."

"Like what?"

"Like trying to get at her father. Like infiltrating the HSC. She always had some plans she didn't tell anyone about." He ran a hand through his thick black hair.

"Could she have told some of these things to Ollie Shimoda?"

"She hardly ever mentioned the girl to me. I heard she was murdered, but that's it. I never even met her."

"Anything with the Co Gang?" I asked.

"Yes. I told you. That was part of it."

"What did she do on her own?"

"I don't know."

I went over everything again.

"You're worse than the cops," Cody said.

"You haven't been through anything yet," Forsander assured him.

After Cody was locked up, Forsander and I left the Hall of Justice to look for a place to have a beer. We found a lot of places to get our bail put up right across the street. It took some more walking to find a decent local bar. I was intrigued. It didn't have a name.

We took stools at the bar. The place was dark, smelled of oiled wood, and was almost empty. The decor consisted almost entirely of old photos of San Francisco baseball players, from the Seals and the DiMaggio brothers to Willie Mays and Will Clark.

We were a little early for drinking, even in the city, but I had a bottle of Henry's and Scott had a Pauli Girl.

"After Cody called him, Boas must have called someone, most likely the killer. Boas must have been worried."

"And the killer was worried because Boas knew who he was." Scott poured half the bottle of German beer into a glass. He watched it form a perfect TV commercial head.

I drank half of mine from the bottle. "Ironically, what could help us with Cody, is a killer who believes there are some more people who're still alive who can finger him," I said.

"So he kills again with Cody safely alibied in jail."

"Or tries. And the cops have to look elsewhere," I said.

"Do you believe there'll be another murder?" he asked.

"I'm afraid so. It's out of control."

"One murderer?"

"I still think so. Someone shutting up people."

The bartender, a tall bushy-haired man in his thirties, came over and wiped the bar in front of us. He was interested in our conversation. Of course, it was the only one going on in the bar this early afternoon. We ordered sandwiches to send him away. That kept him busy for twenty minutes. When he returned with his culinary work, we ordered two more beers.

"Boas' murder could be gay bashing, or a lover's deadly quarrel. We have some possibilities there."

"Maybe." I was skeptical.

"Cody have any money?" Scott asked.

"I have no idea. Worried about his ability to pay your fee?"

"Yes."

"I guess you'll have to find out."

"One thing about you, Jeremiah, you always bring us the most interesting cases."

"Even if they don't pay well?"

"That goes without saying."

The bartender wandered by. I asked him, "What's the name of this place? I didn't see a sign out front."

"Right now it's the No Name. Some pricks stole the sign."

"And so close to the Hall of Justice," I noted.

"The cops have their heads up their asses."

"Good image."

Scott picked up the check and we left the artificial darkness of the bar without ever finding out its real name. We stepped out into the bright sunlight, something that always made me fell slightly decadent.

I drove over to Ness' apartment. This time he was at home and reluctantly let me in after I threatened to rip the guard chain out of the door if he refused. After our last encounter, I had him scared.

"Who else was Boas working with?"

"I don't know. He was part of the CFAF. That's all I know."

"Was he infiltrating the HSC?"

"No. He used to be a student there, but he switched to Music or something."

"Whose student besides Krift's was Boas when he was at the HSC?"

I asked.

"Just Krift's," he said. "But he knew a lot of the faculty there."

"Snokes?"

"Sure."

I left Ness and drove the few blocks to the university and found Krift at work in his office. I went over all the details concerning Boas' death again. No surprises. Instead, he had one for me.

"I knew Boas was dead before you called because I went to see him after you told me he was involved in Claire's kidnapping plot."

"That's not good," I said.

"He was dead," he said.

"This could definitely make you a suspect."

"Why would I kill him?"

"I'll give you some reasons: extortion and revenge for killing your daughter. That's two big ones right there. More than most people have to commit murder. Want any more?"

"Do you believe that?"

"I'm not the police. I don't count. Call your lawyer."

"I thought it was the homosexual thing. Angry lovers. That sort of motive."

"Why did you go there?"

"To find out what really happened to Claire."

"Or to kill the man who. . . What? Turned the staged kidnapping into murder?"

"No. I was angry, I admit. But I just wanted to talk to him. To see what I could find out."

"Call your lawyer. Please."

"Are you going to tell the police I went to see Boas?"

"No. Of course not. You're my client. But that doesn't mean they won't find out."

"He was stabbed with a letter opener," Krift said.

"I know. Remember, I was there too. After you."

"It looked like mine. When I got back to the office I noticed that mine was missing."

"Christ. If you don't call Forsander or Samaho I will."

I didn't mention the conflict of interest concerning defending Cody that I was worried about. Maybe we could get all of this down to just one suspect.

"All right. I will."

I waited until he looked up the number and dialed.

As it turned out, calling a lawyer was a very good idea. After a computer check of the university employees, Krift's fingerprints were found to match those on the letter opener left behind in Boas' chest. According to the ME's preliminary report the stab wounds were inflicted after the victim was strangled, so they were seen by the police as acts of rage committed on the dead body. And rage certainly fit Krift's motive. But I had other ideas.

"So it was another strangling?" I asked Johnny D over the phone.

"Yeah."

"And you think Krift did it?"

"He had motive. We believe he had opportunity. He certainly has no alibi for the possible time frame. And there's the little matter of his fingerprints."

"Are you going to arrest him?" I asked.

"With his standing at the university we can wait. But if he makes a run for it he's finished."

"What was Boas strangled with?" I asked.

There was a long pause. "Forensics says the fibers left on his throat are silk."

"What do you think?"

"That there's too damn much silk in San Francisco."

I put in a call to Krift. I had some more questions for him.

"You said you saw the letter opener?"

"At first I thought it was a knife. Then I got a good look at it. It's just a metal opener. Standard item in every office on campus."

"But this one was yours. With your fingerprints on it."

"I told you. The one in my office is missing."

"Maybe you touched it when you saw the body?" I tried.

"Maybe I did."

"Now you're lying."

"I don't remember. I was in shock. It's possible."

"You're also in big trouble, Krift."

"I know that. I get that from my attorneys all the time. I don't need to hear it from you too."

A little later I got the call I expected. Because of the conflict of interest Forsander and Samaho were dropping Cody.

"Who's going to defend him?" I asked Scott.

"Someone he can afford. The public defender."

"Great."

"We want you to stay on as a defense investigator though," Scott offered.

I agreed to an expenses-only deal, which just about lived up to my promise to Krift not to charge for this work. The good thing about all of this was that I could expect somewhat less hassle from the cops. I hung up and made a call to the public defender's office. I finally got a woman named Marsha Hanes on the line. She was assigned to defend Cody. I explained who I was and that I wanted to meet with her. She agreed to meet me at Monday's, a popular watering hole, after work. I told her how I would be dressed.

"Okay," she said, and hung up without providing reciprocating information.

I killed some time by showering and shaving. Dressed in my blue blazer and a red-and-black-striped sweater, I drove off to Monday's. There was a parking lot in the back and I found a space by a dumpster designated for a compact car.

I went inside the place. It was an old-fashioned tavern with comfortable leather-upholstered booths, wood paneling, and wide-bladed Hunter ceiling fans. The food was eclectic, good, and reasonably priced.

It was also close to the courthouse, which made it popular with attorneys, clerks, legal secretaries, and even with a judge or two. I looked around for someone who could be Marsha Hanes. There was one fifty-year-old woman who looked in pretty bad shape. Probably the public defender, I thought, but she made no move away from the two drinks she had in front of her when she saw me.

I took a seat at the polished bar that gave me a view of the door. I nodded to the bartender, Nelson Bittenbender. He was tall and well-muscled without being overly developed, handsome in a pouting way, and very gay. He sported a good-looking waxed handlebar mustache. In the past he had been a rather reluctant informant for me.

I ordered a Henry's and asked if he knew a public defender named Marsha Hanes.

"No," he said and went to get my beer.

I was watching the door as I poured my beer when I heard a woman's voice behind me.

"You must be St. John," she said.

"Yes," I said, as I turned to face her.

"I'm Marsha Hanes."

She was a very pretty brunette with eyes the color of root beer candy and a stunning figure to go with them. I liked her right off and volunteered my services in defense of Cody. I didn't see any conflict of interest. As far as I could tell both he and Krift were innocent. I hoped.

"One question. How did you get in here without my seeing you?"

She laughed. "You figure it out."

"You were waiting in the ladies' room."

"You'll work out as a PI."

"Not according to the cops."

The murder I feared came Friday night. A woman named Valerie Hong was found strangled in her Chinatown apartment. I heard about it on the late news.

Saturday morning Johnny D called to talk about it.

"What's the connection?" I asked.

"Maybe none," Johnny said.

"So why are you calling me about it?"

"Just the way she was strangled. It was like the others. The fibers were silk. Bruise marks on the face. Apparently no sexual abuse. Also no truth serum."

"But any connection?"

"She used to be a student at the university."

"That's a pretty tenuous connection. What was she doing now?"

"An exotic dancer."

"A euphemism for a nude dancer," I said.

"You got it. Topless and bottomless. She worked those skin shows at the O'Farrell."

"What was her name again?"

"Valerie Hong. A Chinese. Did you know her?"

"No. Why are you telling me all this?"

"Because the media heat is gettin' intense. This is the fourth murder related to the campus and the students are near panic. Meanwhile we got budget cuts up the old whazoo. We're lookin' for any help we can get. Even from you."

"Appreciate the confidence."

"We're desperate."

"And now we have two Asian women murdered."

"The media are calling them the Rice Queen murders already."

"Rice Queen? Why? That's gay for a homosexual who likes Asian men," I said.

"They all know that. But the media just took it over and turned it into something they could use. It's catchy."

"Yeah. Catchy. And a lot more perverted."

"Maybe," Johnny offered. The man started out in Vice busting gays in public bathrooms. He didn't have much sympathy for the boys of that persuasion.

"If I hear anything else. . ."

"You got it Jeremiah. We gotta get some of this heat off."

"But I've got clients to protect, too."

"And I've got a goddam killer to find. With a reduced force."

"Then you're not certain about Zering and Krift?"

"Not when we got new bodies falling from the skies like snowflakes in the Sierras."

"Nice metaphor, Johnny. I didn't know you had it in you."

He hung up on me.

He ought to be nicer to the volunteer help.

21

I decided to try Misty Finch again. I left my office and walked a block to where I had parked the T-Bird. I had been so upset by Ollie's death that I hadn't paid any attention to the bullet holes in the car from her angry fiancé. But now I did. I found three of them in the door, and one in the hood. The car would need some body work that I probably couldn't get my insurance to pay for without a big jump in my premium. Besides, I may have skipped a payment or two, so I wasn't sure how I stood with the company anyway. The damage pissed me off a whole lot. But it didn't affect how the car ran.

The anger felt good. Maybe I was beginning to get over Ollie's death. Maybe not. It would take finding the killer to do that.

I found Misty at home late that Saturday afternoon.

When she opened the door the length of a guard chain, she reacted as if I were an obnoxious magazine salesman or a Mormon missionary. I didn't mention the uselessness of the chain in the face of a determined assailant.

"You again?" she said through the crack between door and chain.

"I'd like to talk to you." I peered in at her.

"I've told you everything."

"Humor me."

"Why should I?"

"People are getting killed," I said.

"What's that got to do with me?"

"Maybe a lot. Maybe nothing. But how about opening the door so we can talk about Claire with a little privacy?"

"I've got to get dressed for a date," she said.

"This won't take long, I promise."

She slipped the chain and let me in. I noticed that her hair was damp, obviously just washed. Her face was clean of makeup. She was wearing the identical clothes she'd worn on my last visit. She sat down on a chair in the small undecorated living room. I took a seat on the old-fashioned couch across from her.

"You ought to get a peephole so you can see who's at the door."

"Then I wouldn't have answered when I saw it was you."

I shrugged. "It's still good advice. And free, from a highly trained and experienced PI."

"What do you want?"

I went over the names of the dead for her.

Except for Claire, Misty didn't know any of them. "I'm in Communications," she explained. "I don't know these scientific types."

"But you knew Claire."

She took out a stick of sugarless chewing gum and started to unwrap it. "She answered an ad I ran for a roommate. She couldn't stand living in that big house with her father. That was all. You want a piece? I'm trying to give up smoking."

"No thanks. Good idea though. Besides killing you, smoke ages your skin. Makes it look like papyrus."

"Thanks for pointing that out. But I'm gaining weight." She put the piece into her mouth and started chewing vigorously.

"You have a career goal?" I asked, not because I really cared, but because I wanted to get her off the subject of getting fat and chewing gum.

"To anchor a network news program."

That was enough talk about Misty for me. "The police went through here before, right?"

"Yeah? So? I told you that." Misty shifted in her seat.

"Did they miss anything besides your little black book?"

She hesitated. "I don't know. They're supposed to be good at what they do. They had a whole crew of people in here going over everything." She twisted a rope of damp hair.

"Are all her things still here?"

"No. Her father came and took them away."

"Did you look through them first?"

"Not really. A little bit after the police were through."

"Did you find anything?"

"Like what?" She snapped her gum.

"Like something they might have missed."

Misty hesitated again. "No. I mean, I didn't find anything when I went through her things."

"You're being evasive."

"I'm not."

"What are you hiding, Misty?"

"Nothing." She folded her hands in her lap and, I suppose, tried to look innocent.

I didn't trust the gesture or the look. "You're not telling me everything."

"But I am."

I smiled. This was not the time for threats or even more probing questions. I just made myself comfortable on the couch, put my feet up on the coffee table, and waited patiently.

"What are you doing?" she said as she got up.

"Getting comfortable while I wait for you to tell me whatever it is you're hiding, or for your date to show up. Do you have a beer? Or, if not, a soda? Asking a lot of questions makes me thirsty."

"No."

"How about a stick of gum?"

She snapped her gum and ignored the request.

"I've got to get dressed." She started back towards the bedroom.

"I'll wait."

"Do you want to watch too?"

"Not necessary. Besides, your date might object."

"I'll call the cops."

"Go ahead. That's just the thing to do if you're in a hurry. You start filling out forms for them and you won't see your date until Spring Break."

Instead of calling the cops she took a deep breath and started talking. Once again a carefully concocted strategy of mine had worked.

"A few days ago I was trying to move the dresser to get a comb I dropped behind it. I bumped the mirror pretty hard and a key fell down. It must have been taped behind it."

That was an old trick, but apparently still effective enough that the Crime Scene Unit missed it. "Where is it?"

She went into the bedroom and brought out a purse. She fished around in it until she came up with a key, which she handed to me.

"This is a safe deposit box key," I said, as I examined it.

"I know." She snapped her gum.

There was a metal tag hanging from it that identified the box number and the bank. Convenient.

"Where were her other keys?"

"I don't know."

"Did the police take them?"

"I don't know."

"What about her father?"

"I'm not sure. I don't think so. I didn't notice any keys."

"These safe deposit box keys always come in pairs," I said.

"So?"

"Someone has the mate."

"So?"

I didn't have an answer. All I could do was thank her for her help.

"I don't know anything else. Can you go now?"

I got up. "Of course. But get a peephole," I advised. "And go get beautiful."

That got her to smile.

I left her snapping and chewing and getting beautiful for her date and took off with the key.

Outside, I thought over my options. I decided I needed to make some calls. Should I go back into her apartment? I had bugged Misty enough for one day. She probably wouldn't let me in anyway. I started looking for a pay phone. Ten minutes later I found one a quarter of a mile away from the apartment complex and the T-Bird. Maybe Mickey was right. We could use a cellular phone. First I called Krift.

"You picked up her stuff. Did she have a set of keys in her apartment?" I didn't mention the safe deposit key I had come up with.

"No. I assumed the police collected them in the motel along with her purse."

"That would make sense. She'd have them with her."

"What are you after?"

"I'm not sure."

"Look. You're working for me. Don't forget that."

"For you and your attorney. To find out the truth."

"That's all I want," he claimed.

I spent another quarter on Johnny D.

"What did you pick up in the motel room?" I asked.

"Whaddya mean?"

"Any of Claire's possessions?"

"Her purse."

"What was in it?"

"Not much. I don't remember offhand."

"Don't move. I'm coming to the police station."

"This is my lucky day. But you'd better hurry. My shift is almost done. Then I'm outta here."

I drove a little too fast to the precinct house, grabbed a space marked Police Vehicles Only, and went up to the bullpen on the second floor. I found Johnny D hiding from me in the john. "Can we go to the property room?" I asked when I located him at one of the urinals.

When Johnny was done we descended into the bowels of the building where Vice, holding cells, and locker and property rooms coexisted. Johnny signed and the sergeant on duty inside the cage limped back to get Claire's marked box and passed it through the opening in the bars to him. We removed her purse. Inside was a wallet with some money in it and a few credit cards. There was a makeup case, pink pearl lipstick, a small notepad, a couple of pens–but no keys.

"No keys," I said.

Johnny shrugged.

"Where's her driver's license? Or her student ID?" I asked, as I went through the wallet again.

"Who knows? Not in her purse."

"Don't you think that's strange?" I asked.

"Yeah. I do. But so was a kidnap victim with a purse in the first place. But what does it prove anyway?"

I had a hunch, but I said, "I'll let you know when I find out."

"Sure."

I thanked Johnny, who turned grumpy on me, and drove back to the office. Even though it was Saturday and late, I called the triumvirate together. The Chief was annoyed because it was a date night for him, but Mickey was glad to cooperate. Since the debacle with Wesolski she had thrown herself into her work.

The Chief arrived first, looking impatient. Mickey arrived carrying a full shopping bag. She looked alert and interested. She put the bag down on her desk chair.

We settled into my back room, the Chief and Mickey on the couch, and me behind the desk. After I ran through my day and filled them in on the possibly related Hong murder, I tried out some ideas on them. "I think this is clear. Whoever killed her took her keys, including the mate to this one." I held up the safe deposit box key.

"And they took her ID to get into the box," Mickey said.

"Exactly."

"So the killer gets the information he wants through the truth serum. Then he gets the key and the ID and goes to the bank and gets out whatever he wants. Very clever," the Chief said.

"That's one murder," Mickey noted.

"The rest will fall into place."

"Even Valerie Hong's?" Mickey asked.

"Possibly," I said, thinking more of Ollie's. *What* could she have known that had gotten her killed?

"So now?" the Chief asked.

"Anybody want to tunnel into a bank?" I asked.

"I think we will wait until Monday. For now, I will get back to my date," Chief Moses announced.

"How about you, Mickey? You leaving too?" I asked, hoping she would stay. I needed companionship.

She pulled a surprise. "Let's have a drink. And then I have some tapes to show you," she said. "They're in that shopping bag I brought."

"I was wondering what you had in there. What kind of tapes?"

She grinned. "Homemade blue tapes. They're the hottest thing on the market these days. The kind of amateur stuff that's putting professional porn actors out of work."

The Chief, who had his coat on and was heading towards the door, stopped. He thought it over. "Tempting. But my lady waits for her football jersey," the Chief said.

"This has to do with my case," Mickey explained to both of us.

"More tempting. But I will take the real thing." The Chief left, despite her comment about the relevancy to the case. He had his priorities straight.

Mickey got the bag and then she and I went upstairs where I had the VCR and the TV. Cinnamon was on the porch, crying to be fed. I fed her and then let her in to watch with us.

"Maybe she can learn something," I suggested.

"She knows too much already. She needs to be spayed."

"I'll look into it."

I got us wine and beer and we settled into my living room couch in front of the VCR and the TV. The cat went to sleep in a corner of the room.

"I bought these at a video place by the campus. In a tiny back room. They actually have a title printed on them: *The Bestiary Set.*"

"Bestiary? Interesting title. What's the point?" I asked, as I turned over the videotapes in my hand. Each was in a plain blue box and marked by a number. Everything about them looked amateurish, but maybe that was their appeal.

"You'll see. First I set the mood." She got up and turned the radio to a hard rock station. "Okay?"

"I'm ready for anything."

I hit the VCR remote and started the tape. Watching a few minutes

of each, which was all we could take, we ran a set which included
women in sheep masks, rabbit ears, Minnie Mouse ears and gloves,
deer masks and high-heeled hooves, cat and dog masks, and one cute
otter head, with nothing much else on except heels, net stockings, and
garter belts, all with naked and unmasked guys. Then we played some
tapes of naked maskless women with men in dog masks, ram heads, a
horse's head, crocodile heads, a gorilla head, even a Caribbean cer-
emonial animal mask, a chameleon head and a painted body to match,
shot somewhere outdoors in Golden Gate park, and a bull's head complete with real-looking horns.

"'The Rape of Europa'," I said, as I watched the bestiary tape of
the bull and the naked Oriental woman. "I get the classical allusion.
These could have redeeming artistic, social, and moral value."

"Sure."

"A Bestiary is a collection of tales about real or mythical animals
with a moral point," I noted.

"Jeremiah! So you went to college. Get real."

"About what?"

"About these tapes. The moral point is how many different ways
you can perform the sex act."

"Are you asking me?"

"No. I'm asking you if you notice anything," she said.

"I've seen better quality. But the content definitely leaves nothing
at all to the imagination. Except for a few faces. Other than that, you
have a a review of the different shapes that breasts and butts come in,
and a count of how many guys were never circumcised. Nice masks,
though."

"These amateur videos sell real well."

"I can believe it. A nice cottage industry. But I thought you said
this had something to do with your case."

"Here. This is what these tapes are about." She handed me several
still pictures. "Remember these?"

"These are the pictures of Vannessa Sable that Jimart gave us."

"And?" she asked.

"What? What am I missing here?"

"A clue. Think of the naked bodies."

I studied the pictures. "She was the girl in the Minnie Mouse ears and gloves and the apron with all the right parts cut out!"

"You got it. It has to be her."

We looked at the tape again, studying it carefully.

"I'm sure that's her," I agreed. "How'd you get this lead?"

"A video fan recognized the picture I was showing around the streets."

"Your next step?" I asked, certain that Mickey had it all worked out.

"We talk to the guy who's selling this filth," Mickey said.

"Right. He has to know who's making the tapes. Let's go over to this video place and make some inquiries."

"We need an angle," she said.

"How about the angle of: I beat it out of him?"

"Very subtle. I thought of reviving my hooker outfit and telling him I wanted to be in pictures."

"What kind of animal mask do you want?"

"A Siamese cat. What else? But I need a partner. These are all couples doing their thing."

"Sounds like the best Saturday night date offer I've had in a long time," I said.

"Then you're in?"

"Of course. But how far do we go?"

She punched my arm.

"This ought to be nothing for a *Playboy* pro like you."

"That was erotic art. This is porn."

I put the cat back on the porch over her meows of protest and an attempt to bite the hand that fed her.

Mickey went downstairs to get the hooker costume out of storage. She had used it to go undercover in the Silverman case when we were flushing out a pimp named Amos Billy. A sweet guy who liked purple suede suits, wide-brimmed matching hats, and an electric blue Eldorado, which I borrowed for a few hours, along with the hat. After Amos came through for us I returned the Caddy. I kept his purple hat as a souvenir.

Mickey disappeared into my bedroom with the old costume and shut the door behind her. When she finally appeared it was worth the wait. She had on a tight, low cut red sweater that revealed the top of her black pushup bra as well as the rounded bare tops of her breasts. Her garter belt straps hung down just below the hem of her skin-tight leather skirt above high black boots. She had put on heavy makeup that made her face look painted. Her hair was teased. She looked ready for the streets, and sexier than anyone on the tapes.

I whistled. "You still look great."

"Nothing fits."

"You're perfect. Don't complain."

"I never lost that ten pounds I gained after I quit smoking." She wiggled her hips. "This skirt is killing me."

When Mickey first came to us, smoking had been an issue. But one quickly resolved. Now she was an anti-smoking fanatic like the rest of us.

"The ten pounds look good on you. A lot better than a cigarette in your mouth."

"I have to put on a warm coat anyway. I'll freeze out there like this." She put on a short fleece-lined jacket that only came down to just below her waist.

We set up the security system and left.

"It's nice to be dating again," I said.

"Shut up," she said. But with a smile.

22

We drove over by the campus and Mickey directed me to the video store. It was a respectable looking place, with all kinds of movie posters in the windows in a respectable and busy shopping mall. At least the mall had a parking lot, so I didn't have to hunt for a space.

"Wonder how long before somebody gets the idea of charging to park at a mall?" I asked.

"Sooner than you think. These are some of the last free parking spaces in the city. If not California."

The video shop owner was a tall guy in his fifties. He had a short gray beard, a few strands of gray hair that looked like pencil lines drawn on his scalp, and dark glasses. Despite the cold, he wore a university sweatshirt with the sleeves cut off, and stone-washed jeans cut off at the knee. He looked like he had spent a lot of time pumping iron, which spelled quality prison time to me.

The man, who didn't give us a name, remembered Mickey.

"We'd like to be in pictures," Mickey said.

"Doesn't everybody?" he asked with a smirk that showed he was missing a few lower teeth. He checked out Mickey's legs.

"Pictures like in *The Bestiary Set*," I said.

He looked us both over. "I'm not in production. I just do sales."

Mickey took off her jacket. He whistled at the rest of her, but didn't say anything. I decided on the money approach. But not mine.

"The guy who makes these ought to spring for a finder's fee for you," I said.

After thinking it over, he said, "The guy who delivers the amateur blue tapes will be here on Wednesday." We got the time, and promised to be there then.

"And dressed like that?" the guy asked Mickey.

"You got it."

"This guy who's coming makes them?" I asked, getting the subject away from my partner.

"Far as I know," the video man said.

"He have a name?" I asked.

"A Chinese guy name of Co."

Ain't coincidence wonderful. "Thanks."

In front of the store I said, "So Co rears his head. Again."

"He seems to crawl into a lot of unsavory things," Mickey said.

As we walked through the shopping mall, with Mickey's short skirt, exposed garters, and legs turning heads, I asked again, "How far do we go on Wednesday?"

Instead of punching me, this time she just smiled and said, "Whatever it takes, honey."

"I think you could pick up a little money tonight. You're attracting masculine attention to your lower zones."

"Shut up, pimp." This time she punched my left arm.

"Ow! That's where I was shot," I complained.

"Sorry." But she didn't mean it. Then she added, "Why don't you wear Amos Billy's purple pimp hat next time?"

"I always knew you liked that on me."

Super Bowl Sunday was warm and clear. I picked up Mickey and we spent the morning playing mixed doubles on the courts in Lafayette Park with Dr. Earnhard, the TV doctor and Mickey's former wooer, and his fifth wife, Gloria, my former tennis partner. It was a pleasure to whip them in straight sets. Ollie and badminton began to fade slightly in my painful memory.

In the afternoon the Chief came out of cover to drink beer, eat sandwiches, and watch the game.

I told him about the blue video connection to Co.

"What do you want from me?"

"You did so good with the animal rights people, see what you can do with Co."

"You want me to infiltrate?"

"Yes."

"This is an Asian gang."

"Your people came over from Siberia. Right? That's Asia."

"I will see what I can do. Now can I watch the game?"

"Of course."

As it turned out, it was one of the better Super Bowls. It took a closing drive by Joe Montana to pull out the victory for the 49ers 20 to 16 over the Cincinnati Bengals in Miami, which had quieted down by game time.

The winning drive became THE DRIVE, to go along with Dwight Clark's famous THE CATCH against the Cowboys that took the Niners to their first Super Bowl. As these things go, I predicted that one day we would have THE INTERCEPTION, or more likely, THE FUMBLE, which would blow a 49er chance at a Super Bowl. But I was enjoying today's victory with some Henry's and my partners, trying to put Ollie out of mind for a while.

After the game we took my car and the Chief's truck and went out to dinner at the Canton Vegetarian Chinese restaurant and had a few more cuts at the case, along with selections from eighty-nine meatless dishes.

"I can be a vegetarian on occasion," I said.

We decided how to handle tomorrow at the bank. It would be tricky getting the information we needed, but at least we had a plan. Mickey and I would handle the bank. Chief Moses would have his own problems with the Co Gang.

After dinner the Chief drove off to his houseboat. Mickey and I got into the T-Bird. We checked the late news on CBS radio. We got sports, weather, 24-Hour Traffic, which was now essential in the Bay Area, but there was no news of any more murders. The City was too busy celebrating the Super Bowl.

I drove Mickey home to her Embarcadero apartment. The white lights of the Bay Bridge outlined the intricate steel web behind her.

"It was nice with you today, Jeremiah."

"A little crazy, but like old times."

"Almost."

"Yeah. Almost."

At the elevator I let her go off without making a move. That felt right.

One the way home I thought of Ollie. And the pain returned. Like a letter opener in the chest.

I really would never see her again. Or touch her. Or hold her. Or love her.

My eyes blurred and I tried to blink them clear. It didn't work. Until I thought of what I wanted to do with her murderer. Attila the Hun would have nothing on me.

Mickey and I were at the downtown branch of the Western Pacific Bank when it opened Monday morning at nine. We were both dressed very conservatively in dark suits, like investigators from the Banking Commission—the roles we were playing—would dress. We came complete with business cards from the Commission, which I had plucked from my very useful collection—something no PI should be without. It was a collection that contained borrowed, stolen, bought, and even printed-to-order cards that had helped us get where we needed to go. We had impersonated everyone from termite exterminators to National Endowment for the Arts reviewers, to US Army investigators.

Today we had to take on Ivy White, a sharp black woman with a perfect coke bottle figure in a short and tight red sweater dress and red-tinged hose, who was the teller in charge of access to the safe deposit boxes. She had dark brown eyes set deep and wide below a smooth brow and hair cut almost into a crewcut. Those dark eyes looked at us suspiciously.

Our cards, impressive as I thought they were, didn't help to diminish her suspicions much.

"You're from what?" she asked from behind the locked waist-high panel that separated her domain from us.

"The Banking Commission. Just like it says on the cards." I tried to get them back, but Ivy insisted on holding on to them.

"I'm going to bring these to the bank manager. I never heard of this Commission." The woman started to march away from us in her spiked red heels that matched her dress perfectly. "Hold on," Mickey said, jutting her chin out over the silk scarf she had tied into a necktie. Nice accessory for her man-tailored suit.

"Why should I?" she asked Mickey.

My partner, who usually handled these situations well, looked at me.

I had to try something. "We can keep this confidential," I said.

Ivy stopped the click of her heels.

"Keep what confidential?"

"We won't use any names. Unless you insist on bringing in the manager. Then we have no choice," I said.

She looked uncertain. She ran her hand over her short hair. Her long and manicured nails glistened with red enamel. She rattled the loose gold bracelet on her left wrist and then tugged at a dangling gold earring.

"What the. . . What are you talking about?"

"We're investigating unauthorized access to boxes," Mickey said, stepping in at just the right moment and pointing at the open steel door to the vault where the safe deposit boxes were stored. The door gleamed like chrome.

That got Ivy upset. "This is a secure operation," she insisted. And then she went on to explain why. In careful detail. And very emotionally.

I interrupted her speech. "We are not trying to single out any individual. We are looking at security practices in general. We promise anonymity. But you must keep this confidential."

"And you must cooperate," Mickey added.

We were both leaning over the low, locked, door.

The woman was shaken, but still guarded.

"You saying I allowed unauthorized access?" Her tone had become angry and hostile. And defensive.

I worked the confidential bit again.

"We are not accusing you of anything. There will be no recriminations."

"No matter what?"

"No matter what," I promised.

"The goal is improvement of procedures. Not criticism of any specific individual. If anything is at fault, it is the procedures, not the personnel," Mickey said.

"I don't like this."

I repeated my offer. "No recriminations."

When we finally got Ivy settled down, I showed her the safe deposit key Misty had found in Claire's room.

"This is the key to the box in question."

She stared at it.

"Will you let us in?" I asked.

Ivy pressed the button that electronically released the panel. We stepped softly into her carpeted domain.

"What do you want?" she asked.

"The record of who had access to this box," I said.

She got out the records for that box number and passed them to us without giving me any argument. Each access was signed for by Claire Krift.

One visit to the box was recorded in late November of last year, and a second visit in December, and a third visit in January, dated exactly one day after Claire was murdered. The third signature was a pretty good attempt to match the first two, but it didn't quite make it.

"Do you remember her coming in?" I asked.

"Yes."

"All three times?"

"Yes."

"Was she alone?"

"Yes."

"All three times?"

"Yes."

"Even the last time?"

"Yes. This is getting annoying."

"Do these signatures match?" I showed her the second and third ones.

"They're close."

"But not a perfect match," Mickey said.

"No one signs exactly the same way every time," Ivy said and shrugged.

"But this is more than that," I said.

A long silence. "I know," Ivy finally admitted.

"Why'd you let her in then this last time?"

"I made a note on the back here. I had my doubts about the signature, so I asked for some additional identification."

"And she had it, of course," I said. Right out of Claire's wallet.

"Yeah. She had all kinds of ID. A license. A student ID. Credit cards. The works. Everything but a note from her mother."

"Did she look like the Claire Krift from the other two visits?"

Ivy took her time. She looked at her long red fingernails as if she had never seen them before. "Who remembers? She wasn't that regular a customer. As the card shows, she was only here twice before."

"What did the woman who came the third time look like?"

"She was all wrapped up. Even though the weather was warming up. And she had a hat on. She did look a bit different though, from what I remembered."

"How's that?" I asked.

"She looked shorter. And she had sunglasses on so I couldn't see her eyes. But I'd bet she was Oriental from the bone structure of her face."

"And you still let her in?"

"I told you. She had the proper ID. And I wasn't sure what Claire Krift looked like. I'd only seen her twice before."

I thought about possibilities.

"I'm not going to lose my job, am I?" Ivy asked.

"Of course not. We're going to take steps to improve security controls in every Western Pacific Bank. This is a structural problem, not a personnel issue." I hoped that sounded convincing to her. It did to me.

"Thanks," Ivy said. She gave us her first smile of the day.

I went back to my possibilities. I pointed to the cameras in the corners just below the ceiling. "You had camera surveillance for her last visit?"

"Of course."

"We'd like to see the tape."

She sighed. "This is unusual." But she didn't fight it.

"And could we have our cards?"

Ivy gave us back the business cards and brought us behind the row of tellers' cages back to a security area where our cards and our act got us access to the tape for Wednesday, January 4th. The three of us watched the tape on a TV in a closet of a viewing room set up in the rear of the building.

"That's her," Ivy said. "The woman who signed in as Claire Krift."

"That's not Claire Krift," I said.

"You're sure?" Ivy asked.

"Claire Krift was murdered the previous day."

"Oh."

We kept rewinding the tape, looking for the best angle on the woman. We finally froze her face about as good as we could ever expect to get it.

"Does she look familiar?" I asked Mickey.

Ivy broke in, "I don't feel too good. I need to go to the rest room." She hustled out of the viewing room.

"I don't recognize her," Mickey said.

"We've got to let some other people look at this," I said.

"How're you going to do that?" she asked.

"Easy." I stuck the cassette down into the front of my pants and we got the hell out of there as quickly as we could before Ivy could recover and return.

As we drove away I saw Ivy come out of the bank and run towards us. But it was too late. She stood in the parking lot either waving or shaking her fist at us. I couldn't tell which. She faded to a swatch of red in my rearview mirror. She had been a great help.

I pulled the tape out of my pants and handed it to Mickey.

"Try not to get too excited."

"About something in your pants? Forget it."

"That's what I love about you. Your sense of humor."

23

It was time to meet with the cops. With even more cutbacks hitting the police, Johnny and Chang had become almost agreeable when it came to volunteer help.

We drove right over to the precinct house with the tape from the bank.

I left my S&W in the glove compartment and Mickey slid her weapon under the front seat so we could make it through the metal detector. We got visitor's badges from the sergeant at the main desk, who was always much more polite when I had Mickey with me. We went up a flight of metal stairs and found the partners in the Homicide bullpen. Winter light was seeping in through gray windows that desperately needed washing.

I noticed that Mickey's presence made Chang and Johnny friendlier, as well.

I explained what we had on the tape and Chang led us to an interrogation room that was equipped with a TV and a VCR. The room smelled of fear and urine, but we all ignored the odors. I turned on the VCR and put the tape in.

After a dozen passes at the relevant footage, Chang and Johnny looked at each other and nodded. Chang said, "She looks like the woman who was just murdered. Valerie Hong."

"So we have connected murders," I said, drumming with my fingers on the scarred table we sat around.

"What was in the safe deposit box?" Chang asked.

"Whatever the killer wanted."

"And got," Mickey said.

"Did you check in the box?" Johnny asked.

"No. This woman got it open. Don't tell me she left anything behind."

"We'll get a court order and check anyhow," Chang said.

"Don't waste your time."

"Procedure."

"Whatever," I responded.

"So what is your take on the motive here?" Chang asked.

"This woman became like Claire and Boas, and maybe even Ollie. She knew too much."

Chang nodded. "She does this job for the killer and is eliminated. Very neat."

"This should clear Krift and Cody," I said.

"Not so fast," Chang said. "We have motive and opportunity."

"Come on," I said. "We have something a lot bigger here. I think we have one killer with a specific motive. And it's not Krift or Cody."

"I was a believer in the serial killer, but Krift still left that letter opener behind," Johnny D said. "Boas is different from the others."

"He's a man," Mickey said.

Another idea hit me. "Whoever took Claire's keys would have the key to Krift's office as well. It would be easy to get the letter opener with a good chance Krift's fingerprints would be on it."

"If she had that key."

"We can find out," I said.

"How? By asking Krift? Of course he'll say she had one and it was stolen."

"That didn't go too far," I admitted.

"No. It isn't a bad idea; we just can't prove it," Chang said.

"You still don't have anything but circumstantial evidence on them."

"Are you going back into the lawyer business?" Chang asked.

"Never."

"Then leave the case to the prosecution and the defense attorneys."

"I'll keep that advice in mind. But don't forget that we're defense investigators." Mickey and I got up to leave.

"One last thing," Chang said. "Let's not let word of this cooperation get around."

"Fine with me," I said. "I wouldn't want to sully my reputation." Mickey laughed. "Sully?"

"That's what I said."

It was a relief to be out of the oppressive room. Mickey and I went down the steps, turned in our visitor badges, and got out of there.

We drove to another Chinese restaurant on my list, this one specializing in Hunan cooking, for a late lunch.

As I sipped my hot green tea I said, "I wonder how the Chief is doing?"

"Probably has Co eating out of his hand," Mickey said.

"We'll see." I had my doubts about that.

We had the murder of two research assistants, Claire and Ollie; a gay activist, Bruce Boas; and an exotic dancer and former student, Valerie Hong. Were they the victims of one killer? The MO was similar down to the silk cord, but there were serious questions. The media was throwing in the Hong murder and pushing hard on the Rice Queen angle; Asian coeds on campus were frightened. Campus police and fraternity volunteers were escorting women around at night. But nothing would really bring things back to normal except finding the killer. Or possibly killers. And even then it would never be the same.

I tried not to think of the way it was with Ollie. I tried not to think of her brief flicker of a life. I tried not to make this too personal.

I had to keep thinking of myself as a defense investigator. Right now our best bet was William Co. First we had heard of him and his gang in connection with the stolen cats and then with supplying cocaine to Claire. The runaway case had brought us to him and maybe we could get a lead on the murders while we looked for Vannessa. Maybe it was just a coincidence. Maybe. But I didn't think so.

Meanwhile Krift was calling. Impatient with how things were going.

"At least you're not in jail," I told him over the phone.

"So far," he said.

Then I had to deal with Scott Forsander.

"We've got some good leads," I assured him.

"I need some results."

"We guarantee satisfaction," I said and hung up.

Staying out of jail was more than I could say about Cody, who, although he had a beautiful public defender, didn't have bail.

I had lunch with Marsha Hanes, that beautiful public defender, when she called and asked if we could talk over the case. We shared a bottle of Chianti and a vegetarian pizza at a small family Italian place downtown, that she recommended. The red and white checked table-cloths were made of real linen, and the dishes were clean. It looked like the place had once been either a candy store or a barber shop, but the family had transformed it with minute attention to detail. The murals of Venice, Pisa, Florence, Rome and Genoa, helped us to ignore the traces of its prior incarnation.

The pizza was good too, but nothing helped Cody's situation much. Marsha was happy to get the information about the bank. That had some potential.

"I think we'll have Cody out pretty soon," she said, with more hope than realism. A wedge of hot pizza in her hand was fogging up the large horn-rimmed glasses she was wearing today. The lenses magnified her beautiful eyes to the size of large marbles.

"Good," I said, staring through the glass at them. "I'll let you know whatever I come across." I attacked my piece and burned the roof of my mouth.

"Unless it damages your client." After watching me struggle, Marsha took a small careful bite.

"That goes without saying. But I'm hoping both Cody and Krift are innocent." I cut a piece for myself on the china plate and ate it gingerly with a fork.

"Cody was in jail when Valerie Hong was killed," she said, pointing out the obvious.

"And Krift was out. But with no motive to kill her."

She took off her glasses and wiped off the steam on the lenses with a napkin.

"No motive that you know about," she said.

We went over the case once more without coming to any conclusions. After that I picked up the check and walked Marsha to her car, an old beat up VW bug that used to be red, the rear engine model they stopped making years ago and never found a satisfactory replacement for.

"Thanks for the pizza," she said.

"Sure. It goes on my expense account with Forsander and Samaho."

She smiled and said, "Good. They can afford it."

"Next time the Blue Fox," I said.

"Now you're talking *lunch!*"

On Wednesday morning Mickey was at the front desk typing on the Mac and I was in my office working on some new juror profiles for an attorney client when the Chief stopped by to give us his report. Mickey followed him back into my office. He was having a hell of a good time at school, but he hadn't made any headway with the Co Gang.

"Why do you like it so much?" I asked.

"No football practice."

"And you're actually going to classes?" Mickey asked.

"Yes. Native Americans are fascinating subjects."

"Good. How about some Asian Americans? Like one named Co?" I asked.

"I told you. No luck yet. Do you have any viable suggestions?"

"Viable?"

"Ones that actually might work," Mickey said.

I thought it over. "Act like one of them. They'll come to you."

"What do you mean, exactly, Jeremiah?"

"Wear the gang uniform. Buy a Raider jacket."

"Just like I'm a gang member?"

"Right. Pretend you're one of them. That'll get their attention."

"They'll be pissed," Mickey pointed out. "That's not the right kind of attention."

"Not to worry about that, lady. I need an in." Then the Chief turned to me. "Who pays for the jacket?" he asked. "They are expensive."

"Put it on the agency American Express card," I said.

"Can I buy the matching hat?"

"No. Wear a black bandanna. That's the gang's style."

"They also wear hundred dollar Nikes."

"Okay, okay. Just don't get mugged for your sneakers."

He grinned and announced, "I'm going shopping."

"Be careful, Chief," I said as he left the office.

"You've made him the bait," Mickey said.

"I know. Well-dressed bait. But he's a big piece of bait who can take care of himself."

"I hope so."

"So do I," I admitted, remembering the time Chief Moses had been shot. Nobody is bigger than a bullet.

"One other thing," Mickey said softly and sweetly.

"Yes?" I asked suspiciously. "What do you want to buy?"

"How can you tell that's what I'm going to ask?"

"I could tell what you were thinking when the Chief was negotiating for his gang uniform."

"I need a new hooker outfit. That skirt was way too tight."

"That's why the video man liked it."

"But the Chief got to go shopping."

"When this is all over with. If I'm not crazy by then. You can buy a new skirt on the company card."

"Thank you. You don't want me to start smoking again, to lose weight, do you?"

I didn't bother to answer. I just coughed.

Our meeting at the video shop was scheduled for noon. Mickey got into her too-tight hooker costume and put on her pound of tart makeup. I put on jeans and a black turtleneck. Mickey decided on a raincoat.

"I attracted too much attention last time," she said, as she covered up whatever the outfit left exposed.

Then we got out of there.

We showed up a few minutes early at the video store and acted nervous, playing up our roles as would-be first-time porno performers. The bald man was behind the counter in his dark glasses. He had on exactly the same clothes as last time. Only difference was they were dirtier.

At quarter after twelve, a young Chinese man wearing a lightweight hooded parka showed up with a brown grocery bag. He pushed the hood back to reveal long black hair tied into a thick ponytail. He had smooth skin and a boyish face, but eyes that were dark and hard. They reminded me of Detective Chang's. I estimated that he was five ten and about a hundred and sixty pounds.

The nameless man pulled down his glasses and winked at us. William Co had arrived. Then they went into the back room together while we waited.

"Lose the coat," I said.

Mickey obliged with a mock striptease.

Five minutes later they came out together. The brown grocery bag was empty, folded up under Co's arm. He walked over to Mickey and me and looked us over like he was in a deli picking out lunch meat. When he made his choice he settled on Mickey.

"So you want to be in the movies?" he asked her, grinning like he was having the time of his life.

"Yes," I answered for her.

"We need the money," Mickey said.

Co nodded without taking his eyes off Mickey. "Who doesn't? What kind of action did you have in mind?"

"Something different," I said.

"There is nothing different in this business." He grinned.

We convinced Co that we had seen this young girl in action on a tape and that we wanted to perform with her *a trois*. While that was hardly a unique proposition, Co liked the idea, and liked Mickey even more, from the way he was removing whatever little clothing she was wearing with those dark and cold eyes.

"How does all this work?" I asked.

He turned to me. "I have a studio. A friend can do the taping, or you can set it up yourself on a tripod with a remote and perform for the camera in private. Some couples feel less inhibited that way. Sometimes I do the taping. For special subjects." He looked at Mickey again. "Like you. Unless you're heavy into inhibitions."

"I'm flattered," she said and smiled at him. "And we're not into any hangups about sex." She looked at me.

I nodded. "What about the girl?" I asked, as if to demonstrate the point.

He gave us an address and said, "Be discreet."

"What about a name?" I asked.

He shook his head.

"And when I find her?"

"Call this number." He gave me a business card that had a phone number on it, but nothing else.

"And how about payment?" I asked.

"When the tape is completed you will be paid."

To make it authentic we haggled over the money. I got Co to spring for a hundred and fifty more than his original offer. I figured it was Mickey who was the attraction for him and that he would be willing to pay bigger for this one.

He ran his eyes one last time over Mickey and then he was gone. We nodded to the grinning proprietor and went out into the hall.

"I feel like I need a hundred showers," Mickey said, as she put her raincoat back on.

"I think a dozen will do it," I said.

She shivered. "It was like he was touching me with his eyes," she said. "I could feel them on my skin."

"Let's hope we come up with a good excuse to blacken them up," I said.

24

It was still early in the afternoon. Mickey and I picked up fast food at the drive-through at a Mickey D's and went out to the address Co gave us. It turned out to be a large old house in a mainly warehouse district of the city. Parking was no problem. I parked across the street half a warehouse building down from the house. There were no other cars close by. We staked it out and ate our hamburgers and French fries

"Those are awfully young girls going in there," Mickey said.

After watching preteeners and young teenagers come and go I said, "It could be a halfway house for runaway girls, or a house of child prostitution."

The middle-aged men who kept arriving gave us the clue. The customers, who were all coming up on foot and with an attempt at disguise—everything from a false beard to huge dark glasses—were very interesting in themselves. If we were into extortion, we would have been setting ourselves up well. We saw at least two of our biggest local married politicians going in to get their rocks off with these kids.

"What's the plan?" Mickey asked.

"Plan? I thought you had the plan."

"Come on."

"All right," I said. "Apparently the girls are free to come and go as they wish. So a stakeout makes sense."

"And then what do we do?"

"We kidnap Vannessa when we see her."

"That could be forever."

I saw a pair of girls coming down the stairs. I grabbed the steering wheel. "I don't think it will be that long."

We had our break. A girl I was sure was Vannessa was coming down the stairs with another teenager. They looked like two kids playing dress-up in their mother's clothes. Only their mother was into hot pants, stretch tops, and high-heeled boots. They passed us and continued up the street towards Mission.

"Drive," I said to Mickey. I got out from under the steering wheel and ran around the car and got in on the passenger side. With a slightly immodest climb over the stick shift, Mickey took over as the driver.

"Damn. That was dangerous," she muttered, as she pulled her raincoat back together on her lap.

We made a U-turn. As we pulled up next to the pair of girls I asked, "Aren't you two cold dressed like that?"

"Nah," Vannessa answered, and started to walk away.

I began talking business.

"You want both of us?" the other, slightly older one, asked. Her voice sounded old and hoarse, as if she were smoking several packs of unfiltered cigarettes a day. Probably a sucker for those Joe Camel cartoon ads.

"Just her."

"Just because she looks so young." The first one pouted for a few moments and then she started to walk away. I saw her stop to take out a cigarette and light up.

"I just got off," Vannessa complained. "And I don't like to do stuff with a woman," she said into the car.

"She's just my driver. Nothing physical with her."

"I don't have to touch her?"

"No way," I said.

"And she's not going to touch me?"

"No. She's not the touching type. I swear."

Mickey was looking at the roof of the car as if she could see through it to outer space. She was probably trying not to throw up.

Vannessa sighed. Resignation. "Okay." She started back to the house.

"No. In the car."

"I'm not supposed to do that."

"You're not supposed to do any of this."

"I mean the lady who runs the joint don't go for free-lancing."

"How's she going to know?" I asked. "I'll pay double the going rate."

She thought it over for a few seconds and then she squeezed into the car. "Jeez. There's no room to do anything in here."

"We'll figure something out, Vannessa."

She stiffened. "How did you know my name?"

"You just look like a Vannessa."

"Bullshit," she said.

"Bullshit is right," Mickey concluded.

Vannessa made a move to escape. I caught her around her tiny waist. Her hand went towards her boot. I caught it by the wrist just as she pulled out a knife. I twisted.

"Ow!"

The knife fell to the T-Bird mat on the floor.

"Relax. Enjoy the ride. This is a classic car."

"Are you motherfuckers cops?"

"Who the fuck taught you to talk like that?" Mickey shot back.

"We're not cops. We find missing persons."

"I'm not missing."

"Wanna bet?" I asked.

She didn't.

Twenty minutes later Vannessa was sitting on the couch in my back office with Mickey, telling my partner her brief life story while she drank a diet coke and ate some ice cream and cake I had found in my refrigerator upstairs. It was what a Norman Rockwell PI would do if he found a lost child.

Up at Mickey's desk, I called Johnny D and gave him the address of the teenage brothel, which he said he would pass on to Vice, his former assignment. He appreciated the tip.

"I like to stay in good with the old guys," he said.

"Never can tell when you'll be back there," I suggested.

"Damn right. Never can tell when people will stop gettin' murdered."

"The story should be hot enough to take the pressure off the homicide investigations for a while at least," I said.

"Unless Vice goes into an undercover sting to get the big time pols. Either way, it's worth it."

After Vannessa finished eating and their conversation was over, Mickey proposed taking Vannessa with her.

"Why?"

"You'll see."

"Where is she going to stay?" I asked.

"Don't worry. I've got room," Mickey said.

"Don't lose her," I said to Mickey in an aside.

She winked. They left together.

I called Jimart with the good news about his runaway, and he said he would fly up that night from San Diego. I went upstairs to work out, shower, eat, and watch some TV.

Jimart's yellow cab pulled up about midnight; he got out and paid the cabby. He looked like he had been sleeping in his suit for a week. He picked up a small suitcase and climbed the steps while I waited for him on the porch. The man had gained a lot of weight and lost a lot of hair. What he had left had gone gray. He was out of breath by the time he got to me.

"Guess you gave up jogging on the beaches to stay in shape," I said, as we shook hands.

We went inside and I made us sandwiches on rye. I had a Henry's, but Jimart started out with the bottled in bond Wild Turkey bourbon and finished with it. We ate, drank, and talked about old times until Jimart fell asleep on my couch. I covered him up with an old blanket, remembered to put some food out for the cat, and went to bed at three o'clock in the morning.

* * *

Mickey brought Vannessa over early on Thursday. Mickey had cleaned up Vannessa for Jimart, and she looked like quite the young lady in the new outfit she had bought for the kid yesterday. It had sleeves, a high collar, and a pleated plaid skirt that hit the middle of her knee. The black boots with the knife were gone, replaced by Bass loafers.

I went upstairs to get the man, and found Cinnamon sleeping on his chest. I put her outside and got Jimart up. He started sneezing violently.

"Is there a cat in here?"

"She must have got in when I put out the food last night."

"What was she doing? Sleeping on my face? he asked, as he blew his nose.

"Just about."

When I finally got him downstairs, he was delighted to see Vannessa. And almost as delighted to see Mickey, whom he had never met before. He turned charming, which he can do when someone beautiful like Mickey is around.

"I like the way you have her dressed," he said.

"We bought some clothes yesterday."

Later on in the day, Mickey took Vannessa to a doctor for a checkup, something that seemed prudent given her recent hazardous occupation. She seemed in good health, with no apparent venereal infections, but they would have to wait for the results of the HIV AIDS test. Then Mickey took her shopping for some "feminine necessities," as Mickey put it. That evening Jimart put her on a plane to San Diego that her parents would meet, and, after paying us off as subcontractors, decided to vacation with us for a few days.

"Until the tan begins to fade." He took out a butt.

"You still smoke? And tan?" Mickey asked. "You have heard about lung and skin cancer?"

"I told him, no smoking in our office."

"Don't worry, I'm going outside on the porch. And nobody tans in Frisco."

"We can work on your diet too," Mickey said.

"Now I remember why I got divorced," he said, and went out.

Since Jimart was with us, I decided to tap into his expertise. I caught him up on the murder cases between cigarettes on the porch. Now we had four of us looking into the collection of cases.

"Where are you on this stuff right now?" Jimart asked.

"Right now I'm waiting to hear from the Chief."

"What the hell is a Chief?"

I told him about my partner and his attempt to infiltrate the Co Gang.

"Man, I wouldn't do shit like that for a client," he muttered.

"We're idealists here."

"And I bet you've each been shot at least once."

"You got me there."

"Hell, I'm like a cop. I never been shot and never fired my weapon."

"My hero!" I kissed him on the cheek.

"You been livin' in Fagtown too long." He wiped his cheek, then smiled. "If you want a cheek to kiss. . ."

Jimart got bored Friday. He considered taking a flight home, but decided to run *The Bestiary Set* instead.

It was his best idea. I watched it with him. Maybe something would leap out from the tapes at me that I had missed before. Something did.

"Hold it," I said, then, amazed, I added, "That's Valerie Hong in 'The Rape of Europa'."

"Nice bull," Jimart said.

"Too bad he's so well-disguised."

"Should we call the police?" Mickey asked.

"Not yet."

I called the Co number and told him Mickey and I were ready to perform.

He told us to meet him at the video store in an hour to discuss the details. He would be glad to help us out with the taping. From the way he had been looking at Mickey I figured he would.

"What if we meet at your studio?" I asked.

"I'll take you there," Co said.

After we told Jimart that he couldn't come and watch, Mickey got into her hooker outfit and I got into basic black. We both put on coats and made a run across the city in the T-Bird.

We arrived at the same time as Co at the video store. Nameless was there in his usual outfit, grinning at us from under his dark glasses.

"You get the teenage girl?" Co asked, looking past Mickey and me.

"We checked out the place you gave us. It was closed down when we got there," I said.

"The police busted the place. I read about it in the newspaper. They beat you to her."

"Too bad," Mickey said.

Co stared at her. "I can get you another young twat," he offered, in a voice that sounded like a challenge. "Just as nice. But yellow instead of white." Then he grinned, and added, "Only difference, the Asian slit goes sideways." He laughed at the bad joke.

The thought of Ollie raged inside me. I put it down for the moment.

"We'll go with two. If you have no problem with that?" I asked.

"What does the lady say?" Co asked.

Mickey pulled her coat tight around her and said, "Forget the kid. This time."

"I like that. Planning for the future."

"Why not?" I asked.

"I imagine you two will be a hot blue video with a lot of potential for sequels. Now. Any special props?"

"I'd like to use an animal mask," I said.

"Ah. We could fit you into *The Bestiary Set.* One of our best sellers. No problem. Nobody looks at the faces anyway. Any special animal?"

"What have you got in the way of a bull?" I asked.

Co laughed. "Try something else. It is time to go."

We followed him out of the store, all of us ignoring the nameless manager. Co led us to a rundown wooden two-story house a block away. It didn't look old as much as neglected. We went up a flight of rotting steps to a porch that didn't look earthquake-safe to me. He unlocked the door to the first floor apartment and led us into his studio, which consisted of a bed, lots of lights, and a Sony Camcorder on a tripod.

"Nice setup," I said.

"Get undressed," he said to us.

"Just like that?" Mickey asked.

"Do you have a better idea?" Co asked.

"I've got to fix my makeup."

"Just like a woman," he said. "No one will care about your makeup. What they care about are buns and boobs."

"I will care," Mickey insisted.

Co, in exasperation, showed her to the bathroom. I noticed a set of *Bestiary* tapes and a TV and VCR in the next room, and went over there.

When Co came back he was carrying a Donald Duck head, a pig's head, and something I couldn't recognize.

"How about these?" he asked, putting them down on the floor.

"Interesting," I said. "But how about if we take a look at one of these *Bestiary* tapes? Might give me some ideas."

"Okay. But these are all the heads I have left."

"You mean the actors keep them?"

"Souvenirs."

I looked at them again. "I'm not surprised these are left over. Who would want one of these heads?"

"Someone will."

I dug out the "Europa" tape and stuck it into the VCR and turned on the TV. Europa and the bull came on.

"Handsome bull," I said.

Co gave me a strange look.

I picked up the pig's head and tossed it into the air like a football. It rose in a tight spiral and fell into my hands just before it hit the floor.

"Be careful," Co said.

"I always am."

25

While we waited for Mickey to repair her face and hair we watched the Valerie Hong performance from two folding chairs that Co set up. The performance was pretty good. I wouldn't say the same for the uncomfortable metal chairs, or the pig's head.

"Too bad about that girl." I had almost said Vannessa, which would have meant problems with Co, since we were not into names with him. I dropped the mask to the floor.

He stared at the pig's head. "What girl?" he asked as if he had forgotten our original plans already.

"The young piece. Minnie Mouse, or whatever."

"You two will be fine. I predict excellent sales of your video."

"What about this woman in the 'Europa' tape?" I leaned forward towards the TV and pointed.

"What about her?"

"Would she be interested in a threesome?"

Co turned cold. "I don't think so. That woman is dead."

"Not much luck with your actors lately?" I asked.

He shut off the TV. "I am getting impatient. Go get undressed. I'll check the camcorder."

I stood up and gave it a shot. "Who was the bull on that tape?" I kicked the pig's head into a corner.

There was a strange flicker, like a struck match, in Co's eyes. "What is it to you who the bull is?"

I thought about trying a bribe. But that wouldn't work and it would only make him suspicious as hell. I tried instead: "Maybe we could use the bull on our tape."

"The bull? I don't handle homo stuff."

"No. I mean the bull and me and the woman. She has the orifices."

He thought it over. "I am beginning to wonder about you. It seems that the pig head is appropriate."

"Whaddya mean?"

"Are you dysfunctional with just the woman alone?"

"No way." I wondered if Co was going to volunteer to join us for fun and games on the tape. He seemed to be considering it.

Instead he said, "Then let's forget about this third party bullshit and get this going." Apparently participation wasn't his thing. But I bet he got a hell of a kick out of watching those B&Bs in motion.

"We need her." I motioned towards the bathroom.

"Where is that woman?" He started to get up.

"Right here," Mickey said, as she swung the bathroom door open. Her hair and makeup looked the same and so did the clothes she was wearing.

"What's with you? You're dressed?" Co asked as he got up. The chair fell over behind him. He pretended not to notice.

"We'll have to make it another time. I was in there fixing my face when my time of the month arrived. Unexpectedly." She shrugged.

Co said sharply, "Plenty of women do it then. Nothing to worry about. Some viewers are even into blood." He turned to me. "You have no objections, do you?"

"Not me."

"I don't care what he says. I feel sick. With cramps. We'll have to wait a few days until I'm feeling better."

"Jesus Christ," Co muttered and slapped his forehead.

"I'll give you a call," I said to Co as Mickey and I started for the door.

He just stared at us. His dark eyes were full of anger and something else. Maybe suspicion. He put his hand behind his head and tugged at his pony tail.

"We can let ourselves out," I said as we maneuvered around him.

"Are you cops?" he asked.

I didn't answer.

"I asked you a question."

"We're not," I said. "If we were we'd be busting you."

"Then who the hell are you?"

A plan suddenly took form. "A couple of people who want to know who is playing the bull on that tape."

"Why?" he asked.

"I'm willing to pay."

No problem with suspicion now.

"I do not know." Co smiled.

"I don't believe you," I insisted.

"I don't care. Now get the fuck out of here."

We let ourselves out into the cold. So much for our brief movie career.

"Now what?" Mickey asked as she pulled her coat tight around her.

"If it works we'll hear from the bull," I said.

"If what works?"

"Co will call Valerie's bull to tell him that someone is looking for him. And the bull is not going to like that."

"You're assuming the bull is her killer?" she asked.

"You have somebody better as a suspect?"

"Not offhand."

"At least we can find out if there is a connection between him and any of the other murder victims." I opened the car door for her.

"At what price?" she asked, as she slid into the seat.

I didn't answer that one. I got in and started the engine. As I pulled away from the curb I remembered my other partner. "I wonder how the Chief is doing?" I asked.

"Better than we are, I hope." Mickey said.

I speeded up to get through an amber light and just made it. Then I noticed a cop at the intersection and held my breath. He could've come after me, but he didn't.

Mickey, who'd taken in the whole scene, said, "You were lucky. He probably had his quota for the day."

I started breathing again.

At the office I called Forsander, Krift, and Marsha Hanes to assure them that I was making progress. I was real vague on the specifics, but real upbeat on the attitude. It bought me a little time, at least.

Later, the Chief called and I had my answer about how he was doing. He had been attacked by the gang for wearing their colors and after a vicious fight in which he inflicted some heavy human damage, he was apparently going to be taken in.

"I am like a fraternity pledge," he said. "I will be tested."

"Don't fail," I said.

"That depends on the test."

"Where will you be?" I asked.

"Some kind of gang headquarters. I don't know where."

I didn't like the way this sounded. "Damn. Be careful."

"I will be as careful as the hunted wolf."

"Good. But unlike the hunted wolf, keep in touch."

"I will call again. As long as there is a telephone."

"What if there isn't a phone?"

"Then look for smoke signals." He hung up.

But he didn't keep in touch with either a telephone or smoke signals. That single call was the only time we heard from him. Which made us very nervous. But maybe he was only playing it safe in the gang world, which made sense.

As for playing it safe, since the Co Gang had blown up a few cars belonging to people it didn't much care for, Mickey insisted that we get a remote starter for the T-Bird. I thought it was a ridiculous and expensive toy, but when Mickey swore she would never ride in the T-Bird again without the device, I had the necessary parts installed by an anti-terrorist auto shop that specialized in that kind of work. I could start the engine by pushing a remote button in a minature control box from almost a block away. Like turning on a VCR.

Mickey, dressed in ski jacket, jeans, and sneakers had come over early in the morning for an attempt to track down the Chief. Our plan was to start on the campus. We left Jimart asleep on the couch upstairs and went out of the office together. We walked towards my car, which was parked unusually close, just about a block away, and right on Octavia.

"Start it up," she said.

So far I had used the remote three times. But not this time. "I left it in the office. Let's skip it."

"Go get it," she insisted, after an initial hesitation.

We argued.

"That car's been out there all night." She was adamant.

So I lost and went back to get the device.

Half a block away from the T-Bird I got ready to press the remote starter.

"There are kids playing right there," Mickey said.

"Go chase them away."

Mickey did and came back. "I know you think this is silly. . ."

She was talking while I was pressing the remote. The next thing we knew we were flat on the ground and my T-Bird was engulfed in flames. The kids were screaming, but from a safe distance. Luckily, the other cars around it had cleared out for the morning commute, so it was isolated. It looked like one of the funeral ships the Vikings would set on fire and send out to sea. Only this one was a Ford, parked on a street.

I was furious. I wanted to shoot William Co. I wanted to bust some heads wide open. I started cursing and raving in the street while Mickey and the children watched me. Suddenly the edge to my anger was off. It had to be when you've lost a woman you loved. Even if it was a great American classic, a T-Bird is still just a hunk of very beautiful metal. Ollie had been life itself. But that didn't mean I wasn't going to get revenge on the Co Gang for this atrocity.

"At least it's insured," Mickey said.

I swallowed hard. "No, it isn't. When I put in a claim for the bullet holes, they told me I'd missed a couple of payments so they'd canceled my policy."

Mickey just shook her head.

"Don't say it. I know it was dumb."

I heard fire truck sirens and decided that we should get out of there. I didn't want to answer any questions about an exploded car right now.

"I just hope they haven't blown up the Chief," Mickey said.

"We're going to find him. And we're going to have to conduct a little business with Co and his boys, as well. One way or another they're going to pay for my car."

"At least you flushed out the bull. Co must have called the guy on the tape."

"This wasn't what I had in mind."

We had a problem right now with transportation. We went over to California Street and caught a cable car to downtown. There we grabbed a cab that took us to Mission Creek and the Chief's houseboat, where I hoped we would find his pickup. It was there waiting for me.

"But you don't have the key," Mickey said.

In two minutes I had the door unlocked and in five minutes I had it hot-wired.

"This could be your new profession. You seem more adept at it than at investigating."

"Thanks for your vote of confidence in the eponymous head of the agency," I said, as we drove the pickup away.

"I looked up that word," Mickey said, as she settled in and made herself comfortable.

"Then you know what it means."

"Of course. It means anyone who uses it is a *schmuck.*"

"Thank you Ms. Webster."

I drove to the campus and we went to our liaison officer Barry Kobida. We found him at his desk in the Public Safety Building. We went over some of our problems, but he wasn't a whole lot of help. He insisted that he had no leads on the Co Gang, which was easy enough to believe, but also disappointing.

"Then what have you been doing these days?" I asked.

"Walking a lot of Asian women back to their dorms at night."

"Keep them alive, man," I said, thinking of Ollie.

"Don't worry. They feel safe with me."

26

We bumped into Dixie on the way out. She was balancing a stack of files and a coffee cup. She invited us to sit down and talk to her and we took her up on the offer.

"Find the Chief. I like that guy," she said after Mickey went over some of the undercover story for her.

"How's the campus scene?" Mickey asked.

"We have frightened women. Some guys came up from L.A. with cartons of mace sprayers and they sold out on the street corner. I hear they went back to pick up some more."

"Is it the Asian women?" I asked.

"Mainly. The Rice Queen junk in the media has them spooked. But I'll tell you, *every*body's scared."

"How's Kobida?"

"Why?"

"No reason. He says he's doing a lot of escort work."

"If you ask me, he likes it."

"Can't really blame him for that," I said.

"It's more than that; he frightens the Asian girls."

"What do you mean?"

"He warns them about their lifestyles."

"And?" Mickey asked.

"That's it."

"It could be good advice," I said.

"Or it's blaming the victim," Mickey said.

"Probably both," Dixie noted. She shifted back to the Chief. "Too bad you don't have a phone number. We could check it in the reverse phone book and come up with an address for the gang's hideout."

"All I have is the number for Co's porno studio," I said.

"Wait a minute. Are you sure that's what the number is for? I didn't see a phone in there," Mickey said.

"I didn't either, now that you mention it. It's worth a shot." I fished out the business card with the phone number and gave it to Dixie.

We went over to a wall of phone books lined up in metal bookcases and Dixie pulled one out. The reverse phone book is listed numerically by telephone number and provides the name and address for that number. Which is what it provided for us. And it wasn't the address of the video studio.

"Damn, this is great Dixie." I gave her a peck on the cheek and Mickey and I were on our way in the Chief's pickup to the Co Gang Headquarters. We hoped. At least it wouldn't be a bunny.

The address was for an auto body shop in the Mission District that was long out of business. The boarded-up brick building was set back from the street with a row of parking places in front of it and a lot full of junks on the side. Around the perimeter was a chain link fence with barbed wire running in coils on top of it. The only gate was electronically locked and hooked up to a digital box with a small keypad of numbers on it. It was much more sophisticated device than an abandoned building would warrent.

"How do we get in?" Mickey asked.

"How do I get in?"

"We. I'm dressed for a little action."

I looked at her ski jacket, jeans, and sneakers. Another argument. I finally agreed that we would try it together.

"I don't think we have a shot at the lock in front," I said. "It's too electronically sophisticated."

"I agree."

I looked in the back of the pickup. There was a folded canvas cover pushed up against the cab. "Let's get back to basics. We can use this canvas," I said.

We went around with it to the side of the lot with the junks. The cover was folded into quarters, giving us a wide and thick cushion of canvas. I reached up and draped it over four feet of the width of the barbed-wire top. On the other side was the roof of a junked '49 Mercury that we could land on.

"That should protect us when we go over," I said.

We checked and loaded our weapons.

"I'd better help you first," I said.

I boosted one of her legs up high enough so that she could step with the other on the wire fence, grab the canvas, and pull herself up and over it. She landed on the roof of the junk with a dull thud and gave me the okay sign.

I took a running start, hit the fence with one foot, pushed off and landed with my butt on the canvas. I didn't feel a thing. I swung my legs over and joined my partner by the car.

"Nice work," she said, as we climbed down.

"Thanks. This is just the beginning," I said as we hit the hard ground. I pulled out my gun and waited for the junkyard dog. But none appeared. A break for everybody—especially the dog.

We made it to the other side of the building without a problem, but we couldn't spot a way in. I didn't want to try the front entrance which would get us immediate attention. So we went around the back of the building where a huge pile of old tires were stacked in the shape of a pyramid. There we found a door that wasn't boarded up and only closed with a padlock. That was easy work for me and my lockpicks.

The door creaked a bit, but it didn't seem to alert anyone when it opened.

"This may be the wrong place," Mickey muttered as she got out her gun.

"I don't think so."

The open space of the body shop had been converted into a series of walled cubicles that were probably gang member rooms, storage rooms, weapons rooms, or rooms for anything else the gang was involved in. It was like making your way through a maze. At least light bulbs were burning everywhere overhead.

"The place seems empty," Mickey said.

"Just yell out 'Hey Chief' and we'll see how empty it is. This is some operation." I raised my arm. "Wait. Hear that?"

Mickey nodded.

I peered around a corner of the maze, trying to see where the voices were coming from. There were two armed Asian men in Raider jackets playing cards with the Chief.

Chief Moses saw me and the gun I had out. And then Mickey behind me. He smiled.

"I will take your guns," he said suddenly to the two men.

"Huh? You didn't even win the hand, asshole." They both laughed.

The Chief laughed harder. "Look behind you," he ordered them.

"Now," I ordered.

The two men spun around to see our weapons aimed at their chests. Not a heart-warming sight for them.

"Now put your guns down on the table. Real slow and easy," Mickey, my ex-cop, said.

They looked at each other, sized up their chances, and complied. The Chief got some rope and duct tape from a storeroom and very quickly we had them hog-tied and gagged in one of the small rooms in the maze. That had been almost too easy.

"They are the only ones here," Chief Moses said.

"Good," Mickey said. "But for how long?"

"How'd they get on to you, Chief?" I asked.

"Remember the Yellow Suns?"

"Of course. How could I ever forget?" The Yellow Suns Social and Athletic Club had provided the weapons and a small Vietnamese army for a military venture we pulled off up in Mendocino County.

"Well, one of the Yellow Suns went renegade a while back and joined the Co Gang. Of course he recognized me as soon as they brought me here."

"Bad luck," Mickey said.

"I must be getting too well known," the Chief said.

"And your appearance is so forgettable."

"Where are Co and the others?" I asked.

"Picking up the day's haul from drugs, extortion, porn, numbers, whatever."

"How much is that?"

"Twenty-five, maybe thirty thousand. Or more."

"What do they do with it?"

"They bring it here to count and band and then they bank it around the city and collect interest."

I smiled. Maybe Lady Luck was with us. "Not today. I've got a better idea for their money. They owe me a car." I told the Chief about our plan to flush out a suspect and the resultant destruction of the T-Bird by the Co Gang.

"Some plan," he said.

"It had drawbacks," I admitted.

"And now we're using your pickup," Mickey said.

"Given the circumstances, that is okay." Then he thought for a moment. "You must have hot-wired it. Did you ever steal it before? I thought it had been moved the night you rescued the cats."

I grinned sheepishly. "I couldn't fit them into my car."

"So you took my pickup?"

The Chief didn't sound amused. I tried a bribe. "I'll pay for a truck wash."

He scowled, but said, "And hot wax?"

"Deal."

"And detailing?"

"All right already," Mickey interjected. "I heard a car pull up in front."

We got out our weapons, including the two we had confiscated from the two hog-tied gang members, and took positions in line with the front door. Co and three Asian gang members, of various sizes and ponytail lengths, and all in Raider jackets, came in. Co was carrying what had to be a sack of money.

As they say in the westerns, we had the drop on 'em.

Unlike the first two, when these four guys calculated the odds, they liked their chances.

Having the drop on them didn't stop Co from throwing the sack of money across the room and into my face as all four of them pulled out weapons and started firing. Once again, something wasn't going as planned.

Instantly, Chief Moses overturned a large wooden table in front of us and Mickey and I fired back. But they were blasting away at it and it was soon going to be in splinters and in no condition to protect anybody. So the three of us crawled backwards into the room behind us. From there we could look around a corner of a wall and get off shots at the gang. Of course, that made us pretty neat targets as well.

They had a similar position across from us in another room. The sack of money was in the middle of the floor between us, on the other side of the overturned table. It looked like a stand-off.

With limited ammunition we were in no position to withstand a seige. There was only one thing to do.

After telling my partners to make sure no one from Co's Gang jumped out there to grab the money, I left Mickey and the Chief firing at the gang to distract them while I crawled back through another door into the maze. My plan was to get behind them and catch them in a crossfire. That would force them to surrender and we would capture them and the money. Brilliant military strategy.

As I came around a corner I bumped into Co, who apparently had the same brilliant plan in mind.

We looked at each other and we both smiled. Did I owe this bastard.

He raised his Magnum, but I managed to swing out with my S&W and strike his forearm hard enough so that the gun went sailing across the room.

He looked like he was going to dive after it, but instead he paid back the favor with a loud grunt and a kick that knocked my gun from my hand. The man had studied the martial arts. I checked to see what color belt he had on, but he wasn't wearing one. No problem, I figured.

Until the next kick connected with my jaw and sat me down on my butt. He went after his weapon, but I stuck out my foot and tripped him. Nice professional wrestling move.

We were on our hands and knees facing each other. From there we started wrestling in earnest. This was not what I wanted to be doing. His jacket was slick and hard to get hold of, but the Raider jacket also made it hard for him to get a good grip on me. I slipped out of a weak headlock and jumped up. Co was right up with me. Another kick just missed my eye. Another grazed my forehead. Co was crouching to deliver one more when I decided I had had enough of kick boxing or whatever the hell it was we were doing.

He started to spin out of his crouch for a wheel kick; I rushed him, caught the kick on the outside of my thigh, and came up at him with a basic knee to the groin. Old no-color belt trick. He doubled over, but recovered enough to try another kick. It was weak and I caught him in the groin again, then cracked him in the jaw with my fist. Blood spurted from his lip and ran down his chin. He licked at it with his tongue.

He wasn't giving up easily. He came at me with another wheel kick that just missed my head. Then he tried to surprise me by kicking with his other leg, but I saw it coming and caught his ankle and twisted it while he was in mid-air.

I heard a cracking sound in his knee, like a giant wishbone breaking.

He screamed and fell to his knees.

Not a good position from which to practice martial arts. A couple of good shots to the chin with my knee and he was down for the count. A pool of blood and saliva formed under his mouth.

I picked up both guns and dragged Co by his ponytail. I had always wanted to do that to someone and I wasn't going to pass up this chance. I kept my gun on his head. His Raider jacket slid nicely across the floor.

After passing through two rooms of the maze, I could tell by the gunfire that we were only a room away from the gang.

"Get up," I ordered.

Co muttered in Japanese, but got up. I got behind Co and steered him around the wall for the gang members to see.

"Drop them or this bastard dies," I said, using Co as my shield.

The three of them looked at Co.

"Do what he says. That's not a fucking toy gun he has pointed at my head."

They hesitated. Maybe considering the odds. Maybe not giving a damn if Co got blown away. Maybe thinking about who the next gang leader might be.

"Throw the guns out into the middle of the room by the table," I ordered.

With a glance towards Co, one by one they threw out their weapons.

"Good boys," I said.

Mickey and the Chief were picking up the guns and the sack of money. Chief Moses turned the bullet-ravaged table upright and put the guns and the sack of money on it. I pushed Co over to the other Raider fans. Even with the help of my push, he limped towards them. Co would be needing some arthroscopic surgery on the knee for sure. I hoped he had a good health plan.

So far I had gotten exactly what I wanted. I beat up on Co and got his money. I took the sack of money and counted the cash out on the table in front of the gang. They had collected over thirty grand.

"Thanks for the contribution," I said.

"You can't take that!" one of them shouted.

"I'm collecting for damages done to my classic T-Bird. Sue me if you want. Or maybe call the cops."

"Fuck you," Co shouted.

I grabbed Co and twisted his arm behind his back. I could inflict a little more pain.

"Let's try to be polite."

"Ow. Okay."

"Who hired you to blow up my car?" I asked.

He didn't say. And he wouldn't say. I applied more pressure.

"Was it the bull on the tape?"

"Fuck you," Co said again, as he spit blood.

I kicked him in the back of his damaged knee and he fell to the ground, writhing in pain.

"Are you going to talk?"

Co sat up, held his knee, and howled in anguish. Tears were running down his cheek, mingling with the blood and saliva at his mouth.

I looked at Mickey and the Chief. Mickey, who was not enjoying this at all, turned her head away. The Chief, who I could usually count on to put on some unconstitutional pressure, was just shaking his head.

Torture is tough. I was facing a moral dilemma. If I kept it up I would be a candidate for condemnation by Amnesty International. I wanted the name of whoever had ordered my car blown up, but the amount of pain I had to inflict would be tantamount to torture. And I wondered if I had already crossed the line. The truth was I didn't have the stomach to do any more—something Co probably realized. However, I did have another option. I could turn him over to the police and they could probably get it out of him with a plea bargain. But then they would impound the thirty grand and there would go my car. Not what I had in mind.

"You want to know so bad?" Co asked.

"Yeah."

"Give me my money back."

So I could get it out of him by turning back the thirty grand. I didn't like that idea at all either. Torture started looking better. But the sad look in Mickey's eyes told me she would never forgive me.

What the hell. I decided we could figure it out without his help and keep the money and my reputation with Amnesty International unsullied.

But I did have a good idea on how I could help out with urban renewal.

First, I counted out enough of the money to buy all of the Co Gang members one-way airline tickets back to L.A. In tourist. Then enough money for Co's knee operation.

"And make sure you buy them, " I said. "Or the Chief and I will come looking for you, and break more knees."

To make sure they left, I used several cans of gasoline I found stored in one of the rooms to wet down the room behind us and the floor, walls, and table where we were standing while Mickey and the Chief covered the gang. The room shined, and smelled like a gas station.

"What the hell are you doing?" Co shouted.

"Making sure you stay out of business here. But you better free your two buddies in that back room over there."

Co, who was having trouble standing up, much less walking, signaled one of the gang members. The Chief followed him to the room. I picked up the sack of money from the table. I noticed a little gasoline had gotten spilled on it.

Co started insulting the untied gang members' parentage and their manhood for letting us get in here and surprising them, when they reappeared. I put an end to his ranting by lighting a rolled-up newspaper. Everyone moved towards the door. I walked across the floor and threw the flaming torch on a pile of other newspapers in the room behind us. In a few seconds the gasoline would catch.

"Let us out of here!" The gang was anxious.

"This is in retribution for my car."

"The place is going to go up!"

I was anxious too. "Well, get the hell out of here. Everybody."

I gripped the sack of money and held it high. I wanted to make sure it was safe from the flames. Mickey, the Chief, and I, threw the gang weapons back into the fire. Co put his arms around the shoulders of the two gang members he had just cursed and they helped him walk out the front entrance.

We all made a break for it. We went in one direction; the Co Gang went in the opposite. Towards the airport, I hoped.

We recovered the Chief's pickup and I shoved the sack of money under the seat. We got the King Cab safely the hell out of there.

My partners and I watched the building burn from a hill a few blocks away. Occasional small explosions punctuated the fire with small orange bursts. Junks in the lot caught fire as well, and some blew up. Huge flames were leaping up from behind the building. This was better than the Fourth of July. Then thick black smoke began to rise, smelling of burning rubber. The huge pile of old tires behind the building must have caught fire. Despite the pollution, I figured this whole action ought to improve the climate of the neighborhood a whole lot, not to mention that of the campus. A lot of weapons and dope and porn and whatever had just gone up in smoke.

The place was so quickly fully-involved that the fire fighters who showed up concentrated on wetting down nearby buildings and putting out the smoldering tires. Fortunately the old building was isolated in the middle of a junkyard, so it could burn to the ground without too much risk to any other structures.

We had seen enough and it was probably better for us not to be spotted in the area.

On the way back in the pickup Mickey put on a rock station. The DJs were having an argument about an actor's rear. Whether after baring it in the first movie, did he bare it again in the sequel? One DJ was arguing that he used a stand-in for the rear end shot because it had gone from flabby to firm. The other DJ was arguing that the actor must have worked out after he saw what he looked like bareass in the first film.

"This is ridiculous," I said as I reached out to change the station.

"Wait. They're asking listeners to call in with their opinions,"Mickey said.

"On the great tush controversy?" The Chief shut the radio off. "My pickup, so I rule the radio," he added.

"At least the Chief has taste," I said.

Mickey looked at me. "Could you have hurt Co any more?"

Not with you standing there watching, I was going to say, but the real answer was no. Some things just aren't worth it.

"I was getting sick," I said.

No one contradicted or consoled me.

Back at the office, Mickey and Chief Moses filled Jimart in on the latest events. After I locked up the thirty grand in my safe, and while they talked, I did some thinking at my desk about how we could flush out the man playing the bull on the tape. At least he couldn't turn to the Co Gang for protection, and I didn't have another car to blow up. Maybe he would come after us himself now.

Suddenly I had an inspiration that went beyond the mundane collecting of information in a Q&A routine. I called Mickey. "I've got an idea. And it's thanks to you and my wrestling match with Co."

"What is it?" she asked.

"You'll see. Let's go back and watch those tapes again," I said.

"Good idea," Jimart said.

"My you are a pair of horny voyeurs," Mickey said.

"The best kind. But this is research. And this time we'll have the Chief with us."

"I can take it," Chief Moses said.

"I bet," Mickey said.

We watched the tapes and concentrated on the bull who performed with Valerie. After slow motion and still frames I was pretty sure I had seen this bull in clothes. Now I had an idea that involved a gym and a video camera.

"We're going to do some body work," I explained cryptically to the three of them.

I called Barry Kobida for some campus police help and got his somewhat reluctant cooperation.

The Chief, Officer Kobida who was a member, and I, went to the University Gym on Saturday. Mickey complained about being left out, but she was still the only one who could go undercover now if I was right about our suspect. Except for Jimart, but I didn't expect him to volunteer for such hazardous duty given his attitude towards anything risky. As for going to the gym, Jimart was going to sleep in and then watch TV or do something that didn't require a lot of energy or movement. So Mickey stayed and caught up on some work at the office, with Jimart either unconscious or relaxing upstairs, while the Chief and I hit the gym. With some help from Kobida's badge and membership, we established our cover and then we were on our own.

The place looked like a yuppie health club with everything from women in Spandex to a heated indoor swimming pool to a weight room that included one of those chrome and black adult jungle gyms that was guaranteed to develop every muscle on your body to perfect definition. There were exercise bicycles and rowing machines and step machines and Nordic cross-country skiing simulators. And aerobics classes.

While we kept alert for our suspect, we had a great day exercising in the weight room on Saturday. On Sunday we were both a little sore and mainly hung around the pool, admiring the perfectly-toned women in their second-skin racing suits. We also couldn't resist joining an aerobics class in which there were only two other men and some two dozen shapely women. Then we spent some time in the steam room and the Jacuzzi. Work can be tough.

On Monday we just hung around, playing some racketball. That was my hustle. I let the Chief beat me at it and then proposed switching to badminton. The Chief scoffed. He also ended up losing two hundred bucks to me at the game.

"Next it is lacrosse for us," he swore. "A real game."

"Some other year." I packed up my badminton racket. Badminton and Ollie. The memories flashed by like a movie. I stopped it on a single frame of the girl. It hurt to think that her killer was free.

As for the man we were looking for, nothing doing so far.

But we remained patient. Not hard to do between the pool, the weight room, and the sauna.

We could get used to this kind of life, except for the complaints we got from Mickey for being left out. Jimart, on the other hand, was just getting bored.

Fortunately, or unfortunately, on Tuesday we got lucky.

We spotted our suspect going into the gym just as we were pulling up.

"I think it's back to serious work," I said.

The Chief got the equipment out of the locked and bolted-down box in the back of the truck and I went into the gym to try out the routine we had planned just for this moment.

I felt a little better about Ollie.

27

The first problem I spotted was that there was someone new at the registration desk. Instead of the out-of-shape bearded guy that Kobida had talked to, there was a short, wiry man wearing a green tank top and black shorts guarding the gate. He had a brush cut, a lined and weathered face, electric blue eyes, and enormous hands. He looked like an ex-jockey who certainly took his job a lot more seriously than the previous guy. I didn't have Kobida here to give me credibility, so I decided not to waste time with truthful, but overly long, explanations. Instead, as the Chief, dressed in a loose tan trench coat specially designed for clandestine operations, brought the camcorder in, I showed the jockey at the desk my business card for a TV commercial company. Whenever we do anything with a video camera I carry that card. It opens most doors.

"A commercial?" The guy at the desk scratched his scalp through his crewcut.

"Right," I said as the Chief quickly moved past me.

"Hold it!" the guy ordered the Chief.

Chief Moses stared, but the man didn't blink. He had probably wrestled at 120 pounds when he was a kid, or maybe had taken on wild horses as a jockey, so the Chief didn't scare him. Wrestling and racing horses obviously didn't do much to develop brain power, though.

"What's the problem?" I asked, and smiled warmly.

"Who set this up? What are we supposed to be selling on this commercial?" He frowned.

"The Alumni Office in conjunction with Development. Part of their new joint fund-raising campaign. They're pushing the benefits of belonging to the Alumni Association. And this gym is a big one. So we're going to show it on video." I indicated the exercise and weight room. "We did the pool already when the other guy was here." Another smile.

"Yeah. Great. He doesn't even check IDs. I don't know about this." Another frown.

I cut out the smiling. "Look. We're doing this as a freebie for the university. You want to call the Development Office and explain why you kicked us out of the gym? Next time we show up it's cash up front. No more favors from us. They'll probably deduct it from your paycheck." I turned to the Chief. "Okay, let's pack it up. I've had enough of this *schmuck*."

"Okay, okay. Let me just call the Alumni Office."

"Go ahead. But we're out of here. We can't waste any more time. I've got a shoot to do for Pier Thirty-Nine. And you want to know how much that's costing them?"

He hesitated. "Oh go shoot your goddam commercial."

The guy looked skeptical, but sat down and shut up. What more could you ask for?

"Get to work, Chief," I ordered.

"Yes, boss. Right away, boss."

"Now that's what I like. A cooperative employee."

Chief Moses turned to me and whispered, "Fuck you, White Man. We do not forget the Trail of Tears."

"What's that?"

"Something I learned about my people in class last week. A forced march to hell."

"I'm sure you'll do well on the test. But for right now. . ." I discreetly pointed out our subject and the Chief took off his trench coat and went around videotaping the action in the weight room while I went to the health drink bar—which turned out to operate much like a

North Beach singles bar, but with better-looking people wearing less—to hide out. I didn't want to be spotted by our video star, who at least didn't know the Chief by sight.

Twenty minutes later, after I had, with regrets, turned aside the advances of a beautiful young blond woman held together only by blue lycra, and while I nursed a blender protein concoction of celery, tomato, egg, and six kinds of vegetables, the Chief appeared bearing the gift of a videotape. He looked down the bar at the woman in blue, who was now hitting on a guy that looked like a finalist in a Mr. Universe contest.

"At least she tried me first," I said.

"Obviously the muscled one was not here yet."

"True, but irrelevant."

Chief Moses grunted and I got back on track. "You got it?"

"What are you drinking? It smells like horse piss."

"Old Indian drink. Horse piss in vegetable juice. Can I order you one on the rocks?" I asked cheerfully. "Or maybe you'd rather just finish mine. I'd appreciate it."

The Chief ordered a glass of water with a slice of lemon.

"You're not helping the drought," I noted.

"I am also not poisoning myself with horse piss."

"A Seminole Standoff." I pushed my drink away and stood up from the bar. "Why can't you get something like beer here?"

The bartender looked at me and said, "Blasphemy, man." Then grinned. I had the feeling he had something a little more potent hidden behind the bar. His private reserve.

"Try a diet drink," the Chief suggested to me.

"No way," the bartender said. "You ever read the shit that's in there? Everything from saccharin to aspartame to sodium."

"Right. Considering the ingredients, I'll just stick to Henry's—when I can get it." I turned to the Chief and rephrased my earlier question. "Any hassles about the camcorder?"

This time I got an answer. "Not after I explained about the commercial. The men all started flexing their muscles and the woman started fixing their makeup and pushing their breasts up to their chins and everyone was asking when it would be on TV."

"Did you get our main man flexing?"

"He's the star. Right up there pumping iron for me, although he did cut out rather quickly to the sauna, as if he had second thoughts about TV exposure."

"Suddenly struck camera shy," I said.

"Apparently."

"He's probably in the showers. Shall we see if we can get lucky?" I suggested.

"Some idea of luck. This calls for the trench coat." The Chief put the loose coat back on and slipped the camcorder into the custom holder sewn into the lining. The camera would shoot on automatic through an opening created by an oversized buttonhole. Ingenious. Good for parties, too.

We slipped into the men's locker room. We were lucky. Our star was singing in the shower.

"Go to it," I said, as I ducked behind a tile wall.

The Chief sat down on a bench in front of a row of lockers and got the camcorder going while he pretended to be tying his shoes. We were getting some great shots of our man naked in the shower. Assuming nothing went wrong with the battery or the tape.

"We have enough," Chief Moses said, as he got up.

The shower went off along with the singing. We got the hell out of there.

We took the Chief's pickup back to the office, got Mickey, who told us that Jimart had gotten bored hanging around and had gone out to a movie, and the three of us watched *The Bestiary Set.*

"What are we doing?" Mickey asked.

"We're going to be making comparisons."

"Where did you get this crazy idea?" she asked.

"It's not crazy. I got the idea from those DJs you had on the radio, and their contest about that actor's rear end in the two movies."

"What?"

"You remember. Whether he used a bare butt stand-in in the sequel or not."

"Chief, is he sane?"

"Some days," the Chief said.

"Like today. Pay attention."

After *The Bestiary Set* I put on our workout videotape, but it didn't start out as we expected.

"Damn it, Chief. What the hell is this?" I asked.

"It's obvious, isn't it?" Mickey said. "The Chief and his playmate at bedtime in his houseboat."

"Damn. I apologize. I thought I had taped over this sequence." He moved to fast forward the tape.

"Don't do that," I said. "We could sell it to Co's blue video operation for some cold cash."

"Get this adolescent garbage off," Mickey said. "Men. Not only are their brains in their dicks, but so are their eyes."

"I like the image," I offered.

"Sorry," the Chief said sheepishly as he hit the fast forward button.

"Men," Mickey repeated.

I decided not to counter with a comment about women who let it all hang out in entertainment for men in high-class skin magazines.

We watched the workout videotape, going through the lifting and the candid shots in the shower.

"What do you think?" I asked Mickey. "Is it the bull?"

"What, am I the expert on the nude male body?"

"Who else?" I asked.

"This isn't of great interest to me Jeremiah. I can swear to that." She considered. "Look, Jeremiah, I need to see them side by side so we can freeze the frames and compare parts. I've got a friend in a camera and video store who'll let us use a couple of VCRs and TVs, side by side."

"Let's go for it."

The store was close enough to walk to. The weather was mild and we just wore light sweaters. Sometimes it was colder in July than it was today. The sky was a faded denim blue and there was almost no wind. As we climbed the California Street hill, I said, "We ought to walk more often."

They looked at me. "Makes sense when you no longer own a car," they said in unison, as if they had a script.

"You were waiting to deliver that line," I said.

"Not us." In unison.

The Witt's Video Store was near the top of the hill. A pleasant young man named Ralph, with bulging colorless eyes, very light skin, and a case of premature balding, was happy to help us out at Mickey's request.

"Only you need to wait until the boss leaves. Maybe another fifteen minutes."

With fifteen minutes to kill I let him go through an enthusiastic spiel about the new 8mm handcams that were going to revolutionize the market. He spoke like a true believer. The 8mm camcorders were impressively light and compact, and the tapes were smaller and produced clearer pictures.

"These go on my list," Mickey said, as she swung a new camcorder around in her hand.

"I figured they would."

"Your VHS camcorder will soon be obsolete," Ralph assured us.

"I'll wait until that happens."

Ralph eyed his boss, a heavyset man of about sixty, who was staring at Ralph.

"I'm taking too long with this sale," Ralph said. "He wants me to try to close the deal."

"That's hard to believe, considering what these cost," the Chief said. "I remember when you could buy a new car for the cost of one of these camcorders."

"About the time of the Little Big Horn?" I asked.

Mickey squeezed my left arm.

"Ow. It's still sore."

"Don't be such a baby. Men are always such babies. Just buy something from Ralph and maybe the boss will leave."

"Give me some VHS tapes," I said. "The Chief here needs a new supply for his houseboat library."

I bought three tapes and Ralph rang them up. The boss wasn't real pleased with such a small change deal, but it was enough to get him off on his break.

"How long will he be gone? This could take a while," I said.

"Don't worry. This is a different kind of coffee break. He meets the black woman from the donut shop in his van in the parking garage down the street. We won't see him for a while."

I looked out the store window and saw an attractive black woman of about thirty, in a long gray coat and black heels, hurrying in the direction of the garage. She was about half a block behind the boss. She was much too good-looking for him. I said to Mickey, "I'm all out of moral judgments. All I've got is a camcorder to objectively record human events."

Ralph set us up with what we needed in the rear of the store. He went up front to carry on with business. A young couple came in, pushing a kid in a stroller. The woman was pregnant, and they were talking about wanting to record the birth of their next child in living color. I heard Ralph begin his sales pitch for a Sony 8mm Camcorder.

We went to our business. With two TVs next to each other, and with the frames frozen, it was much easier to study the tapes. We compared notes on the naked man in the shower with the bull in the *Bestiary Set.*

"I don't think we have to watch this any longer. It's turning my stomach," Mickey said.

"And I always thought women were dying to get into the men's locker room," I said, just to bug her, as I hit the play button.

Mickey made a barfing gesture by putting a finger on her tongue in response. Then she said, "The man in our tape and the man in the bull tape have to be the same. Look at the endomorphic body structure. Identical. And the height is apparently the same. And also the feet and hands. And yes, Jeremiah, that's the same rear end."

"But you ignore the most telling similarity," I said.

"I knew that's what you were looking at. I'll leave that to you and the Chief. You should be towel-snapping locker room experts."

"Chief," I said, "you're the Love Dick specialist. Give us your analysis."

Mickey muttered, "Adolescents."

"Probably identical. Approximately three inches flaccid and five inches erect, which would be an appropriate proportion, but not much of a tool."

"Skip the editorial. And the most obvious point?"

"The man is not of the Jewish persuasion," the Chief noted.

"Exactly. An uncircumcised penis is not that common," I said.

"But is all this proof of anything?" Chief Moses asked.

"No," I said.

"Then what are we doing?" Mickey asked.

"I'm not sure," I admitted. "Except for making some connections." I ejected our tapes from the two VCRs.

"Thanks, Ralph. That was a big help," I said, as we walked out past him and the young couple that were about to buy a new 8mm camcorder to record the birth of their next child.

From down the street I saw the boss returning. He had a smile wide as the grill on the Chief's pickup on his puffy face. The coffee break must have gone well for him.

"I'm never listening to that station again," Mickey muttered.

"But at least we know who the bus is," I said.

"What made you think of him/" Mickey asked.

"Wrestling with Co brought him to mind."

"Another leap of logic?" the Chief asked.

"That's how I do my best work."

28

It was Wednesday, the first day of February, and the mild weather had changed overnight with a front that had descended on Northern California from the Gulf of Alaska. It was freezing cold again, breaking a low temperature record for that date in the early morning hours.

I was up at six, making notes on the murders. And trying to fit Ollie's death in. By nine, I had a stack of notes, but no solution. I needed to get out.

I left Jimart still asleep upstairs, shivering under three blankets. I didn't think he was going to last here too much longer.

I spent the day walking around the city, going through Japantown, walking the docks, retracing the way I had gone with Ollie. And thinking. Late in the afternoon, sitting in the cold on a bench in Lafayette Park as the sun set, I drew up my conclusions. On paper they looked plausible. It was time to try them out on my partners and Jimart.

All three of them were in the office waiting for me.

"Where were you?" Mickey asked.

"Working," I said.

"On what?" Chief Moses asked.

"On a park bench," I said. I realized that I had not eaten all day. I felt slightly faint. "Let's talk about it over dinner."

Everyone agreed to that.

"I know just the place to go," I said. "If we can get a car and a driver."

Jimart, who had just rented an ancient Cadillac from an outfit called Rent-A-Junk, wanted to show off his clunky bargain.

"I'll drive," he volunteered. "I want you to see my fifty-seven Caddy. Did I get a deal."

"You're on," I said.

They put on their heaviest coats, while I checked the office security systems. Then we walked three blocks to the huge Cadillac that looked as large as a dinosaur. A dinosaur with rockets attached to its giant skyscraping fins.

"I thought these gas guzzlers were extinct," I said.

"Like a lot of things, you're wrong about this one, Jeremiah," Jimart shot back.

"Indians love cars like these," Chief Moses said.

"Nice to drive around in on the reservation and pick up squaws?" Jimart asked.

The Chief glared at him. "Indians love oil wells and oil stock, as well as fire-water. Cars like this keep the price of oil up there with the Great Spirit." Although when he started the gesture, it looked like he had another finger in mind, the Chief was content to aim a forefinger upward to make his point.

"And I thought you liked the big back seat," Mickey said.

"Only in my younger days, as a brave. I can afford better places now," the Chief noted. "And better women."

"We could tell from your videotape," Mickey said.

"What videotape?" Jimart asked.

I looked at the Chief, who actually blushed. I hoped he appreciated how Mickey and I refused to answer.

The car was that sickly gold that Detroit used to think was attractive as hell to somebody or something. Maybe to overflying birds, which had done a pretty good job on the hood and windshield. Certainly not to any human buyer who wasn't color-blind.

Jimart cursed out the feathered bombers as he looked at the condition of the car.

"What is this street? On some kind of flight pattern for migratory geese?"

"It's that dull gold color. It's been scientifically proven that it attracts birds," I said.

"Shut up and get in," he said.

The three of us hesitated. "No remote starter?" Mickey asked.

Jimart looked at us. "I couldn't afford to rent a car with a high-tech gimmick like that. I'd have to go to one of those places that rent anti-terrorism vehicles and shell out a fortune. This thing costs me under twenty bucks a day."

"And worth every cent. But that gimmick saved my life," I said.

"And mine," Mickey added.

"I don't care. Nobody's trying to blow me up. But go up the street when I start the car if you're so damn scared."

The Chief took it as a test of his Indian manhood and got in the front seat. Mickey and I got in the back because there didn't seem to be much choice—Mickey as gracefully and modestly as possible, considering her short wool skirt under the heavy coat. No cowards here. Just fools maybe.

"Nice leather seats," was about the only good thing I could think to say about the garish interior as Jimart turned on the ignition.

I held my breath. I could tell Mickey was doing the same.

The Cadillac started without blowing up.

The Chief turned to us and said, "I checked under the frame earlier for explosive devices."

"You could have told us," Mickey said.

"I let you be brave."

I cursed to myself.

Jimart sailed the huge boat away from the curb and worked the washers and wipers to clear the windshield.

"Where are we going?" he asked.

"Dante's Corner."

"Good choice," Mickey said.

The Chief agreed.

"Need directions?" I asked Jimart.

"Come on. I'm from The City." He said it like it was in caps, the way our local newspapers refer to The City. "What I need is to clear the damn window." The droppings had smeared under the wipers, into something thick and white that looked like Elmer's Wood Glue. He blasted the windshield again with the washers and this time opened up two fans of vision under the wiper blades.

Jimart only made two wrong turns—and only twice tried to light up a Marlboro, but the old car lighter wouldn't work—before he let us off on Green Street in North Beach, while he went to hunt down a parking space in which the Caddy would fit.

"Hope he's back by dessert," I said, as we went in.

Dante's Corner was definitely a great Italian restaurant and rumored to be a pretty good sports bar. But not the kind with a giant TV to watch sporting events, a dart board, and pictures of every NBA, NFL, NHL, and National and American league team on the walls. In this case, a sports bar was a polite way of saying you could lay down a sporting wager on your favorite race horse if you were so inclined. The sideline had been going on for years in a back room, so no one thought to put an end to it. It lent charm to the establishment and it didn't hurt that a cop could always get a free meal here, too. Or place a bet.

Dante's had red and white tablecloths that could be wiped off, faded photographs of horses and jockeys, and more horses and more jockeys—and not a hockey or basketball player in sight—curtains in the colors of the Italian flag, ersatz leather booths, dice cups at the bar, and a real roaring fireplace to ward off the winter cold.

I tipped someone in a black suit and tie who looked like he was in charge, and got us a table in the No Smoking section by the fire. While we waited for Jimart to make it back, I ordered drinks.

Ten minutes later Jimart walked in and appreciated the Wild Turkey bourbon waiting for him.

"Cold out there," he complained. "And no parking spaces I could fit the damn boat in. I had to put it in a garage. They'll rob us with those rates. But at least this place throws in a car wash."

"Good," Mickey said, as she got up to go to the ladies' room.

"At least I got to smoke a couple of cigarettes without you guys around." He threw up his arms in a sweeping gesture. "I bet this is a No Smoking section. Right?"

"You got it."

"Fucking ridiculous with a fire going right there."

"That smoke goes up the chimney, not in your lungs," the Chief said. "Just like in a teepee. That marvel of Indian design."

Jimart shook his head in disgust. "You guys are going to die in good health. I'll say that for you. You'll make great organ donors."

When Mickey returned and the four of us were finally settled in with our drinks and warming up, I asked, "Ready?"

"For what?" Jimart asked.

"My theory, or theories," which I proceeded to unleash upon the world, or at least upon our table in Dante's Corner.

"This is what I was working on today. As we saw on the 'Europa' tape, our wrestler Dwight Snokes knew Valerie quite well. From the way Co operates, they were most likely a couple that came to him. That gives us a connection beyond the porno video, which is important to my scenario. Now let's go in reverse from there. Say he used Valerie to get the contents of the safe deposit box. Then he had to be the one who killed Claire to get the key and her identification. If Valerie caught on, she had to go, too."

"But what did Claire have in the safe deposit box that Snokes wanted so much he had to kill for it?" Mickey asked. "What's the motive here?"

"How did he know about Claire's kidnapping?" Chief Moses asked. "He had to know where to find her."

"One question at a time, please. Chief, I'd say Ness or Boas. Boas I'd guess, since he's dead," I said. "Another victim of his own knowledge."

"Makes some sense," Jimart threw in, while he scratched his head.

"What about Ness? Where does he fit?" Mickey asked.

"Ness gave Claire the keys he had for the office, and Claire used them to get in. He sold out for what he thought was love."

"But he came back," Mickey said.

"Probably got consoled by money," I noted.

"What did she take from his office?" Chief Moses asked.

"Now we're talking motive. She had to get copies of something incriminating that he had in his files. The filing cabinets were scratched up. Almost certainly because they were broken into, because Ness wouldn't have a key to them. And there was a copy machine right there. Real handy."

"And now Snokes thinks these copies of something or other have all been destroyed," Mickey said.

"I'm getting lost," Jimart said.

"Hang in there," I said. "We may not be much better off than you."

"You guys work too hard." Jimart ordered another round of drinks.

"Of course he thinks they've been destroyed. He murdered Claire to get her copies, then he burned the originals and the copies from the safe deposit in that office fire. Makes him feel awfully secure," I concluded.

"What do you think was in them?" Chief Moses asked.

"The big question. The motive for all of this," Mickey said.

I took the plunge. "It's a guess, but I'd say evidence of cheating the government out of thousands of dollars on his grant, at the same time that he was lying about the results of his experiments. And Claire was going to make him pay for what she found out. Now we have the specific motive Mickey was looking for."

"Thank you. But how do you know all that?" Mickey asked. "You don't have any proof."

"I know I don't. But it's what makes sense."

"That ain't enough," Jimart noted.

"Why did she go after him like that?" Mickey asked.

"Who knows? Maybe she just hated older men. Including her own father," I noted.

"Maybe he came on to her," Chief Moses suggested.

"You would think of that, Chief," Jimart put in as he paid for the round of drinks.

"That's possible," I said. "And there's always greed."

"You haven't mentioned Ollie," Mickey said softly.

"I know."

"Well?" the Chief asked.

It was still hard to accept. "I assume that she knew some or all of this. So he had to take her out of the picture." It was a cliché and a euphemism, but it was easier for me to put it like that.

"What do we do now?" Mickey asked.

I pulled myself together. The professional PI. "Easy." I pointed to our waitress standing by the table in a white outfit with white stockings that made her look like a nurse. "We order."

Jimart went for meatloaf, the Chief for lamb shanks with lentils, Mickey for *gnocchi* Alfredo, and I ordered the *osso buco* with *polenta*.

"Jimart, meatloaf is not Italian," I said.

"Hey, they put tomato sauce and Romano cheese on it. What do you want?"

"Some wine," I said, and ordered a bottle of the reserve Chianti and four glasses.

Jimart kept us off the subject by talking about life in San Diego and comparing the warm weather there to what we were experiencing in San Francisco.

"You have to come visit me," he ended up saying to Mickey. "And warm your body."

"We'll be there," the Chief and I promised.

Jimart grunted. I wasn't sure what he meant, but I took it as a welcome. Then he talked about how well he thought the Padres were going to do this coming season.

"Sure," I said and ended up making a hundred dollar bet on where they would finish relative to the Giants.

The meals came quickly and the portions were large. My *osso buco* pieces were as big as baseballs. There was no room on the plate for the *polenta*, which was served on a side dish. I tasted the Chianti, then let the waitress pour it around.

As she filled Mickey's glass, I asked, "How would you like to set another trap?"

Mickey waited until the waitress was gone before answering. "It's getting old."

"You won't have to wear a hooker costume," I promised.

"Gee. And that was my favorite part."

"I thought so."

"I'd like to see this," Jimart tossed in.

Mickey forced a smile at him. She swirled the Chianti in her glass. She held it up against the fire and watched the orange flames thread through it. She took a swallow and put the glass down hard on the table. "Tell me about it," she said to me, as she picked up her fork and began to attack her *gnocchi*.

"You're going to talk to Snokes, the man who killed Claire and the. . . others," I said.

"How nice for me." She stabbed a stray *gnocchi*.

"And then you're going to bring him in from out of the cold, so to speak."

"That's even nicer," Mickey added.

"Let's hope so," I said, as I dipped some *polenta* into my plate and tasted the rich brown sauce in which my *osso buco* floated like islands.

"One thing you have overlooked," the Chief said.

"What's that?" I asked.

"The man has a substantial alibi, according to Johnny D, for the time of Claire's murder."

"What're you trying to do? Spoil my fun?" I asked.

"I am looking for the truth."

"We'll spend tomorrow morning looking into the truth of that alibi."

"It was his wife who swore to it," Mickey reminded me.

"Start with her, Chief."

"I will do what I can."

"That's what I like. Confidence. Enthusiasm," I said.

"Pass me the Chianti," Jimart said. "This conversation is too much like work."

"Shouldn't we be bringing the police in on this?" Mickey asked.

"No. This is personal," I said.

Mickey nodded and said, "But let's hope this clever plan doesn't lead to another vehicle blowing up."

"My King Cab!"

"Not this time."

29

Like the day before, today's low temperature set a record for that February date. It was so cold that I let the cat sleep indoors. Unfortunately, she ended up sleeping on Jimart again. It was so cold that Jimart turned in his Caddy and flew back to San Diego to get away from the cat, and to try to warm up. I would miss the old guy, but I sure didn't blame him.

After dealing with the police about the destruction of my car, assuring them I had no idea who would want to blow it up, and paying a towing charge for the twisted steel remains to be hauled to a junkyard, we were back to normal, back to our smooth operating agency of three.

The Chief spent the morning working on the computer network, coming up with some interesting facts about our suspect's wife.

"It looks like Snokes brought her over from Japan," the Chief said.

"I wonder if she was one of those Asian mail-order brides?" Mickey asked.

"I bet that alibi she provided won't hold up," I said.

By the afternoon we were ready to put our plan into action. It was a masterpiece of simplicity. Or it was the best we could do.

I got ready for it by pulling on my heaviest sweater, a red crew neck from Scotland, and wearing a Harris Tweed sport coat over that and my gun. I felt like I could hardly raise my arms.

First, we tried to take over Misty Finch's freezing apartment. She didn't make it easy. She wanted to stay, even after we explained our plan and even though she knew it would be dangerous for her.

"I'll do it," Misty insisted. "It'll be a real kick."

I indicated Mickey, who was standing in the living room dressed in her coat, rubbing her hands together. "She's a professional. She gets paid to do this kind of thing."

"And I have a lot of experience at it," Mickey noted. "Can't you do anything about the temperature in here?" she added to Misty.

"I can't get any heat up today." Then Misty went back to her argument with me. "What about him?" She pointed to the Chief, who was sitting on the couch, dressed in a bulky black and white ski sweater that would keep him warm in the Arctic. He was at work attaching a recording device to the phone in the living room. Lately the Chief had become quite interested in high-tech equipment—especially when he discovered how much time and work it could save him. We were going to preserve for posterity the conversation we were trying to set up. "He'll keep me safe if you can't," Misty said.

"That's not the point." I sighed. "Let's make a deal. I notice you're getting your ski equipment ready." Skis, wax, poles, assorted brightly-colored ski clothing, and boots for skiing and boots for hanging around the lodge, were spread out on the living room floor.

"I'm going to Tahoe this weekend."

"Go now."

"I've got classes."

"Cut them."

"I can't."

"The trip is on me." I counted out two one-hundred dollar bills. Then without flinching I added a third. Since I was going to charge them to Forsander anyway, I could afford to be generous.

She studied them carefully for a second or so. Then she pocketed them. "So who cares about a few missed classes?"

"I thought you might see it that way," I said. "*Carpe diem,*" I added as an afterthought.

"Huh? What's that?" Misty asked.

"Latin for let's hit the ski runs," I said.

A half hour later Misty, her suitcase, and her ski equipment, were all on their way to the Sierras to *carpe diem.*

"Ready?" I asked Mickey.

"No. It feels like the temperature has dropped another ten degrees in here. I can't take it."

"Ignore it," I said.

"The woman would not make a good Plains Indian."

"Oh stuff it you two tough guys. You've got enough clothes on to keep you warm in an Alaskan dog sled race. Now how does this work?" She was fiddling with the thermostat controls on the wall.

Obviously, as Misty had said, they weren't responding. But I gave it a try and so did the Chief. No luck.

"Call the manager," Mickey said.

"Probably not a good idea," I noted. "Considering that we don't pay rent here."

"The cold will keep us alert as the wolf," the Chief noted.

"All right. I freeze," Mickey said, as she pulled her coat tight about her.

"Next time, wear something under that coat," I said.

"What? And not be alert like the wolf?" she shot back.

"Here, take my sweater," I offered. I pulled it off and she pulled it on over the tight turtleneck she was wearing. "Now can we get to work?" I asked.

"I'm warming up. Let's go for it."

"Is the recorder set?" I asked the Chief.

"It will voice-activate."

"Like the lady said, let's go," I said.

Mickey made the critical call and I got on the extension in what had been Claire's bedroom. Snokes answered his phone after three rings.

Mickey, whom we had kept out of this case, identified herself as Misty Finch. There was no possible way he could recognize her voice.

Or even recognize her, if it came to that in the latter stages of the plan. But I was betting it wouldn't get to that point.

"Yes? Do I know you? Are you a student of mine?"

"No. You don't know me. I was Claire Krift's roommate."

"Oh. Yes. That was a terrible thing that happened to Claire. It must have been an awful shock for you. What can I do for you?"

"Actually, I can do something for you."

"Such as?" His voice sounded cautious now.

"I've got something you want."

He forced a laugh. "What exactly is that?" The voice tried to be suggestive and sexy, but it cracked just a bit.

"I've got the same set of copies that Claire had."

There was a long silence. Finally he said, "How could you? She would have told me."

I had expected him to deny everything. He was getting reckless. Maybe that's what happens to you after three or four murders. And we were getting it all on tape. Not that it would admissible in court, but it would be very useful nonetheless to those of us not bound by judicial or any other kind of restraint.

"She didn't know anything about it. I copied them before she could put them in her safe deposit box."

A long, palpable, pause. "Why did you do that?"

"Because I saw what was in them. Because she said she was going to use them to get a lot of money from an old fart professor." Mickey rolled the insulting words on her tongue. Let her have a little fun with the guy. That was probably what Claire would have said anyway.

"She did, huh? And you thought they might be useful someday for the same purpose? With the old fart?"

"Exactly. And it turns out I was right. That lucky day has come."

"Maybe. Maybe not. Things didn't turn out too well for Claire, you recall." The voice had turned harsh.

"Is that a threat?"

"Oh no. Why would I do that? Just a reminder about your dear departed roommate."

"Can we cut the bullshit?" Mickey said, sounding just about right for an impatient coed. "Do you want these papers or do I shop them elsewhere? I'm sure I could find some other interested parties."

"Who else would pay you for them?"

"I think the news media would make an offer. A tabloid for sure. They love a university scandal. Especially one they could tie in with murder."

Another long silence. I listened to Snokes breathing heavily into the phone.

"What do you want?" he finally asked.

"Are you talking in dollars?" Mickey asked.

"No. Fucking pesos."

"Let's say twenty thousand dollars then."

"That's absurd."

"Not for a one-time payment, it isn't. No bleeding you dry month after month. I'm too nice for that. You get all the copies for your money and it's finished."

"How can I be sure there aren't other copies?"

"Trust me. I'm not greedy. I just told you, I'm nice. I just want one quick sale. You'll get everything."

"I'd better."

"Oh you will. I promise that."

They discussed a time for him to bring over the money to the apartment. Mickey said right now. He said it wouldn't work. Since the banks were already closed, he insisted on Friday morning for time to get the money out of his bank.

"Unless you want to take a check?" he asked.

"I'll wait for the cash."

It was also all the better for the trap.

"But are the papers there?" he asked nervously.

"Of course."

"When I get the money I want them in my hands."

Mickey baited the trap beautifully. "I'm holding them in my hands right now." She shook some papers she picked up from the floor into the phone.

"Just keep them there." He hung up.

I hung up and came in from the other room. "Nice touch, shaking those papers."

"We strive for authenticity. Now what?" she asked.

"Now you are truly the tethered goat," the Chief said.

"Huh?" she said.

"It is how we attract the Everglades panther," Chief Moses said.

"Nice analogy," Mickey said.

"Fair. But the panther is an endangered species," the Chief added.

"Murderers aren't. Did we get it all on tape?" I asked the Chief.

"We shall see." He played it back. We had it all.

"Now what?" Mickey asked.

"We put on the TV and try to stay warm. At eleven o'clock it's lights out."

"And tomorrow I play Misty Finch in the flesh," Mickey said. "Good thing he's never seen me before."

"You'll be able to pull it off, but somehow I doubt that'll be necessary," I said.

"The panther does not wait," Chief Moses noted.

"Well, at least I'm a nice and warm piece of bait in this sweater." I shivered under my sport coat.

"Can we work out the logistics?" Chief Moses asked.

"I take him alone. This one is personal," I said.

"That's not a good idea," Mickey said.

"Maybe not. But I don't care. Snokes is mine."

30

After midnight we waited in the darkened apartment for a surprise early visit. As we expected, Professor Dwight Snokes came in the middle of the night and opened the door to the apartment with Claire's key. The incriminating evidence was right there in his hand.

When Snokes stepped into the living room and shut the door, I jumped him from behind, as we had arranged, and tried to take away the keys. I managed to knock them from his hands and they flew across the room. That ended my success.

I should have remembered the man was an NCAA champion wrestler in the '50s, because he sure as hell didn't forget that fact, or any of his moves. As I grappled with him in the dark, I began to agree with Mickey. Maybe this wasn't such a hot idea after all.

I decided to implement the backup plan before I got killed or badly maimed. "Chief! Help!" I called, as Snokes pulled a reversal and pinned me to the rug. A sharp stab of pain ran all the way up my spine. I had visions of myself sitting in a wheelchair. I had visions of myself never walking again. "Chief! Goddam it! He's crushing my spine!"

The light came on, and so did the Chief. "Why didn't you say so?"

A moment later Snokes was dangling in space above me and then he was bouncing like a medicine ball off the apartment door more than a few times. That took the wrestler right out of him. And so did the S&W .38 I held on him. Mickey came out of the bedroom and watched the last few rebounds.

Someone in the downstairs apartment was banging on the ceiling and yelling for us to keep it down. No problem. Things were under control.

The Chief pulled a silk cord and a hard plastic case containing a hypodermic syringe out of Snokes' coat pocket and held them up in triumph. He pushed Snokes down unceremoniously into a chair.

"The murder weapon," he said, as he dangled the cord in front of the intruder.

"And the sodium pentothal, I'm sure," Mickey said.

I picked up the keys. "With the cord and the hypodermic needle this covers everything tied to Claire's murder. You have the safe deposit box key too. And the key to Krift's office, which explains how you planted the letter opener implicating Krift in Boas' death."

"You don't know what you're talking about."

"Oh no?" I went at him. "Boas, your mole in the CFAF, called you in a panic after Cody Zering talked. Boas knew you were with Claire at the motel and you had to kill him before he talked and put the cops on you for her murder. And you had to kill Valerie Hong for the same reason after you used her to get Claire's safe deposit box."

He grunted. Which wasn't much of a response.

"You got anything to say?" I asked.

"Why would I do this?"

"Why would you come here to get papers you thought you destroyed in that fire you set in your office?"

He repeated his grunt.

"What's in those documents?" I asked.

Another grunt.

"I'd say evidence of cheating the government, at the least. Maybe lying about the results of your experiments."

"Bullshit," Snokes blurted out.

"Listen to this. Go ahead, Chief."

Chief Moses played back the recorded telephone conversation.

"That's illegal."

"Tough shit. So is murder," I said.

"I've got an alibi," he said weakly.

"You think your wife will stick with it? Whatever you threatened her with, we can protect her. You're finished Snokes," I said.

"I want my lawyer."

"You're going to need a good one. I'm counting three murders I can understand. And a fourth that I can't. Here's for the fourth." I hit the bastard right in the mouth for the fourth. "For Ollie. And for trying to mash me into the living room rug. And for having Co blow up my goddam car!"

"You can't do that," he complained as he rubbed his jaw.

"The police can't do that. But I can do whatever I fucking want." I hit him again. "See?"

"Take it easy, Jeremiah," Mickey said.

The Chief just smiled. He liked it when I did some of the heavy work myself. It saved his hands.

"Tell me about Ollie. Why'd you kill her?"

"I don't know anything about that."

I hit him again and motioned for the Chief to come over. He shrugged and moved towards Snokes. I stuck the gun up under his nose.

"I didn't kill her," he still insisted.

"What did she know? Or what did you think she knew?"

"Nothing. She wasn't involved in anything, I swear."

"One last punch for Ollie," I threatened.

He flinched and I held up. As much as I didn't want to, I found myself half-believing him about Ollie. Besides, I didn't want him in too bad of shape when we turned him over to the cops. Anyway, my hand hurt like hell from those punches.

I picked up the telephone and dialed Homicide. I got Oscar Chang. That turned out to be a break.

"You're working late," I said.

"With all these cutbacks, all I have is overtime and damn little enough of that," he complained.

"I've got some news that should cut down on your workload," I said.

"That would be appreciated." Chang had mellowed.

I told him who we had, and why.

Twenty minutes later he was at the apartment with Johnny D, who was complaining about being dragged out of bed in the middle of the night. What surprised me was that for the first time, Chang looked almost as disheveled as Johnny. And he hadn't come from his bed.

As usual they were a little unhappy with our methods, especially when they noted the bruises on Snokes' face, but they were too tired to make a fuss about it, and accepted the results more or less gratefully when I explained: "He was resisting a citizen's arrest. Violently."

"Of course," Chang said. "Very understandable, considering who the citizens were."

Then we played the tape for the detectives.

"That recorded conversation ain't worth shit," Johnny D couldn't resist sticking in. The man was obviously cranky because he had to get out of bed at an ungodly hour. But he was getting a murderer handed to him.

"It's worth something to me," I insisted.

For the first time since the police arrived, Snokes spoke. "It's not legal."

"Nobody said it was. I just said it was useful."

"He hit me," Snokes complained to Chang.

Oscar Chang just stared at him with those anthracite eyes.

"Why don't you file PI brutality charges? I understand there's a board somewhere in Sacramento that reviews them," Johnny said, with a laugh as he cuffed Snokes' wrists behind his back. He shoved Snokes towards the door. "Let's go, Professor." He said the title like he was hitting a spittoon with it.

"What about my alibi?"

"We will be talking to your wife about that. Don't worry," Chang said, "she will tell us the truth this time."

Finally the man became talkative. If you considered an unending stream of expletives a garrulous performance.

They took away the bitching and screaming Snokes in the back of the squad car.

It was after two in the morning, but I decided to make some calls anyway. Why not share the good news, even at this hour? Mickey decided to go lie down in the bedroom, to try to get some sleep, while the Chief went out to get some fresh cold air in his lungs. I woke up Scott Forsander and let him know what had happened. Through his grogginess he expressed mumbled appreciation. Then he started to hang up. "This is all just a dream," I whispered into the phone before he went off. Then I called and left a message on Marsha Hanes' answering machine not to worry about Cody. I even gave my client Krift a call. I was surprised to find him up. He was shocked about Snokes, even though he said he had had some suspicions about his work. He sounded relieved to have it all over. Then he asked me a dozen questions before I could get him off the phone.

"Go to bed," I said and hung up.

Case closed.

Almost. Almost.

Snokes had no motive I could verify for killing Ollie. But she had been murdered. So if it wasn't Snokes, which I wasn't quite ready to buy yet, there was another killer out there. A copycat. I had to find out the truth. If it wasn't Snokes, I wasn't going to let the real killer stay out there. I told myself it was to make sure that he didn't strike again and leave another young and beautiful girl dead. But I knew my motives were far purer. Like driven Sierra snow. I wanted blinding white revenge.

Chief Moses drove me back to the Victorian and then left to drop Mickey off. The first thing I did was get some ice from the refrigerator for my swollen right hand. I was paying for the fun I had punching Snokes around.

I took a plastic bag full of ice into the office, stuck my hand in it, and tried to figure out the rest of the case.

After some frustration in that attempt, I at least found a new use for the ice when I was through with my hand. I poured myself some Stoly on those melting rocks and started going over the entire case in my head.

After a couple more drinks, at five in the morning, I fell asleep on the couch without coming up with a single new worthwhile idea.

My unremembered dreams were dead. And with my partners off that day, so was the rest of Friday. Almost.

I did manage to finish up some overdue executive screening reports on the Mac, and I called the black messenger who would deliver them by bicycle to the firm. Along with our bill. This time he had his name shaved into the back of his head under a high flat Afro.

"Nice cut. Who does your hair?" I asked, as I handed him the papers fresh from my printer, but about a month later than promised.

"This blood I know does it real cheap. Learned the trade in Folsom. Can throw in a tattoo if you want. Like this one."

He showed me something on his forearm that I didn't recognize, except for what could have been a half-eaten heart.

"I'll remember that if I'm ever in the market."

"Me, I don't recommend the tattoo," he said. "Hurt like hell when he done it."

Then he was gone with the reports. I watched him cycle up the street, barely missing a Mercedes and a BMW as he rode with no hands and lit up a cigarette. Talented guy.

The work on the reports had taken my mind briefly from Ollie's death. Now that I was through, her murder returned with a vengeance that I found physically painful.

I wanted her killer. Snokes or whoever. The taste was like blood in my mouth.

31

I woke up early Saturday to another cold morning thinking of what I had to do. I owed the Chief a washing, hot waxing, and a detailing as restitution for hot-wiring the King Cab, so he had left the pickup with me last night with the following injunction: "Do not get my vehicle blown up."

"Not to worry," I promised. Then I added, "You do have insurance?"

"I do not believe in insurance. My pickup is in the hands of the Great Spirit."

"And in mine."

"Maybe I should consider insurance," the Chief said, as he left for another of his football jersey dates.

I didn't believe for a moment that, despite the Great Spirit talk, the Chief didn't have a full-coverage policy on the pickup and the houseboat, in contrast to my situation with the T-Bird. But at least I had the thirty grand to buy a replacement thanks to the generosity of the Co Gang.

The cat wanted out of the cold, and I let her into the kitchen and fed her. I ate a bowl of Wheaties while she chomped on her own bowl of Friskies. I tried to read the morning paper, but I kept going back to Ollie. Even the Sporting Green of *The Chronicle* couldn't hold my attention, so how the hell could world events or national or city news about more budget cuts for the SFPD? I tried the comics, but even that didn't work.

I poured myself a second bowl of Wheaties. Michael Jordan was soaring through the orange air, but he only distracted me for a moment. I spent another few seconds reading the fiber content on the side panel and then my mind went right back to the last part of the case.

Why had there been no signs of a struggle? No attempt by Ollie to fight off the attacker? I didn't seem like Ollie at all. Of course, she could have been taken by surprise, but that wasn't enough of an explanation for me. Surprise would still create some kind of evidence of a struggle. It could have been someone she knew. Someone she was comfortable with? Her fiancé was an obvious choice there. But he had his alibi too, although Snokes had shown us what an alibi could be worth. And then there was her summer lover, about whom I knew nothing at all. Not even if he was real.

I finished the bowl of Wheaties.

The cat rubbed up against my leg and then curled up under the table. Perfect trust. She was only inches away from my foot. I could easily step on her by accident. Or worse, intentionally. The way Ollie could have been taken.

I was desperate for a clue.

I got up and went over to the VCR and TV, and started watching *The Bestiary Set*. I didn't know what I was looking for, but the tapes had given us leads before. I didn't expect to find Ollie performing, but even that was a remote possibility. Maybe behind a sheep mask or a deer mask or cat mask or whatever. I watched the women, but only one or two could possibly have been Ollie, but not likely. I looked for the fiancé. Nothing doing. I watched a young man in a chameleon head, his naked body painted to blend with the outdoors scene where the video was shot. Suddenly I had my idea. This was what I should have thought of before. The answer to Ollie's murder could be a chameleon that fit in perfectly with the background. *The Bestiary Set* had come through again, I hoped, but in a very different way than I expected. I didn't find the right naked bodies, but I may have stumbled upon the naked truth.

Maybe there was something to the morals to be drawn from a bestiary after all.

I called Johnny D and found him working the morning shift.

"Could you get the Ollie Shimoda file?" I asked.

"What else have I got to do?"

"Right. When I've solved your biggest case for you," I said.

"I'm going to hear about this for the rest of my damn life," Johnny muttered into the phone.

"Come on. You owe me."

"Okay, but we're gonna get even fast."

"That depends on the performance," I said as Johnny put me on hold. No music on the police lines yet, I noted.

When he got back on the line, I asked, "How long from the time of death to the discovery of the body?"

"Let's see here. I got it. Hard to say. But very brief. The campus cop must have just missed the killer."

"And he stated that he saw no one in the area?"

"Right. He called it in and then conducted a search."

"What about the fiancé? Any change there?"

"Obvious motive. But that alibi held up good as gold. A dozen witnesses. Looks for real, unless the whole family's in on it."

"What about the lack of evidence of a struggle?" I asked.

"She was apparently overpowered."

"Or something."

"Yeah. Or surprised."

"Or all of the above. One more thing. That silk cord was kept out of the newspapers, but it was in the autopsy report. And that was available to police agencies?"

"Of course."

"Like the University Police?" I asked.

"Yes."

"Thanks, Johnny."

"That it?"

"For now."

"I figured the 'for now' part."

I thought again about what Ollie's former fiancé said about someone she had been dating all summer. Again, assuming it was real, what had happened to that summer romance? He was apparently out of the picture by the time I came along. Or was he?

I was going to try to find out. Too bad about the Chief's King Cab. The washing, waxing and detailing would have to wait.

Since Ollie didn't seem to have any close personal friends she might have confided in, I drove the pickup to the address I had for Ollie's family to try them. It turned out to be a four-story apartment building in the Sunset near Golden Gate Park. The Shimodas lived on the first floor. The other names on the inside mailboxes appeared to be Cambodian, Chinese, and probably Rumanian. A typical San Francisco multi-cultural apartment.

A beautiful Japanese child, who had to be Ollie's sister, answered the door before her mother could stop her. I looked into an immaculately-kept apartment.

"I told you. Call me," the woman scolded the child, then looked at me. Mrs. Shimoda was dressed in a lovely black silk kimono, tied with a silk cord. It was the way Ollie would have looked in middle age.

"Sorry," I said. Then to the girl, "Your mother is right."

The girl ran off crying. What a way to begin.

I introduced myself as an investigator and friend of Ollie's, and asked for help. "Could you tell me anything about who she dated last summer?"

The woman didn't have a clue. She kept talking about the fiancé. That wasn't getting me anywhere.

"Anything? Letters? A memento? Something from last summer in particular?"

The father came in from the bathroom dressed in a gray bathrobe and slippers. He was older than his wife and didn't look too healthy. He coughed a few times, then sat down in a recliner and lit up an unfiltered cigarette. I went through my routine again. He was sad and uncooperative. The mother was sad, but helpful.

"Was she going out with anyone last summer?" I asked him.

"She was going to be engaged," the father said, as if that settled the issue.

"Mrs. Shimoda?" I tried again.

Her answer changed slightly. "I do not know. These children these days."

The father gave her a harsh look, but said nothing.

I repeated my question about letters or mementos from the summer.

"I will show you what we have," the woman said sadly.

The father did not protest. He opened a newspaper instead.

She led me down a dark hall to a small room with a large, softly-curtained window. The room was meticulously neat and clean. Stuffed animals sat in a precise row on the carefully-made bed.

"This was her room," the woman said.

It looked like she was expected back soon.

She let me dig through all of Ollie's stuff. I found what I was looking for in a shoe box under a pile of books in the back of the closet. I went through the items looking for my clue. What I found was a start: desperate unsigned letters, a picture of Ollie that wasn't much help at first, and the initial "K" on some notes. And the badminton charm I had given her.

I studied it all. Over and over. The letters were dated from the Fall, when Ollie was obviously dropping the guy. I checked the fiancé family name. It was Kakashi, which I took as a coincidence. But the picture. Something about the picture. I finally recognized the location. It fit in with my evolving chameleon theory.

It was coming together because of *The Bestiary Set.* And an autopsy report for a copycat.

I thanked the Shimodas and left with most of the evidence. And the badminton charm. They didn't object. Outside I got to a pay phone as fast as I could.

I called Dixie Wynne at campus public safety and she gave me the address I asked for. It was in a trailer park south of the city. I drove over in the King Cab, parked it several blocks away, and broke into the tin-can trailer with ease.

It was a narrow boxcar of a trailer with a kitchen and eating area up front, a bathroom to one side, and a bedroom at the rear. The place was a mess. Dishes filled the sink and there were plates still on the table with crusted food on them. The place stank of stale tobacco and smoke. An ashtray of butts sat on the tiny kitchen table.

I pulled aside the curtain and looked into the bedroom. The bed was unmade and clothes were piled up on the floor. But the walls proved that I had found Ollie's summer lover.

The filthy walls were covered with photos of Ollie. Most of them candid shots, and a few of Ollie with her admirer. Then we got into the other stuff. I found myself staring. Pictures shot with infrared, catching the girl undressing. I noticed that there were a few partially-nude photos that she apparently did pose for, and these were blown up to poster size. They weren't pornographic, but they were *Playboy* erotic, and half-innocently self-conscious. Most of the others seemed candid: a shot coming out of the shower, a shot where she was trying to cover up her breasts. I read the pictures like a history of the affair. In the end the girl-woman had wanted her dignity back from a sick voyeur.

In a cardboard box I found a cheap wedding ring. Perfect for bruising the face of a dead woman. And a silk cord. Perfect for a copycat killer.

I went out into the kitchen.

I waited with a can of Lite beer from the refrigerator. A sealed can was the only thing I would touch in that moldy box where food looked like it was left over from last summer like everything else in the trailer.

And I waited.

The door to the trailer finally opened early that evening. By then I had finished two more cans of the Lite. Not bad, but not Henry's. I was ready.

Officer Barry Kobida stepped into the trailer. He was still dressed in his campus cop uniform, complete with service revolver. That was going to make this a little tougher.

"Welcome home, Barry. Tough day?"

"What the fuck. . ."

"Want a beer?" I lifted one of his cans.

"What are you doing here?" Kobida asked angrily.

"I came to drink some beer and admire your erotic picture collection."

"Fuck you, rice queen."

"Chaperoned any women on campus lately?"

He looked around as if there was someone in the trailer who could help him. His hand moved closer to his holster. So did mine.

"You were with her that night. What did you try to do? Get her back after she dumped you?"

"Asian bitch. Wanting a white guy. Wanting you. They're all alike."

"So you killed her when she wouldn't go back with you? And since you had access to the autopsy and knew about the silk cord the strangler used, you used the same MO as the other murders to bury this one. Clever."

"Social-climbing bitch. Willing to put out and give out until something better comes along." He made a disgusting sucking noise full of obscene suggestion.

"You killed her because she didn't want you anymore."

"Prove it."

"I can try."

"Try this."

He went for his service revolver. I rolled on the floor and pulled out my S&W. The bullets from both weapons ricocheted off the metal walls like miniature billiard balls.

When the noise stopped, I was bleeding from the left chest and shoulder area and in a hell of a lot of pain. Kobida, however, looked even worse. He was bleeding a lot more and he wasn't moving at all. I dragged myself along the floor and got to the phone. I dialed 911 and got an ambulance and the cops.

What a way to solve a crime.

"For you Ollie," I said softly, then blacked out.

I regained consciousness to find myself being rolled along the sidewalk strapped to a gurney. Shot once again, and on the same case. Jimart would have been disgusted.

Kobida and I were taken away in the same ambulance. He was the unconscious one.

"Is he going to make it?" I asked the attendant.

"Fifty-fifty."

In the white heat of revenge I wasn't sure which half I wanted. I blacked out again before I could ask about my chances.

32

The bullet had missed my heart, and did just nick a few much less vital internal parts on its way through the St. John body, but I ended up in intensive care anyway, connected to IVs and a wall of green-blinking and beeping monitors. Good thing my partners and I kept a supply of our own blood in storage, just in case. An extra safeguard against HIV infection. I had to put up with isolation in the ICU and bossy nurses for three days before I could convince the overly-cautious doctor, who kept telling me how lucky I was to have so little damage from the bullet, to move me into a regular private room. With flowers and sunlight and visits from Mickey and the Chief. And visits to the rest room. And a smuggled-in six-pack of Henry's, courtesy of my partners. Better than a blood transfusion.

"Who's taking care of my cat?" I asked my partners as soon as I could.

"We're taking turns feeding her," Mickey said.

"And changing her litter," the Chief said.

"My mind is at ease."

Johnny D and Oscar Chang visited. Along with some old clients, old friends like Rita, attorneys like Forsander and Samaho, and new ones like Marsha Hanes, the public defender, and of course Krift and Cody.

I learned that Snokes was saying little, but his wife had changed her story. It turned out that she was a Cherry Blossom mail-order bride illegally brought to the US after Snokes responded to a magazine ad. Apparently he had threatened to send her back to Japan if she didn't lie for him. Now the government, with Samaho representing her in the INS hearing, was likely to allow her to remain in the country after she testified in the case. Obstruction of justice charges were possible, but Samaho was confident that he would get her immunity.

As for Snokes himself, porno performances and Asian women he could lord it over apparently obsessed him. When his wife refused to "act" with him in a blue video he paid Valerie to be his partner, and later his mistress. The police also discovered a Cambodian mistress he was keeping in an apartment near the university. Love is strange. And expensive. Which explained why Snokes got into the business of cheating on his grant. And ultimately into murder.

The actual evidence kept mounting up against him. The police had physical evidence from fibers and hairs taken from the crime scenes that placed Snokes there. The fibers of the silk cord we caught him with matched the fibers from the necks of all of the victims—except Ollie's. Ironically, Snokes had used the silk cord from one of his wife's kimonos for the murders. In addition, the motel manager where Claire was murdered was suddenly able to recall what the older man looked like and picked Snokes out of a lineup, and a number of canceled checks linked him up to Boas as well. The professor looked on course for promotion to the gas chamber.

On the other hand, he was white, middle class, smart, and one of the best and most expensive and obnoxious defense attorneys in the city was defending him. I wouldn't bet too much on the San Quentin gas chamber trip.

Meanwhile, the government was working to untangle his finances and was having a hell of a time trying to conduct an audit of his grant activities.

His assistant, Wayne Ness, had been located in Hawaii, and admitted faking transgenic experiments with Snokes without Ollie's knowledge. In fact, they were glad to get rid of her whenever they could. I remembered that first night, when Ness seemed relieved that Ollie was leaving early with me. Now I understood why she could spend all that vacation time with me away from the lab at Christmas. According to Ness, Snokes was using the old needle and thread method because success of the gene transfer with sperm had not come near to expectations. All along Snokes was defrauding the government with padded expenses, phony invoices, and downright embezzlement. The love-struck Ness also admitted giving Claire, who it turned out, had a pretty expensive cocaine habit, the key to Snokes' office last November. He didn't have a key to the filing cabinets and that explained the scratches by the locks and how Claire had managed to get them open. At least we knew what she needed the money for.

On the other, more personal, side of the story, Barry Kobida was going to live. At least for now. With the copycat use of a silk cord and bruises inflicted after Ollie was dead to make the murder look like the others, it was going to be easy to prove premeditation. This also looked like a death penalty case. About which fact, I, a believer in capital punishment, especially when people I love are involved, had to admit I was pleased.

Since Kobida had confessed to Ollie's murder and had supposedly been hit with the ricochet of his own bullet—which I didn't for a moment believe—the DAs office had decided not to file charges against me. That was with a little help from Chang, who declared to me that we were now even, when he and Johnny D came to visit. Bringing flowers, no less. Having solved this difficult case for him, I didn't feel that way. Then he mentioned not pushing a certain arson investigation involving Co's Gang headquarters. And although the bullet that hit Kobida was in very poor shape, it was possible to run a few more tests to see if they could prove that perhaps my gun did in fact fire it.

"Even, friends," I said.

Chang smiled. "Even, Jeremiah."

Maybe things did balance out after all.

With Snokes and Kobida locked safely away, fear had passed quickly from the campus. The Co Gang, without their headquarters here, were back in L.A. where they would blend in nicely. Their absence helped the campus climate too. Drug arrests were down. Coeds were turning in their mace cans and their whistles. Escort services were reduced, but not eliminated and women did not walk alone at night. Sensible precautions. As for the other players, Cody was back in school and Krift was back conducting his research and driving Heather around openly in his red Porsche. The rumor I heard was that they were actually engaged. Maybe he would keep his hands off the other coeds now. But I doubted it.

One final sad item came from Jimart. When I called from the hospital to let him know all the good news, including my survival, he told me the bad news. Vannessa had tested positive on the ELISA diagnostic test for exposure to the AIDS virus.

"Tough break for the kid," I said.

"You can't save them all," he said.

"Hell, you can hardly save any of them."

"Now you're wising up," he said.

"Maybe," I said. "I don't feel any wiser."

"Don't worry about it. You never will." Then he asked, "You keeping that damn cat?"

"Yeah. She's a pet. I'm going to have her spayed."

"Don't count on any more visits from me."

"I'll visit you. I'd like some warm beaches."

"Help you recover."

"Yeah," I said, but I felt depressed about Vannessa and what the future held for her and her parents.

I healed quickly and I was getting out of the hospital sooner than the doctors predicted. But I was warned that I had to take it easy. I promised to try. Anything to get out of there.

When I actually got out on the street, I found springlike weather that rejuvenated me. There was no reason to make plans to do some recuperating with Jimart in San Diego. My city and my partners would do just fine.

It was still part of the long Chinese New Year's celebration and Mickey, the Chief, and I, went to the Khan in Chinatown to celebrate the Year of the Snake and my survival. Appropriate, I thought. And to celebrate the ten grand we got from Krift as a finder's fee for the money we lost. Not bad. Not to mention the thirty grand from the Co Gang that I was going to spend to replace my blown-up classic T-Bird.

The Khan was another of the restaurants on my list of Chinese places to eat. It turned out to be one of the better ones.

They were playing Christmas music, mixing up the holidays in some strange way that must have made sense to them. Music and holidays by association, I guessed. If we played Christmas music at our New Year's so could they at theirs. I liked it, especially when "Rudolph the Red Nose Reindeer" came on with Burl Ives. It gave me an appetite for the tea-smoked duck I was eating in ornate red and gold Oriental surroundings.

We did a little talking about the case, but not much. Mickey wanted to know what finally put me on to Kobida.

"First I got a moral lesson about camouflage from one of the *Bestiary* tapes."

Then I went over the brief differential between the time of death and discovery of the body, the lack of struggle as if it were someone she knew or trusted, the mystery of her summer lover, the shoe box of memorabilia, the initial "K", the picture of Ollie, and access as a campus police officer to information about the silk cord murder weapon in the autopsy.

"It took me a while, but I realized two things. She was wearing a light summer dress in the photo, and the car she was leaning against was a campus police car. She almost completely covered the insignia, but I caught a piece of it behind her. A campus cop would be perfectly camouflaged. I took a chance that it was Kobida, and when I saw his bedroom walls covered with her pictures, I knew I had the killer."

"So he was punishing an Asian woman for what?" Mickey asked.

"For being with a white man."

"No comment," Chief Moses said.

"Not funny, Chief," I said.

"Sorry, Jeremiah."

That was the second time in recent history that the Chief had apologized. Amazing.

"How did he know about you two?"

"Kobida claims she told him when he came around trying to get back with her. It's probably true. It was Kobida who told Chang about Ollie and me after she was killed. I didn't know that before."

"Why did he tell Chang about the two of you?" Chief Moses asked.

"So I'd be a suspect. In fact, Chang looked at me that way at first."

We each went for our drinks.

"Going with me got her killed," I said softly.

There was nothing but silence at our table.

I looked at both of them and worked up a smile. "I don't want to depress everyone. Let's crack open these fortune cookies."

We broke them open and took out the thin slips of paper with the wisdom of Confucius on them. However, these were different. They turned out to be the kind that give you so-called adult humor rather than philosphy. I wasn't in the mood for it and passed mine to the Chief, who got a good laugh out of what it promised him in bed.

Mickey blushed and wouldn't show me hers. It must have really been something.

On the way out, I told the waiter that they must be giving out fortune cookies left over from a stag party by mistake. He ran in a panic back into the kitchen.

The old Chinese manager rushed out to apologize and we got promises of a meal on the house or pagoda or whatever next time. And no sexy fortune cookies.

The Chief offered me a ride home, but I turned him down. He and Mickey argued with me about it. I was supposed to take it easy, they reminded me, but I was adamant. I had something I needed to do. So Chief Moses took Mickey home.

I had a ghost to exorcise and I wanted to do it alone.

I walked around The City. Slowly. Sometimes physically painfully. Retracing the path I had walked with Ollie. Bringing back the few and beautiful memories. I didn't think of her dead, or her posing for nude pictures for Kobida. I thought of holding her and kissing her and loving her.

Looking for catharsis.

At the waterfront, I watched the stars glitter on black velvet from the same stretch of dock. I looked off to the west, unhampered by fog or clouds, past the Golden Gate Bridge towards the land of her ancestors. I imagined her spirit free now, floating above the towers, her murderer incarcerated. With Kobida caught, her story was over too. A tragic opera. A revenge tragedy.

Looking for catharsis.

The girl was gone. I rubbed the badminton charm between my fingers for a long time. I wanted to keep it. To hold on to it all. Instead, I threw the charm into the bay and watched it sink into a swath of moonlight cut into the gently foaming dark tide.

Be free Olivia.

Be free Jeremiah.

The pain in my chest intensified, but I knew it was only the damaged pectoral muscle that was aching. At least physically. With no fountain around, I gulped down some pain pills with no water and sat down on a wooden piling. After a few minutes I felt better and started to look around for a cab to get me back home.

What I saw were Mickey and the Chief pulling up in his King Cab pickup.

"You followed me," I said.

"After the ransom episode we figured we needed the practice," Mickey called from the passenger side. "Now get in. You're going home to bed."

I moved slowly to the pickup and slid in next to Mickey, leaning against her.

"What were you doing?" she asked.

I waited a long time to answer. "*Sayonara,*" I finally said. "Saying *Sayonara.*"